PROMPT
GENERATION 1

GUIDEBOOK

BLUE FORGE PRESS
Port Orchard ☸ Washington

Prompt Generation 1 Guidebook
Copyright © 2020
by Blue Forge Press

First eBook Edition March 2021
Second eBook Edition January 2025
First Print Edition March 2021
Second Print Edition January 2025

ISBN 979-8-89439-039-0

Cover and interior design by Brianne DiMarco

For information about film, reprint or other subsidiary rights, contact: blueforgegroup@gmail.com

This is a work of fiction. Names, characters, locations, and all other story elements are the product of the authors' imaginations and are used fictitiously. Any resemblance to actual persons, living or dead, or other elements in real life, is purely coincidental.

Blue Forge Press is the print division of the volunteer-run, federal 501(c)3 nonprofit, Blue Legacy (EIN 83-4307421), founded in 1989 and dedicated to supporting artisans marginalized due to race, age, disability, economics or other factors. We strive to empower storytellers from all walks of life with our four divisions: Blue Forge Press, Blue Forge Films, Blue Forge Gaming, and Blue Forge Sound. Find out more at www.BlueForgeGroup.org

Blue Forge Press
7419 Ebbert Drive Southeast
Port Orchard, Washington 98367
blueforgepress@gmail.com
360-550-2071 ph.txt

*dedicated to the nine authors
brave enough to take this journey*

TABLE OF CONTENTS

PROMPT

GENERATION 1

GUIDEBOOK

JENNIFER DiMARCO

HOW TIME UNRAVELS

I remember my first jump. Standing there naked and proud. A brush stroke of chestnut skin among a spectrum of complimenting Earth tones. Like someone had taken a box of Colors of the World crayons and stood them all on end in perfect formation. Bare as the day we were born, we marched in cadence—a Battalion of four Companies, eight Platoons, sixteen Squads—one thousand souls all moving in tandem for a single purpose. Confident in our lockstep march into the linear. Ever onward. Always forward.

Eyes ahead, solider.

The Maw left us speechless. It was terrifying and empowering, inspiring awe and dread in equal measure. A thing, an event, a location, an origin story formed by human hands guided by godly endeavors emerging from a world that no longer believed in any god but science. This was the multi-flavored flash point that ignited the preons within the quarks that wove the veil between dimensions. The algorithms had spoken and numbers don't lie.

Four-point-six-six-nine. The soldier in front of me had it

tattooed on the back of his neck. A fundamental constant. A goal to obtain.

The quantum well required sacrifice (a prerequisite for any god) and had eaten four hundred thousand by the time it ate me. For all I know, it feasts to this day. We're a patriotic variant of lemming where we 're not mindless but driven by purpose over the precipice.

I watched without watching as my comrades before me moved to the edge of star-encrusted oblivion and dove, fell, floundered or flew, taking that literal leap of faith into the near-infinite hall of mirrors that was our multiverse. Four-point-six-six-nine million versions of our own dimension and this was the only way out of ours and into all the rest.

Then it was my turn. I was standing on the brink—literally and figuratively—and she touched the small of my back. Not a push or a pull. Not a question or a statement. Just a truth shared: We would never be together again so we could be together forever. In a way.

I jumped.

It was white-hot pain for not quite long enough for me to scream. I was unraveled down to my consciousness, the physicality of me spooling out into the well of the Maw, fueling the jumps to come after mine. Like Taja's. The heat of her final touch was stolen from me as my body deconstructed.

I had known it would be this way; nothing had been hidden from us. But what no one had told me—not my recruiter, not my Commander—was that inside the white-hot pain was wonder. When the nanoscopic whirling dervishes, those gluttonous quantubots that were citizens of the Maw disassembled my meat-brain and body, they left me a gift. The almost instantaneous act of my physical deconstruction corrected my every flaw, explained my every fear, unpacked my every neurosis. The mysteries of me were solved. I was made whole and perfect and the pain was washed away by a tsunami of gratitude. I was whispered the secret of me, the reason I existed, the meaning of everything.

Why wouldn't I keep jumping?

(I know why I keep jumping.)

I don't remember the next time, or rather I don't specifically remember it as the second time. After that first leap, it was all more routine. Never again was I part of a Battalion to stand with. Each of us were, now and indefinitely, on our own; no more than one of us could inhibit a dimension simultaneously. Alone together.

But that first time... the sight of those before me vanishing into a myriad of equations; my beloved's illicit touch at the final moment, and my truths handed to me like golden armor even while my body was taken away forever? I will never forget or regret that first time.

When I arrived on the other side, having passed through the eye of the needle into another dimension, I wept. And every time I jumped again, every time I opened my eyes in another variation of home, I confirmed the leap was successful, and I wept again.

But over time, after twenty or thirty or two hundred jumps, the reason I wept changed.

It was getting so much harder.

I blinked. It was raining. Hard. I'd left a bright, searing Dwarka in summertime and dropped into the wet, riotous monsoons along the western shore of the Okhamandal Peninsula on the right bank of the swollen Gomti River. I was grateful it was early in the season.

Often identified as the ancient kingdom of Krishna, believed to be the first capital of Gujarat, and one of the four sacred Hindu Chardhams, I'd never seen Dwarka outside of Taja's childhood photos until I jumped. Now I know the city as I know no other. I've lived in hundreds of Dwarkas with their subtle differences and nuanced parallels. In all the variants, in every dimension, the word Dwarka means Gateway to Heaven. I'm not surprised this place was identified as one of the pivotal nodes.

I inhaled sharply and started to move. That first breath often felt strained. The rain hid my tears but not the look of loss in my eyes. I was, at least, dressed for rain; or rather, the woman Remington Valentina, the woman annexed or colonized by my consciousness a moment ago, had dressed for rain. I never felt bad about that—the commandeering of the vessel. After all, I *am* Remington Valentina.

The only Remington who has seen the universal algorithms foretelling the Great Compression and enlisted.

I started to walk. I've never been here before and I've been here every day of the last twenty years of my unaging life—lives? I know this city—six times submerged, swallowed by the Arabian Sea—as my life's (lives'?) work. I think only Krishna himself with his hundred and eight names must know Dwarka the way I do.

So I walk. Across the Sudama Setu, the suspension foot bridge crossing the Gomti River. Away from the Rukmanidevi Temple, legendary dwelling of Rukmini, Krishna's chief queen; a temple which itself impressed me as the aspiration of all sand castles with its base carved with naratharas and gajatharas in alto-rilievo, haut-relief.

The spires, domes and ancient walls of temples and mosques surround me. The blonde stones and darker cobbles seem more a texture laid over a familiar wire frame than they seem like actual buildings. I have to keep walking until I know for certain.

Until I see something new.

The rain is cold and salty today. The tide pushes back on the river. There are a tenth as many people on the streets as in the summer. And that's still an alarming number of people given we'll all be drenched to the marrow in a week or two.

There are as many street markets as there are temples and

even some of these still display their wares—silk saris, brass works, ghagra-choli—beneath dripping awnings of russet and gold, some shielded behind sheets of clear vinyl. Where wet, the luxuriant colors are deepened by the rain and the rich voices of brass bells meant to please the gods are the sights and sounds of the only home I have known as a soldier.

I stop.

There it is. Or rather, there is isn't: Daavat, the corner open-air storefront with its red and orange awning, is instead Vankol Krupa selling roti samosa with chutney. I turn in a circle to make sure I'm not lost. I ensure I'm seeing what I'm not seeing, beyond a shadow or a doubt. If the jump was unsuccessful and I have been here to this dimension before, I must deactivate immediately. Unpleasant, always, but I can't take the risk of undoing my work and toppling a domino chain of suspicion.

I walk up to the vendor. "Kachori?"

From beneath impressive brows, the man forces a tight grin. I am not Indian but my accent is right and my clothing are native, not tourist. "Samosa."

"Moong dal kachori?"

Kachori are most commonly made with dried fruit but Daavat sold them with moong dal.

The shopkeep's grin becomes a frown. I see myself as he sees me for a moment: Average height, nondescript build, ringlets of hazelnut hair dripping down my back. My angular nose and wide, caramel-colored eyes might give me away as Greek but other than that I'm unmoored, a creature of the world(s) on the streets of Dwarka.

"Nahi." A hard no. I don't say thank you because that would offend him; he hasn't really been of help. Except he has and just doesn't know it.

As I turn and walk away, he calls after me, making a sound of sudden recollection, "Ah! Daavat! Shri Ram Bazaar."

I immediately return and pay for a large take-away order of samosa. You don't casually say thank you in India; gratitude is assumed and reciprocal action speaks volumes. As the deep fried phyllo triangles stuffed with potato and onion are wrapped in parchment, I contemplate this unexpected shift: Daavat is at Shri Ram instead of on Tin Bati Chowk. How... insignificant.

I pay with rupees and find my key. It's unchanged from what I've come to expect, even has the scuff from when it fell down the bathroom drain and I had to fish it out with a metal hanger. But that doesn't really matter because Daavat is at the bazaar so I'm somewhere new. The proof is not in the pudding but in the location of the best moong dal kachori in Dwarka.

I let myself into my apartment (the first flat on the third floor) and lock the door behind me. I put the packaged samosa in the fridge, strip out of my wet clothes and walk, barely looking, into the bedroom.

I sleep and cry for three days. I mourn for what and who I was. I mourn for the loss of life—my life—and for the loss of love—my love—but also Taja's. I mourn for her and for me and for us as a couple.

At least... that's the usual plan.

"Remi? I know you're in there. Your scooter's in the courtyard."

My eyes open. I'm lying face down on a single bed that's familiar and totally new to me.

"Remi."

Not a question. A statement of fact.

It's Taja.

But it's not.

It could be Rebecca, Yua, Naomi, Adaku. My ears hear her voice as almost identical despite her variant nationalities, despite how and why and when she came to be here in Dwarka. She has never been Taja Tangali but she has always been Taja Tangali. She has worn more faces and forms and names than even Krishna.

"Remington. I swear. Open the damn door."

Taja. Her name means crown. Mine is a weapon.

For hundreds of jumps I have followed the same routine. I developed a pattern that allows my newly occupied meat-brain to wrap itself around what's happening. Its native consciousness has been overwritten and there's a time of adjustment for both of us—my new flesh and my ageless... intention. (I don't want to say 'soul' because possession is such a tabloid-tier taboo.) I retain most of the memories of the Remington this body was this morning before I arrived but they are memories like a novel I read starring someone relatable and familiar but not someone real and not someone... me.

I sit up in bed. Breathing is an afterthought. It comes in small bursts of gasp and release. I'm not ready to start anew.

Once, decades and hundreds of lives ago, I could arrive, confirm, and begin. I could complete my mission in a week—once in just four days—and jump again. I told myself we'd made our decision and chosen humanity. Altruism was its own reward.

The sound of a key in the lock.

Does this Taja already have my key?

Sometimes we haven't yet met. Sometimes we've been lovers for a month. Other times we've been married for years. I search the novel part of my brain for memories that are and aren't mine.

I'm not ready yet. I need to drown myself in sorrow, a baptism of mourning to be born again, to rise and commit the same sin.

When had it become a sin? And what archaic nonsense was sin?

A door opens and closes.

The door is not my own. It's my neighbor's. This Taja lives across the hall.

I lay back down and stare at the ceiling. I calm my breathing. I recite prime numbers quietly in a voice not quite steady but getting there. I imagine everyone and everything I've ever loved forgotten and erased from the slate of the universe. I imagine every place and every word I've ever held sacred rent to cellular ribbons and thrown to careless solar winds. I imagine the end of everything and then I allow myself to mourn the end of us because, after all, that's what a successful jump means: I've broken her heart.

After another two days of indulgent, opulent, self-preserving reflection I come to the same conclusion I always do: The loss of the human race out weighs my loss of her. I get out of bed. I shower. I get dressed. I eat the roti samosa from Vankol Krupa. Tonight I'll knock on her door.

Enrapture. Rend. Repeat.

"You've got some nerve."

I try to respond but words won't come. My mouth gapes like a koi, opening and closing with false starts.

Taja's lips are parted, her tongue pressed against the back of her clenched teeth. I have never known a variant of her to do this. As she did.

I should be leaning in, seizing this day and channeling her anger into my cause instead of standing here like a carp without the diem. I thought I was ready. Had stood and stared for an hour at the photos of us stuck to my fridge. We'd known each other for a year but a lot of that has been spent apart because she's—

"I turned down National Geographic for you. *National. Geographic.*"

—a photographer. Like my Taja before we learned of the Great Compression and enlisted.

"Hey!" Her eyes flash fury and she jabs an accusatory finger into my sternum. "Are you listening to me, Remington?"

"Not really." My voice cracks under the Herculean effort to do my damn job.

Taja recoils. She's the speechless one now. She steadies herself against the fact of her own doorframe. I wish she'd just slam the door in my face and end this.

We stand like that in silence for three or four days or maybe for six and a half seconds and I know I should just walk away, cross the hall, open then slam my own apartment door. But tears are welling in her green eyes shot with bronze and I can't look away.

"You…" She finds her voice but it shakes.

My novel memories inform the moment. So mundane. So everyday. We'd planned a long weekend together but instead I'd hidden in my apartment and ugly-cried for a three days. Recycle. Reuse. Reset.

"If you didn't want me," she finally hisses but it's venom-less, fang-less, submerged in loosed tears. "You could've just said so."

I should say, *You're right. I don't want you.* I should say, *People change. I've changed. We're over.* But I'm thrown, unsure. I've ended hundreds of us but not like this and never an us that seemed so much an us.

Instead I say, "Taja."

And something goes wrong. A storm cloud of emotion envelopes her expression and she draws herself up. Her pulse is leaping in her neck. My heart is pounding in my chest.

She closes her door in my face.

I stand staring at the unit number, wondering what I'd just seen, wondering how I should feel. Was I over-thinking this? Was I under-thinking it?

I run a quick checksum and yes, her name here is Taja. Not common for me to find but common enough.

I look down at the concrete floor. Perhaps my job here is done? Perhaps, for once, this love affair has already happened. I'm just here to see the end for once.

It's later that night and I'm still there. Not in the hallway but on the same world. I'm sitting on my low futon-style couch with dinner untouched and cold on the coffee table before me. I found black Levi's in my closet and a red V-neck tee. My feet are bare and my toe nails are pedicured and painted black.

From the moment I knocked on her door and she answered I've been off my game. The three day adjustment? Standard for me. But this dumb-founded inability to think clearly?

This Taja is just too close to my own.

Aren't they all my own? Or are none of them?

But I know this woman. I know her blue-black raven hair. Her full lips and thick brows. Her green-bronze eyes, full breasts and hips. Her job. Her voice. Her ferocity.

What else is the same?

I replay each word exchanged and analyze her intonation and body language. I try to stay detached and clinical. It certainly felt like we were—they were before me—deeply in love. Is that enough? Do I move on?

I shake my head hard. Get in the game, soldier! Buck up! Was I wearing thin? Was I becoming a shade of who I once was? Was I even that person anymore? My original body was long-since dead—as dead as this one will be when next I jump. (The normal reason for heartbreak.) Was it even possible to wear thin under these constantly renewing circumstances?

20

I knew that wasn't it. It wasn't so complicated and psychological. It was simple: She was too familiar.

If you didn't want me, you could've just said so.

I jerk ramrod straight. My not-my memories whisper to me. I cover my face with both my hands.

My job here is not done.

I can tell she's been crying but she answers the door anyway.

"May I come in?" I hold up a bottle of brandy bought in London and saved for the weekend I ruined.

Taja steps aside and pushes ribbons of hair back from her face. She says nothing. She looks paler than her olive complexion normally allows. Like she's had a freight.

I walk to her couch—brown and gold with soft cushions—and lift snifters from the sliding drawer under the center table. I tell myself I'm not disconcerted that I've done this before, a hundred lifetimes ago with a woman alarmingly the same.

Taja comes to stand at the entrance to the room, her arms crossed, her eyes wide as she watches me like one would watch a bird that had flown in the window.

I pour two fingers into two glasses and offer her one. My hand is steady. "Taja." I'm watching her intently. "I want you."

It isn't a come on. It isn't a sexual thing. It's an apology.

She should shake off her sense of abandonment and dread. She should reach toward me with long, strong hands that I know all too well. But she just watches me—the wild thing in her living room.

I set her snifter down on the table and sit down on the couch with my own.

"I got scared, love," I try the endearment on; not surprisingly, it sounds natural. "I'm not the brave one here."

I look at her. There is no pretense written on my face. I have an objective, yes, I have a mission but I also have a heart in my throat and a blush to my cheeks that's only partially from the two glasses of brandy I drank before coming over.

Taja's left eye twitches a little and she slowly cocks her head to the side. Who's the bird now?

"Say it again."

I stop mid-sip and look back up at her still standing in the archway. I hazard a guess, "I want you." But she's already shaking her head.

"Say my name."

I'm nervous, growing paranoid. I check not-my memories again. I inhale. I exhale. "Taja."

Her eyes close. She is so still I'm afraid something has gone terribly wrong. Some glitch in the matrix of space/time. Some hiccup or—

She sits down beside me, picks up her snifter and drinks.

I watch her look into her glass (it's good brandy) and then at me. She is unreadable but also more beautiful than I have ever seen her.

"I forgive you."

It feels like she's saying so much more.

The moon has risen and set and Taja's blouse is open, her long hair free, her head on my chest as we sit entwined with our empty bottle of brandy, the last two figs, and a single nankhatai on a cobalt plate.

"You're a good listener," she says, tracing the deep collar of my tee with her fingertips. Her words blend together just a little bit and I know she's drunk.

"Sometimes."

She makes a wordless sound of forgiveness. Love makes us forget as often as it makes us remember.

"I should probably get home," I murmur gently, able to lean in so easily now, to sink into this embrace of me wrapped around her.

I can't help my own small sound of pleasure as her fingers trail up my neck, along my jaw, and come to rest—butterfly-light—on my lips.

"I don't want you to leave." She whispers it so softly, so sadly.

I kiss her fingertips and draw her tighter. "Taja."

Her eyes sink shut. I feel her shudder. I reach for the cotton-soft embroidered wrap across the back of the couch but she turns in my arms and kneels between my thighs, facing me in our embrace.

"Remi." Her eyes search my face like she's memorizing me or searching for something she's not sure of. "I don't want you to leave."

I shudder this time. The room feels cold. Her eyes do not. The double meaning she can't possibly know is like something arctic or paranormal. Like a specter, lifeless and merciless.

I force a smile and touch her face. "It was the lark, the herald of the morn, no nightingale, my love."

Taja smiles back at me and her smile is genuine and so sweet my heart aches. How many decades have I missed that smile, seeing so many variations but never one quite as *right* as this. "You and your literary illusions."

"Those are the best ones."

"You're such a charmer."

"Prince Charming will come back and make you breakfast in the morning."

"I'd rather you be my princess."

Don't I know it. In all my jumps, I've only been a man twice and both times so was she.

We kiss goodnight and she tastes like brandy, figs, and shortbread with violet petals.

I close my door but don't lock it. My head is spinning and not from the brandy. Okay, maybe a little from the brandy. I don't want us to sleep together. I mean... *I do.* More than anything else in this moment I do but it feels... *wrong. Really* wrong.

This time.

I open my eyes when I realize I've closed them. Desperately my gaze darts. I busy my mind in the academia I find around me; I'm not surprised by the eight over-populated bookshelves crammed into my studio apartment. The colors printed on the spines form a collage of memories—half of which are mine across dozens of worlds—and lure me into a place of calm.

You and your literary illusions.

Once, when Taja's name was Kiki and her hair was lilac and teal, she said the same thing to me but followed it up by saying, *Half the time, I can't even find the book!* Because reflections don't always get the details right.

I've always loved to read. I don't actually remember learning how. It's just something I've always done. I feel solace with a book in my hands. Before I enlisted, I watched as Bradbury's *Fahrenheit 451* and *1984*'s Orwellian nightmare proved true. I watched humanity bend away from altruism and unity into demagoguery. The centre cannot hold.

I close my eyes again. I recite Yeats in my head and remember that in his early 1919 drafts, *The Second Coming* was called *The Second Birth*; if written today, it might have been *The Second Jump* or *The Thirtieth Leap.*

The age old question: Which is more valuable? Words or numbers.

While Shelley's 1826 *The Last Man* or Orwell's 1945 *Animal Farm* were alarmingly prescient in their insight into government fallibility during a worldwide pandemic and the willingness of the people to grant assumptive obedience in the service of tyranny, the numerous volumes of fact, fiction and foretelling penned by futurists did not, humorously enough, stand the test of their most invaluable commodity: Time.

In 1993, a futurist predicted we'd create super computers that so far surpassed us that human function would be irrelevant. In 2005, another futurist proposed that machine cognition would render common institutions needless.

In turns Pollyanna or Doomsayer, these town criers were forecasting the rise of Artificial Intelligence—a neuroscience/technology hybrid concept—that since its inception in the 1920s and subsequent popularization in the 1950s—has persevered as the Holy Grail and/or Boogeyman of moneyed men with too much time on their hands. Which is interesting since one prominent proponent of the destructive AI theory once said, *Time is meaningless when there's too much of it. Time is only valuable in limited supply.*

But the futurists were wrong. About everything.

I walk to my couch, almost forgetting to watch where I'm going. Maybe it's not exhaustion that closes my eyes; I dread bearing witness. I sink down and lie back.

AI didn't turn out to be our executioner but rather our liberation from universal extinction. It was a reservoir of algorithms that showed the watchmen approach was flawed, that solved global problems on a universal scale, that predicted the coming of the Great Compression. AI gave us data. And a data-driven society can make colossal change.

Instead of abandoning the Monster (because remember, Victor Frankenstein left his creation nameless) humanity rose to the maternal occasion and embraced what terrified us the most: We would accept the inevitability of dimensional collapse in a way we never fully accepted the climate crisis or the infertility epidemic. The odds were against us but Battalion after Battalion would deploy to align our reflective dimensions. If we could coordinate 4.669% of our closest parallels, they would consolidate into one and come out the other side intact.

When first I jumped, we were at T minus four hundred fourteen years until the Great Compression. Where are we now? Does it really matter? I'll jump and keep jumping until there's no reflection to jump into.

I just have to do my job.

It's just... my job seems especially hard today.

Exposition wears me out. That's why I love waxing academic; it's the best sleep aid I've found.

I fall asleep on the couch and dream of Arnold Palmer. Not the golfer (though once he said, *The most rewarding things in life are those that look like they can't be done.* which is quite apropos) but the Cambodian-American private that I trained with at Parris Island.

Palmer was a friend. As much of a friend as one could make when you know you only have days until your body unravels. We shared a desire for continence even while we shared the connection of kamikaze soldiers.

Palmer was scheduled to leave the day before me. He was the first person I knew more than casually who was scheduled to jump and I wanted to say goodbye. I snuck away to the Maw (the nickname we'd given the quantum well) and Palmer was outside the building, leaning back against the whitewashed concrete wall and looking... amused.

"Care to share the funny?" I leaned back beside him. We both stared straight ahead. No sound escaped the building at our backs.

"Got my mission," Palmer offered, still with a crooked grin.

"I'm…" We'd all been told we weren't allowed to share our missions. Not with friends, family, lovers. But Palmer continued in his amused denial, "I'm killing a butterfly."

"No." My tone was ridiculously incredulous on several different levels. Palmer had never broken any rule of command; he wasn't one to be amused by anything. And killing a butterfly couldn't possibly save the human race.

"Yes."

Then we were both laughing. Laughing so hard I thought I'd pee my fatigues. It had to be a code or a hypnosis of some kind. It couldn't possibly be… that a trucker would emerge from a rest stop restroom and spot a Monarch, dead, on the sidewalk. Always having been a superstitious man, he would call dispatch and make up an excuse to abandon his rig, quit his job, and return home in time to stop a hate crime across the street. And the little boy he saved would grow up to be the man who wrote the final line of code that awoke our first AI and unfurled infinite algorithms.

Big or small. Sadistically insignificant or monstrously masochistic. Our missions were doled out in binary, translated by a second machine, then given to us without human intervention or opportunity for explanation, compliment or complaint.

Palmer turned to me. "Maybe they'll ask you to kill Krishna."

I think we laughed again but this time I just woke up.

Taja was standing in my open doorway holding a new bottle of Chhaang rum and a bag of masala dosa take out. She was soaked from sheets of rain, her wet locks like streaks of midnight sky plastered to her like a painter's strokes. She smiles at me, sweet and adoring. "You missed breakfast but how about dinner?"

I don't remember crossing the room but I do remember kissing her.

I wish the binary had told me to kill a god.

"I want you," I tell her. And this time, she knows exactly what I mean.

She is a molten creature beneath me. A living flame herself nonetheless caught in the light of two dozen (and one) fiery tongues. The candles around the room are red, orange, and buttercream. Her voice, her dance, her rise and fall are arresting, captivating, and so precisely, perfectly the Taja I know that more than once I forget when/where/who/what and with whom I am. If quicksilver were olive-gold, she would be an alchemist, transmogrifying my deep state strategy into carnal desire so sharp that I find myself willingly flayed.

She lays me bare and the only things between us are secrets.

I kiss her nape, her jawline. I weigh her hair, dry of rain but damp now with sweat and the tears that fall when you're turned inside out by passion. Unprompted, surprising myself, I ask, "Would you rather be romanced or ravished?"

She laughs at the unexpected and tugs me down beside her. "You want to talk?"

I play with her hair. "I want to know you better."

"You know me very well." She lifts one eyebrow, amused by me.

I wet my lips. Taste her. Fall in love. I tread carefully. "Never enough," I whisper over her ear and it's true. I am insatiable when it comes to her. All of her. Every aspect cast wide over countless dimensions.

"Ravished," she confesses, watching my expression. I think her favorite part of talking is watching my reactions; I've been told I have no poker face.

She continues, her eyes on my parted lips, my dilated pupils, the fast rise and fall of my chest. "Romance is so archetypal. Not contrived but filled with troupes like flowers and chocolate and candles." We both laugh a little as she motions to the candles she lit around her bedroom. "When you take me...." Her voices trails away and now she looks only at my mouth, her gaze cast down not in modesty but memory. "You make me feel wanted, desired, sought after. And somehow both sexy *and* strong!"

She laughs harder and I touch her face. "You *are* both."

"You're so controlled, so restrained normally," she adds carefully. "My lit professor love."

We kiss slowly, savoring each other. I think I taste like rum but Taja tastes like homecoming.

"You say my name differently."

I hold my breath but she says no more. We're so close, face to face, and she's watching me again more intently than I think anyone has ever watched me.

"Just... a little," she adds.

I manage to swallow. I manage to breathe. I don't manage to speak.

"I answered your question." She traces my collar bone, making it real to me. Shadows pool beneath her fingertips and in those small places I imagine secrets lie submerged like Dwarka under the sea. "Will you answer one from me?"

You just asked a question, I almost tease her in my nervousness, my apprehension. Instead I grow a spine and answer, "It's only fair."

I expect her to mull her options, to consider and contemplate. Instead, she asks immediately, "Should I feel safe with you?"

Ice water in my veins. The manifestation of dread. The tangible beast of fear.

I want to cry, *No! Run! Get up and leave me instead of loving me.*

But I say nothing. And that's how I knew I was still in it. I was shaken, bent low, but not broken.

"I will love you until the end of time." My not-answer satisfies her.

A month later, I'm still there—not in her bed but in her world—and she tells me she wants us to have a baby. Together.

I really need to leave.

I really can't.

We spend the weekend driving for hours both ways to spend thirty minutes in a new bookstore that dares to have a tiny section of queer books in the back corner of the shop. I love the way books are laid down on the shelves in India. No tilting sideways to read titles. No bowed or bent books even in humid environs.

We get chai on a busy street and walk together without touching. It was illegal to be gay in India until 2020.

"Your turn to start," I tell her. Our *Getting to Know You* game has continued these six months. It still amuses her and still surprises me.

"What does my name mean?"

"Crown," I answer without thinking.

Taja stops walking. Hers is a ghost smile, thin, obscured by something unspoken and invisible. "A brief moment in time."

I walk two steps before I realize she's stopped so now we face each other with four feet of empty space between us. We have moments like this one occasionally. Moments when she seems to be waiting for me to... what?

"What does Remington mean?" I counter with a jaunty smirk, deflecting, playing it off.

"Nothing," Taja tells me. "Just pretty sounds together."

She starts walking again and then we walk together. This world is more divergent and less divergent in the strangest ways.

What does that mean for me?

For us?

It's been a year. The monsoons have come again. We're wrapped in each other, angles and curves fitting like a single creature supine. Taja is luxury, royalty, reward. I am forgetting myself. Forgetting everything else. Everything but her.

I let go of my flat eight months ago and stacks of my books have grown like tree trunks of papyrus in every room of Taja's apartment. I listen to the rain, a constant roar like the ocean. I imagine a rain forest made of books. I imagine sheaves of paper instead of leaves, bookmarks instead of birds.

"Have you read about bifurcation theory?"

I shake my head but of course I have. Gods be damned. Just when I think I can forget....

Taja smiles and settles closer to me. This is the kind of thing she loves to do. To share some piece of newly discovered intellectual property. "It's a fundamental constant," she explains perfectly. "Anything with parabolic growth."

"Like life itself," I murmur.

"You *have* heard of it."

"Tell me more."

Taja shifts up on one elbow. Even naked and revealed, she is poised, composed and elegant. It's not easy to be elegant when unbuttoned. "You tell me."

I drown in her eyes. I don't want to speak. I want to lay beside her and fantasize about forests of books; I don't want to lie. So I don't.

"Periodic doubling," I explain, "occurs naturally. Until totals reach a saturation percentage and the doubling branches into two distinct patterns."

"Everything is patterns. Repeating," she adds, her gaze even more intent than a moment before.

What's happening?

"Then four branches, then eight. The branches grow at a set rate until—"

"Chaos."

I'm looking directly at her and yet she feels fathomless, endless, branching herself even as I watch her, becoming more complex with every moment. "Yes. Eventually, growth descends to chaos. But then it comes back. It simplifies and begins anew."

"It compresses."

"Where did you read this?" I blurt the words.

She doesn't look away from me. "I don't remember."

She's lying to me and I think it's the first time.

"Should I make us dinner?" I'm a master of deflection, breaking eye contact and turning away before she can—

"Stay."

I stay.

Taja is struggling. I see it now. She isn't fishing. She isn't searching. There's something she needs to say, not something she needs to hear. Her eyes study the sheets as if looking for just the right words.

"Remington..." Taja takes one of my hands in both of hers. She sits up straighter. Our touch imparts strength but still she hesitates. For long moments, we are still, together, while the world rages outside this room and inside my head.

"Remington," she starts again, then looks up at me. "I want this."

How powerful to hear that from someone. That proclamation of authentic desire. I wonder why she seems so unsettled.

"I want this more than anything I've ever wanted in all my life and it's about time I do something for me!" A rush of words and emotion.

My heart sings. I shift to reach for her, to pull her back down beside me but she continues.

"But…"

Why is there a but?

"…I have to ask…"

Does she?

"…just so I know for sure…"

Know what?

"What will it be like without you?"

There it is.

Taja ignores the tears that fall down her face. Her body language, her tone of voice, nothing betrays her heart like those tears.

"Taja."

Her eyes close and a tide of additional tears are forced down her cheeks. "Remi. Don't speak."

I don't. She continues in another rush as if she's afraid she'll lose her nerve: "When the time comes, what will it feel like? Like being eaten up or drowned or pressed back into clay?"

I can't answer her but still she asks: "When all is done and there's only one world left, will I get to live my life with you? A you who isn't you… a me that isn't me."

"You know."

"I do."

And so we stare at one another in a way I have never looked at another human being for a century or more. "What gave me away?"

She can't or won't stop the grin that tugs up the corner of her mouth. "Two dozen languages are spoken in India with more than seven hundred dialects.”

“The way I say your name.”

Small wrinkles around her eyes. When did those appear? How long have I loved her? All my life it seems.

I sit up as I ask, “How long have you known?”

“As long as I’ve lived. My parents told me the story.”

“The story?”

She takes my hand in a way I know so well. “The story of Taja Tangali. My namesake. Their gurumayi.”

The bed, the floor, the building, the earth beneath the foundation gives way beneath me and only me and I feel myself falling. So unexpected. So new.

“She came to them during the monsoons when first my parents were married. It was late at night but my father was a very spiritual man and he let her in. He knew she was something... *other*.”

“What—” I choke on my shock. “What... did she look like?”

“A lot like me.”

“But you’re not...?”

“No, Remington.” Her smile is sad; I regret implying. “I’m not the Taja from your timeline.”

I can’t help it. I don’t want to hurt the woman before me but my eyes sink shut and I ignore but can still feel my tears. For just a moment... for just a moment.

“You want me to be.”

Not a question so I don’t answer.

I feel her shift beside me on the bed. “She could be somewhere still. Out there in the world.”

“No.” I open my eyes already shaking my head. “There can be only one.” Only one jumper in a dimension at a time. Only one variant of a person at a time.

Taja nods. Understanding enough. “I’m sorry.”

I am without words. I just look at her.

She asks without accusation, "You're used to this? What you do."

"I've had a lot of time to adjust."

My fingers have closed around the sheet, grabbing fistfuls, white-knuckled, perhaps trying to anchor myself, perhaps trying to cling to the past... to an hour ago... to ten minutes ago before this conversation.

Taja places one hand over one of mine. "Time heals all wounds but not if you keep cutting the same place."

I flail. I'm not good with spontaneity, with unplanned and brutal blindsiding. (I'm also a hypocrite.) I blurt, "Why would she do this?"

"You tell me."

But I can't. My mind is completely blank. My senses under water or beneath a heavy layer of fog. I look down at her hand on mine. I wait.

Taja says more, "She told my parents someone would come. During the monsoons. After they were gone. And we would fall in love."

I sneak a look at her. Her expression isn't hurt or sorrowful but resigned, melancholy.

"And because of us, because of small things—the streets we walked or things we bought, children we'd raise or books you'd write, photographs I'd take—humanity would survive chaos."

No pressure. The thought blooms with disparaging sarcasm. *No self-importance.*

Aloud I say, "The Great Compression."

Taja nods once. Adds, "Somehow those small things would help this world *align and...*"

Silence. We meet eyes. "What else?"

"She said you'd leave me."

"I'll never leave you." Said automatically, autonomously. And also not true. Only partially true. Not true at all in any way. "I always return to you." Amended.

"But it's not me."

And there it is.

She sees me. I see her.

"Not her either."

She's right. I don't want her to be but she is.

Again with the confusion, the shock, the blurting, "Why would she tell you?"

"Because she wanted me to choose, Remington."

"But we did! We—"

"But *I* didn't."

Right. Of course.

She bows her forehead to mine and whispers, "Perchance to love."

Her own literary illusion and a dark one at that. Perchance the dreamless sleep after death? Perchance the sleepless nights after love is lost.

"A chance you're willing to take?" I ask her.

Taja leans back a little, sizing me up. "Now you ask consent? After how many worlds?"

Touché. That expression, that sass. So familiar. "Are you sure you're not—"

"Yours?" She smiles at me. "I am. Her? I'm not. And you're not my Remi."

My mouth opens. No words. Then only, "I'm sorry."

"I wasn't in love with my Remington."

Haven't I had enough surprises for one day? A hundred lifetimes?! "But—"

36

"She was my best friend. And she was also very straight."

I erupt with laughter and Taja joins me. We both know it's awkward and sad but that part remains unspoken and we laugh because it's a release we can manage.

We wind up shifting closer together, moving into one another's arms—for the last time?—and leaning back against the emerald green pillows I bought her at the bazaar.

I try for honesty, I reach for transparency for the first time in too many years. "Each mission objective is different. The same end goal but different means of getting there. I... I just have to love you."

Taja leans her head down a little lower; she's a head taller than me, after all. The green of her eyes is amplified by the silk pillows. "And leave me. Over and over again."

Collateral damage. But I don't say it.

"Is my heartbreak what keeps us all alive?"

Her honesty puts mine to shame. "I don't know."

Taja nods. She doesn't move away from me.

"Perhaps," she's thoughtful, pondering. "*Her* mission was to tell me. To let *me* choose." Taja looks at me pointedly. "To let you choose. Again."

I hear my own gasp. *Pick again, Remington.* "Oh."

"Remington." She kisses me. "Don't leave."

It may be that love will be our downfall. It may be that Taja—my Taja—has gone rogue across the timelines. That she exists in the fringe of chaos. That she's rewriting the rules. I have no way of knowing.

All that I know is this: I can cease to breathe but I cannot cease to love her. No longer can I walk—or fly or fall or jump—away from her side. To hell with everyone else.

"I want you."

Let stardust run through the hourglass. Let humanity go to

seed. And let those seeds plant a hundred million new worlds.

Time can be unraveled but not Taja Tangali.

Never my love.

AN INTERVIEW WITH JENNIFER DiMARCO

When did you start writing and why?

I started writing seriously (six to ten hours a day) when I was ten years old and my first therapist suggested I try journaling to help me communicate better. My parents—I have two moms—bought me a 300-page blank book and I decided to write a 50,000-word novel where women were oppressed for generations but finally rose up in both peaceful and not so peaceful ways.

(If you're wondering how a ten year old had that much time to write every day and still attend school, I will admit that it was this same time that I started sleeping less and less and it was only about a year before I was bussing an hour to and an hour from school.)

Why this all began was touched on in *Terms of Service*, my story for Prompt November which appears in the Prompt Autumn edition. What I didn't touch on was: I was an incredibly late reader and never learned phonics.

The elementary school I attended believed in the

memorization approach to reading. Hanging from giant jump rings, students carried "keywords"—index cards hole-punched in one corner. A teacher would write a word we liked on each card. At any time, any teacher (the entire school—first through sixth grade—was open concept without walled classrooms) could ask us to start reading (reciting) our keywords and if we "read" one of the words wrong, the card was ripped in half and thrown away. Looking back, I'm not surprised I couldn't read a sentence—let alone read (or write!) an entire book until I was in fifth grade.

I wrote that first novel in a personal shorthand—building sentences and characters with misspelled words as much as with symbols and personal cues that would remind me what word I wanted there. My vocabulary was thick with words parroted from adults and I was constantly being praised for my eloquence and comprehension… but my ability to both encode and decode were severely lacking. And while I continued my educational experience at small, alternative, arts-focused schools, it wasn't until taking Latin in high school that words started to really make sense.

It probably comes as no surprise that I was adamant that both my children learn phonics—even though they both hated it! I'm very pleased that both of them spell better than I do.

Which authors or books influenced you the most as a writer?

Before I answer this question, I would be remiss not to mention: I love science fiction because I love science. Science has always turned on my creative brain; it excites and incites me. Physics, chemistry and mathematics concepts have been the flashpoint of all of my best work.

And now for an answer: While I enjoy a good action adventure or mystery novel as much as the next reader, I do see these as escapism and I don't read to escape. (For escapism I tend to turn to painting, boxing, hiking, or woodworking.)

Because my greatest literary love is surrealist science fiction (what has come to be called "New Weird" in the industry) my rare and precious pleasure reading is also the reading that inspires and incites me. Namely:

Richard Calder (*The Dead Things Trilogy*)
Jeff VanderMeer (*The Southern Reach Trilogy*)
Charles Stross (*Singularity Sky, Glasshouse, Accelerando*)
Clifford A. Pickover (*Time: A Traveler's Guide*)

Before someone calls out the fact that there are no women on this list, yes, I am very aware of that. I wish there were more women writing in the field of surrealist science fiction. And while I adore the arching ideas and characters in work by Octavia E. Butler and Nnedi Okorafor (specifically The Xenogenesis Trilogy and The Binti Trilogy, respectively), Butler and Okorafor feel familiar and welcome to me, and when I read, I want to be unseated, to question what I know and expand my perception.

I will say that I recently read Amal el-Mohtar and Max Gladstone's novella, *This Is How You Lose the Time War*, and will absolutely be exploring more work by both of them so perhaps Amal will be the woman writer I've been looking for. (Though I'm very glad the phrase "woman writer" is no longer bandied about the way it was when I was younger and was afraid to write under my name, opting for the genderless "J. DiMarco" for the first ten years of my career.)

I will admit, I'm not someone who reads or enjoys everything written by an author; I can't stand campy, B-grade humor or high fantasy or formula mysteries or romance—the list goes on. There are way more genres I don't care for than I do! I am far more inspired by specific books and stories than by authors themselves and their entire body of work. But this may be because I tend to enjoy eclectic authors who create in diverse genres.

I think the only other authors I would add to my list of influences would be the poet Adrienne Rich (*Fact of a Doorframe*) and the novelist Jeanette Winterson (*Written on the Body*). I suppose there are two women for my list of authors who made me see the world in a new way.

Which authors or books had the biggest impact on you as a person?

In contrast to the work that influenced me as a writer, the authors and prose that were influential to me personally are a bit more wide-ranging in several ways. With sociopolitical commentary, explorations of power and recovery, and authentic journeys of grief and isolation, these are novels, nonfiction, and short stories by a spectrum of authors.

Neal Stephenson (*Snow Crash, Diamond Age*)
Leslie Feinberg (*Stone Butch Blues*)
Patrick Califia (*Doc and Fluff*)
Minnie Bruce Pratt (*S/He*)
Katherine V. Forrest (*Emergence of Green*)
Camille Paglia (*Sexual Persona*)
Lauren Wright Douglas (*In the Blood*)
Herb Montgomery (*The Apple and the Envelope*)
Taro Yashima (*Crow Boy*)
Katsuhiro Otomo (*Akira*)
Philip K. Dick (*Do Androids Dream of Electric Sheep*)
James Patrick Kelly (*Think Like a Dinosaur*)

I think, more than anything else, the inherent dichotomy of my life is on display in that list. What a wonderful sense of freedom!

For more than thirty years, I've run a 501(c)3 nonprofit dedicated to bringing the work of marginalized authors, musicians, filmmakers, and game designers to the public. All work that speaks to the human condition honestly and that strives to break stereotypes and clarify misconceptions is eligible—whether created by a conservative Christian or a liberal social justice activist. And while I don't think any of my artisans wish me ill, I am very aware that many of them would not hesitant to vote for a candidate who would consider it a great victory to annul my marriage to my wife.

To say that I have dedicated my life to empowering and amplifying the voices of storytellers who are dynamically different from me—all while presenting only the G-rated "Earth Mother" side of myself to them—would be an oversimplification but also true.

Which of your original twelve Prompt stories are you most pleased with?

When the Prompt project began, we were told the goal was to turn in our best prose every month. I took this very seriously. On average, for work, I write 45,000 words a month. (Which was a fun average to find over ten months in 2020.) The grant applications, emails, letters, reports, and scripts that make up that word count often leave me wanting to do anything except write more. I willingly dive into every CFO task on my desk—from taxes to budget sheets— just for a chance to play with numbers for a change. Yet every month in 2019, the first project I completed was my story for Prompt.

My goal was always the same: That each story be better than my last… or at least be the best thing I wrote that month. So while I consider "When Time Unravels" or "When Wanda Woke the World" my best stories, it was "Social Box" that was made into a feature film in 2020 and it was "Unilateral Agreement" that I'm most asked to present as a guest author.

If I absolutely had to pick a personal favorite, it would have to be "Lost in Translation."

Which of your original twelve Prompt stories did you find the most difficult to write?

This question is a little easier to answer. When writing "Fireworks" I stalled about five hundred words in. I knew exactly the story I wanted to tell but my own life experiences kept wanting to infiltrate and obliterate the character's. It took me longer than I care to admit to excise my demons so I could write about Geraldine's.

The strange thing is that while the hardest to write, "Fireworks" is not my least favorite story nor do I consider it, ultimately, unsuccessful. That backhanded award goes to "Statement Island." I consider "Statement Island" to be a failure because the medium is indisputably wrong.

The story is set adjacent to a fictional locale my wife and I considered exploring together in a team-written, episodic novel. The characters might reappear but the focus would be on the lawless wonderland Faregrounds. I was so enthralled with my original concept of Faregrounds that I couldn't get it out of my head. But I also knew the full arch I wanted to explore wouldn't fit in a short story and I'd promised to develop it with Brianne—not craft it alone for a solo project like Prompt. The resulting compromise with my own brain was "Statement Island" and perfectly illustrates why I'm not a big fan of compromise.

What book on writing do you recommend?

This is such an intensely personal choice. Instantly I want to say Natalie Goldberg's *Writing Down the Bones* and William Strunk Jr.'s *The Elements of Style*. But I think far more important than which book or books you read is that you actually take the time to educate yourself about your craft.

This is perhaps my biggest pet peeve in this field. So many people think being a writer is just writing. (Others think that just having a "one of a kind idea" is being a writer.) And maybe writing is indeed all it takes. But the way I was raised and educated in this particular art, anyone can be a writer… but being a writer is very different from being an author.

Arrogant? Stuck up? I hope not because it doesn't take a degree or special tools or an expert editor in your back pocket to become an author. It does take discipline, research, more research, and growth. But I'll get to that in the next question.

What advice would you give an unpublished writer?

It amazes me to this day how many people (how many published writers!) don't perform their due diligence. If a lawyer or doctor slacked off the way I see so many authors do on a daily basis there would be hell to pay or even lives lost. These authors are very lucky that their only consequences are tiny royalty checks.

I suppose, ultimately, these are writers, not authors. They are willing to write—maybe even write up a storm!—but they are not willing to handle the myriad of other tasks that make a writer into an author.

"Some people just want to write. They just want to be writers. Not everyone wants to be an author." My seventh grade creative writing teacher first said that to me. And this is why I still count many writers among my friends. Because some receive all the joy and fulfillment they want just by putting pen to paper, just by crafting with words. I value and appreciate their passion for prose.

But I'm going to pretend that this question is asking: "I want to transform from a writer to an author. How do I do that?" This is my advice—just my opinion—on exactly that.

1. Take a creative writing class... without telling anyone you're published already (if you are). Don't go into the class thinking you know everything and don't share your laurels or you'll wind up on a pedestal and won't get real feedback. Pick a night class, community college class, or continuing education class with lots of peer critique and sharing. Go into the class determined to learn at least one invaluable thing.

2. Select and read at least two books on the craft—one written by an author that touches on the writing life and one written by an editor. Keep in mind that you need to know the rules of punctuation, formatting and grammar so that you know when it's okay to break or bend them.

3. Research! Research! Research! When writers say they don't read in their genre, I immediately consider them to be immature. Imagine a doctor saying, "I didn't do an internship. Or talk to other doctors. Or research the procedures I'll be specializing in. I just do my own thing." What I really hear when writers don't read is, "I don't like to read. I'm better than anyone else out there already. There is nothing more for me to learn."

Not only must you be educated in your genre but you must also be knowledgeable about the publishers and supporting magazines and blogs who publish in your genre. That's the second kind of research.

The third plea for research: God—and good fiction—is in the details. One of the most cringe-worthy things I've run into is when a writer will quote a statistic in a story that has been disproved or worse: Debunked. Hearsay is not fact. As a matter of fact (pun intended) if your boss at the cafe says, "Cherry pie is the most popular pie in America. Pitch the cherry." That may sound like a statement of fact but it's still just opinion. Until the fact has been verified by a third party or accepted as an industry standard across an industry, you're just spouting opinions (at best) or fake news (at worst).

Did you work as a zoo-keeper for thirty years? You can say, "In my experience as a zoo-keeper between 1973 and 2003, the penguins were the most popular animals." But you shouldn't make the statement, "The year was 2020 and penguins were the most popular exhibit."

Due diligence. Do your research and know the truth. Not just opinions, hearsay or rumors. Not just what you want to be true.

4. Write every day. It can be a journal entry, a personal letter or email, or on-going work on a story. (Technical writing, marketing copy, reports or writing for work doesn't count.) Do not allow yourself to have days when you don't write. Remember Malcolm Gladwell's statement about 10,000 hours of practice resulting in mastery? I think we all realize that's simply not true but it is a great start. Every minute helps.

5. Quality. Not quantity. I used to feel jealous when a peer was writing 6,000 words a day while also working an eight hour job. Then I saw their work.

Slow down. Edit and revise as you go. Don't be afraid to delete and start again. I call this my "active draft."

6. Struggle with spelling? Grammar? Punctuation? Or maybe you just want to catch more mistakes and create cleaner work? Consider a paid subscription to Grammarly (which catches more than the free version and can be applied to a word processing document).

7. Read your work aloud slowly and dramatically to yourself and revise more. I call this my "second draft."

8. When completed with a story or novel, take a week or more away from it completely and then come, read it over silently and revise it again. If you're finishing a story on the deadline, you're already a week late. I call this pass my "final draft."

9. Send your "final draft" to at least two people who love to read in your genre and who are willing to give you controlled critiques. What is a controlled critique? This is when you send your final draft and five to ten specific questions for someone. Examples:

- Do you find Susan likeable?
- Did you come across any plot holes or things you felt were unrealistic?
- Does Tony need a dog or cat to soften his image? A turtle?
- Was it believable that Kate didn't call the police right away?

Don't make your beta readers work too hard by giving them generic, nonspecific questions. Be smart enough and know your work well enough to spot where problems might lie and ask those questions. How will you know how to spot these problems? By being well-read in your genre.

I call these readers my "master readers" and I select them carefully so that I know and trust their insight. Make any changes suggested that you agree make the story stronger... even if it means you have to throw out a whole chapter or make another major change. Don't be afraid of hard work.

10. Last but not least, I never hire a freelance editor and I have never been asked to. My work has seen three drafts (plus any revisions made after your master readers make suggestions) before it ever goes to the editor at my publisher. Only the opinion of that editor matters to me. He or she will determine if the work is publishable.

Do you have a "dream project" as a writer? What would it be?

I think every fan reading this interview is shouting, "The release of *The Wind Trilogy*!" While all three volumes of the trilogy were actually written as one tome in 1989, the original publisher (and both subsequent publishers) divided the epic into three books and only the first two were ever released.

And while life (raising and educating two children, facing illness, having a time-consuming job) has delayed the final "Author Approved" edition of the work, I gently like to remind people that I wrote *Escape to the Wind*, *Fall Through the Sky*, and *Drinking Silver Wine* when I was sixteen. How would you feel about internationally publishing something you wrote when you were sixteen when you're forty-seven?

If you haven't grown and changed and matured and improved as an author, you might feel excited and delighted to release your teenage prose. But that isn't who I am or where I am in my career.

At first, I told my current publisher and editor that I would not feel comfortable releasing *The Wind Trilogy* until I had a current novel ready to publish simultaneously. In this way, people could see the journey I've taken over the last thirty-one years.

But in the end, *Body of Work*—the compilation of my thirteen stories written for Prompt—will be the work released alongside the trilogy. Another compromise. But one I'm more comfortable with.

My dream project would be a novel I began several years back that explores what it means to be sentient and why happiness and contentment are not synonymous. I wrote the first 10,000 words and then made the mistake of allowing the work to be read by another author who said, "The quality is astronomical. The tension and richness of the language is almost painful to read. You'll never be able to keep this up. Dial it back. Phone in a few scenes."

Never, ever, tell someone to dumb their work down. Why?

Because too many writers will listen to you and do it! The "dumbing down" of art—specifically prose—adds to the dumbing down of us as a people. The National Center for Educational Statistics reported in 2020 that 21% of adults in the United States (about 43 million) are illiterate or functionally illiterate. That statistic breaks my heart.

The original twelve Prompt stories were written in 2019. In 2020, we all experienced a global pandemic. Did the pandemic impact your writing? How?

I definitely had less time to write during 2020. My focus had to shift to paying the bills, aiding our at-risk artisans at work, and spending every remaining hour applying for grants, creating safe events and platforms, and organizing a rotation of the Board of Directors at Blue Legacy.

But all the same, I managed to sneak in some projects that were very special to me: In March, I wrote a children's book, *When Longneck Learned to Love*, about a small dinosaur learning self-love and my son, Maxwell, illustrated it. Then in August, my daughter, Faith, illustrated my children's poem, *Take Flight!*, about cute little fruit bats and it was published as a children's book. Finally, in October, *My Patchwork Heart*, a children's book about a woman who finds a dog who may or may not be real but who, nonetheless, teaches her that the things we love don't wear out, they just get worn in, was released—also with illustrations by Faith.

Of course, I also wrote *When Time Unravels*, my final story for Prompt. And I was hired to write two feature films in 2020 and seven short films.

Overall, I found writing hard in general in 2020 because my head was full of noise. This resulted in me needing to tuck myself away into absolute quiet when writing. I normally have a song that matches the ambiance of the piece I'm writing and I'll listen to that through headphones on repeat until I'm done writing but that wasn't possible in 2020. I hope that skill returns as the world heals and we all slowly start to move forward because my home is rarely quiet!

P.S. As of March 2021, I am able to write to music again and was moved to tears by the return of this skill; The return of my personal normalcy.

LAUREN
PATZER

THE YEAR THAT WAS

Captain Damien Strontum absently flipped his long pony tail back over his shoulder. His dirty blonde hair was tied up with a piece of fabric similar to the reflective blue tunic he wore. He reached forward and pressed the record button.

"Captain's log January fifteenth, I think. For purposes of keeping track here on Unity, it's the Terran year 2055. I confess I haven't been following the Terran Space Authority guidelines with keeping a log every week, but considering TSA ceased to exist a year ago, I didn't figure I would be in much trouble for it."

Damien paused and took a sip of the hot liquid in his coffee mug. The tea composed of varying spices they could grow in the hydroponics bay tickled his nose. He looked down at the tea and swirled the cup around, causing the tiny leaves floating in it to create a small liquefied tornado. He smiled for a moment and then set the cup down. He looked up at the recording camera.

"Unless something extraordinary happens on our journey, this will likely be my last entry. Beyond leaving a record for whatever intelligent race finds our ship, I don't see the value in making these entries." He cleared his throat as he rubbed his beard thoughtfully. "I know the children aren't going to listen to them."

He leaned back in his chair and looked around the room. "A year ago, something happened on Terra. I thought we'd gotten past war especially after the Mycean outbreak of 2026 that wiped out nearly half the world's population. That event brought a long lasting peace as well as a temporary break to the stress on the planet's resources. Twelve billion people dropped to just under six billion in the space of a few months, but those left behind continued to prosper and breed, so within twenty years, we were again reaching population levels that stretched the resource capabilities on the planet. That's why ships like the Grayson were built. Long range harvesting ships capable of mining and extracting other resources from the asteroid belt and beyond."

Damien looked down again and shook his head. "We had such a bright future ahead of us." He seemed to zone out for a few moments and then blinked rapidly and returned his attention to the camera. "Something happened. Director Sheppard—"

A knock on the door interrupted his train of thought.

"Son of a—" he muttered and reached forward to turn off the recording.

He set the drink down on the desk and took the five steps to the door. He opened it and frowned at his second in command, Lieutenant Victoria Driesen. She stood at attention and held up her chin. Her blonde hair was tied up tight in a bun, not a strand out of place. Damien stroked his unruly beard absently, but didn't say anything.

"Sorry, Damien. It all came at once and I felt a little overwhelmed," she said and winced a little.

Damien sighed. It had been a trying voyage to say the least. "What's going on?"

"Emergency beacon has come up for the Tennyson," Victoria replied. "It appears to be drifting and hasn't responded to any hails. There's an atmospheric leak in a rear storage module on the Orion where we were joined. It's already sealed off – nothing perishable in that section. And, Doctor Tanjea has called three times for you in the last hour."

Damien rubbed his eyes and took a deep breath.

"She said she'd just find you on her own, so…"

"So, if you didn't interrupt me, she would've anyway," Damien finished. He stepped out of his room and shut the door. "Let's walk."

Victoria fell into step next to him as they headed to the front of the ship.

"Get Bowers and Simpson on the repairs since they're the ones who connected the ships in the first place. They should be intimately familiar with their own work."

"I've already notified Bowers," she nodded. "Simpson is still, um…"

Damien stopped and Victoria took two more steps before stopping as well. "Okay, it comes into focus a bit better why you came to get me. What's the status of the Tennyson?"

"Just the signal. Weak at first, but stronger as we've locked in on it and maneuvered in that direction. No response to our hails. But we do have a location now. Better than we've had for weeks."

"Set a course to intercept. If she's disabled, we may have to match her trajectory so we can dock. If you can handle that, I can handle Simpson. Get Bowers and his team on that leak. We'll see how the engineering team he's built can handle this. Probably more revealing than test welds in the shop."

"He's been a little gruff with them," Victoria said.

"Our options are cantankerous or drunk. I'll go with

cantankerous for the moment," Damien said. He turned around and headed aft.

"What about Doctor Tanjea?" Victoria shouted.

"I'm certain she'll find me," Damien replied and waved. Victoria turned away and headed back to the bridge.

Damien walked on for maybe two more minutes before he observed a certain brown eyed beauty heading his way. Doctor Illyana Tanjea was on the warpath and he knew why. He slowed his walk as she barreled toward him.

"Damien, why haven't you come in?" she hollered at him before she'd reached him.

"Illyana, so nice to see you," Damien replied.

She came to a stop in front of him and looked up at him. She was six inches shorter than him, but he suspected she could take him in a fight. She wasn't just a brilliant doctor; she was also tough as nails. He looked into her eyes and regretted it almost immediately. He could get lost in those brown pools so quickly.

He smiled and pointed in front of him. "I'm just going to see our resident drunk. Maybe having you along would be good for diagnosis and treatment?"

"Fine," she replied and stepped to the side so he could continue walking. She fell into step next to him.

"I've been busy," Damien started.

"We need to start planning the next generation," she replied. "I've made the lists. We need to review them together."

"It just seems so clinical and sterile," Damien replied.

"We can't treat the future of the human race lightly," Illyana replied. "We can't afford randomness. We need to plan this meticulously."

"But there's no romance, no personal connection," Damien said as he walked. They passed by the hydroponics bay and he glanced in to see several crew members tending to the budding plants growing there.

Illyana grabbed his arm and stopped him. She pointed into the hydroponics bay. "The human race faces the same possible extinction as those plants in there. If not cared for meticulously and planned to the last detail, we'll face the end of our species."

"I prefer to think of humans as a little more complex than plants," Damien chuckled.

"Damien, we need to start soon. Several females are entering their cycle and the time needs to be soon to get this process going."

Damien sighed and resumed his walk. "See, just that. Entering their cycle. You talk like that and it seems so…"

"Scientific?" Illyana replied.

"Detached," Damien replied.

"Look, I know you're feeling loss for Doctor Shepard's passing," Illyana said.

A cloud passed over his face and for a moment he was back on the moon base, going over technical details and smelling her freshly washed hair tied up in a towel. It had taken the sting out of the loss of his family on Earth. In a moment, he recalled the sidelong glances, the smiles and the inevitable hookup in her quarters on the base. They'd found solace in each other's arms even though they had different reasons for doing so.

"We've all lost family and people we care about," Damien said.

"You need to be with Anna Callen tomorrow," Illyana said.

"Our botanist?"

"She has already begun her cycle. There's a small window of opportunity for a successful pregnancy," Illyana said.

"Look, I know we can't store the sperm, but I've said maybe two words to her since she joined the crew from Delta. Isn't there someone I've at least talked to more that I might be better suited for?"

"This isn't about romance, Damien. We have four hundred fifty-nine humans from which to propagate the rest of the species. We have to differentiate our offspring as much as possible to reduce birth defects and maximize—"

"I know why, Illyana. It's just... we're all still human. We're not lab rats." Damien sighed.

"We're going to have to adjust. Our society will need to be comfortable with this for a few generations. At least until we get somewhere permanent to settle."

"This may be our permanent settlement," Damien said.

Illyana looked down. He glanced over and could see her breathing harder than the walk required. He stopped. She stood up tall and wiped her face. On impulse, he pulled her in for a hug and she didn't object.

"We're all human, Illyana. Even you," Damien whispered.

She relaxed into his embrace and cried into his shoulder for a minute.

"I guess I'm just concerned that because we're human, this will lead to some complications of the emotional variety among the crew," Damien said as Illyana sniffled and stepped back.

"We're not designed for space travel, Damien. There's no telling what will happen to us once we've been in space for several generations. It may change us so much we can never go back to a planet's surface."

"That doesn't encourage you to wait?"

"We can't wait. Every moment there's a possibility someone will die and we'll lose that genetic diversity our future may depend on," Illyana said. "Maybe a ship wide conference to explain we can't tie ourselves to antiquated societal norms anymore. Child birth and child rearing will be different for a while, maybe forever. I don't know. I'm sorry, I can explain the technical details, but the emotional aspects are just a little beyond me."

"Well, we may have more diversity to choose from soon. We've found the Tennyson," Damien said.

"You still need to start the process with Anna. We can manipulate genetic diversity with these choices, but we can't choose the sex of the children. We are looking at an uncertain breeding future. It will take a while to obtain and review the genetic profiles of whoever we get when we connect with the Tennyson. Anna should be pregnant before then."

"OK, matchmaker. I'll plan a rendezvous with Anna. Do you think she'll want flowers?"

"She's a botanist. I'm sure she would if we had the capacity to grow such things." Illyana smirked.

"I was thinking of looking up a picture of one," Damien said.

"She may enjoy the thought even if it wouldn't be much of a surprise to show her some of her life's work," Illyana replied.

Damien came to a stop in front of a nondescript door. The number 179 next to it seemed a little dusty. "Hmm, I think we may need to check the air scrubbers," Damien said as he ran his finger along it and collected a small amount of dust. He shrugged his shoulders and knocked on the door. The door opened and a disheveled redhead stared out at them. The reek of alcohol was immediate and overpowering. Damien and Illyana wrinkled their noses.

"Oh, hi, asshole," Alan Simon said as he gave a flippant salute to Damien. He nodded to Illyana. "And the good doctor." He burped and turned around, walking back to his bunk.

"What the hell do you want?" Alan said as he sat down.

"Ahem, we're concerned about your state of mind. Clearly,

you've been drinking again," Damien said.

"Fuck if I care, asshole. Anything else? I'm busy," he said as he pulled out a small bottle and took a swig.

"How did you even get alcohol?" Illyana asked.

"It's amazing what you can do with a couple potatoes, a little yeast and some sugar. I brewed it back on Delta. Got a couple years worth stashed around the ship. You can stop by for a little nip any time Doc," Alan said and then looked at Damien. "But not you, asshole."

"Alan, you need to stop drinking," Damien said.

Alan jumped up from his bunk. "Or what, asshole?" Alan shouted as he got in Damien's face. "You gonna throw me off the ship, big guy? You already took everything I loved, why not take my life too?"

"You lost her long before I came into the picture because of your drinking," Damien hissed.

"Big man on campus gotta fuck my wife? We still had a shot until you pushed your big cock in her face," Alan growled.

"Jesus, Alan," Damien said. "You become a real charmer when you're drunk."

"Well, it's all I got left, asshole," Alan said. He turned around and slammed the cabin door.

"That seemed to go well," Illyana said as she turned from the cabin and started walking back in the direction they'd come from.

"We're all human. Alan's perhaps more human that any of us," Damien replied.

"I didn't realize Doctor Shepard and he were—" Illyana began. Damien held up a hand.

"They'd been divorced for two years before everything went to hell on Earth," Damien said. "The only one imagining them getting back together was Alan."

"He lost everything in the accident on Delta, then," Illyana said.

"Well, clearly not his precious alcohol. Now I know why he volunteered to recover all the supplies we could gather from Delta after the accident. He must've smuggled it aboard in the legitimate cargo," Damien scratched his head.

"We've all had to adjust to circumstances beyond our experience, Damien," Illyana said. "Alan was an alcoholic, a welder and now a useless piece of the crew."

"You have him setup with someone on board? Maybe a little time in the sack will chill him out. Give him something else to live for," Damien said. "A little sex might break him out of his funk."

"There are side effects to increased alcohol consumption on the male reproductive anatomy," Illyana said. "Given his history and continued consumption, I didn't put him on the list at all. The likelihood of him producing any viable sperm is incredibly low."

"Damn. He really has lost everything."

They came to a fork in the hallway. Illyana nodded to Damien.

"I expect to hear of a successful coupling within twenty four hours," Illyana said.

"Coupling," Damien chuckled. "So romantic."

"Promise me," Illyana said, looking at him sternly. He looked into her eyes and felt that yearning for real connection again. He smiled.

"I promise," Damien replied holding up his hand. "On my honor."

"Good," Illyana said. She turned and walked away. Damien stood there for a moment watching her go and his imagination took a small flight of fancy for a moment.

"I'd hack that list, if I could," Damien murmured. When Illyana had turned another corner out of sight, Damien returned to his progress toward the bridge.

Minutes later, Damien walked onto the bridge to the chatter of technicians and scientists debating the status of their wayward sister ship. Victoria approached him as soon as she had a moment.

"Still no communication with the Tennyson. We've established an approach vector. Should be around twenty-six hours before we get close enough to attempt a docking," Victoria said as she stood at attention.

"At ease, Victoria. We need discipline on board but not that much. How are the repairs going?"

Victoria brightened up at this.

"Mister Bowers is suiting up now with two other maintenance technicians. He said it shouldn't be a problem. This is exactly what they'd been training for."

"Good. I want them back inside before we start any docking procedures with Tennyson. It's going to be complex enough without worrying about losing someone on a space walk."

"Of course. As for the Tennyson, we'd like to use the same remote drones that found the external leak on our own ship to look for any external damage on her as well," Victoria said as she pointed at a visual schematic for a drone on one of the bridge monitors in the science officer's area.

"That's great initiative, Victoria. You're going to make a fine Captain one day." Damien grinned and his second in command noticeably blushed.

"Not any day soon, I hope, sir," she replied with a grin.

"Maybe sooner than you think," Damien said with a sigh. "I'll be heading up the boarding party on the Tennyson. You'll be in charge back here. Space isn't very forgiving. Something goes wrong over there, you may need to make some hard decisions."

The lieutenant looked down for a moment and then back up

at Damien, a firmness present in her face that he hadn't seen before.

"We don't leave our people behind, sir," she stated.

"You do if they're dead and there's nothing to be done," Damien said. "We don't know what's happened on Tennyson. We're going in literally blind. We'll get some ideas on her status from those drones, but not what's going on inside. That's a big mystery. I don't like mysteries in space, but she is chock full of them."

"No argument there," she replied.

"I'm going to go help Bowers if I can. Just keep track of things here and…" Damien frowned. "You know, if you could go tell Simon he's been selected to be on the Tennyson boarding party that might get him out of his funk. It would be great to get him engaged in something other than his own misery and stashed vodka. Be complimentary, flattering even. He's a valuable asset if we can get him back on track."

"I'll do what I can, sir."

Damien nodded and exited the bridge.

He made a side trip to the hydroponic facility for a short chat with Anna. On the way, Damien mused that it may be the first time he'd ever been with a woman he didn't have to woo and impress in any way. It was a simple scientific transaction for the survival of mankind. So clinical, so detached. Did that make it worse or better?

He entered the module and looked around at the opaque tubs filled with plants. Several people filled the room with varying levels of activity. He watched a young man simply cocking his head quizzically at a tub of greenery and another woman lifting a tray filled with plants and hanging roots while another technician examined clear tubes going into the tub below.

A blonde walked up to him and smiled nervously.

"Captain," she said with bowed her head slightly. "I'm Anna. You're here about our, uh…"

She frowned.

"We need to set an appointment, I'm told within the next day," Damien replied.

"Yes, it's just that," she looked up at him with tears in her eyes. "John's quite upset."

"John?"

"He heard there would be coupling going on and when he found out I was selected…" Anna wrung her hands.

"Are you dating?" Damien asked.

"We've had a few sit downs. We haven't even kissed yet, but… I'm afraid this will mess everything up with him."

"This is a purely biological connection. There's no romance. Not that you're not lovely, but I can assure him I have no designs on continuing a relationship outside of this encounter."

"Well, I'm not sure he's going to just forgive a one night stand or one week or however long this will take."

Damien noticed the dark circles under her eyes.

"You're not alone. This is a big adjustment for everyone. I'll make an announcement."

"He doesn't know it's you," Anna said as she looked down.

Damien gently raised her chin with his fingers. She looked him in the eyes.

"Honesty and openness is going to be more important than ever now. We've only got each other to rely on in a harsh universe. I'll take the worry out of revealing this for you by making it public for everyone. This isn't something that should be hiding in the shadows."

"Are you sure?"

"It's a new day. We can't just do things the old way. We have to adapt or die. Like the plants you take care of every day. They change to accommodate their environment. Change with the times, if you will," Damien smiled grimly.

"But, some people will hate you."

"Some already do," Damien sighed and winked his eye. "I'll see you in eight hours. It will be respectful and only last as long as it needs to."

Anna nodded.

"If it doesn't work out with John, I apologize for that. I wish there was another way, but our resources are limited as you well know."

"I know," Anna said. "I think he does too."

"I'll see you at the announcement hopefully," Damien said and patted her hand gently. He turned and left.

Halfway to the airlocks, Damien located one of the communication terminals. He pressed a button and got a single line comm-link to the bridge.

"Lieutenant, I need you to make an announcement. We'll have a ship wide all hands in two hours. The meeting will be broadcast across the intercom system to essential personnel who can't leave their duty stations."

"What's the subject of the meeting?" Victoria asked.

"Our upcoming rendezvous with the Tennyson and the future of mankind," Damien said.

"Light subject," she replied.

"Funny," Damien laughed. "If you could make the announcement, I'd appreciate it."

"Right away, Captain."

Damien clicked off the comm-link and sighed. He sniffed and turned back to his brief journey to the airlocks.

The ensuing space walk turned out taking more time getting into space and back from space than the actual work on the exterior of the ship. A few bolts had been missed during the original melding of the ships and a strut had come lose, lifting other components out of place. Replacing the bolts, tightening them down and applying some instaseal before welding took care of the issue. The repair wasn't just good as new, but better than new. On the matter of the instaseal product itself, it was one of a number of resources that was finite and irreplaceable. It was yet another factor pushing them to find somewhere habitable in the universe besides their temporary space ship home.

The morale boost for the maintenance crew at having the Captain take a personal interest in their work was a big bonus. It might have been different if the repair hadn't been successful, but for now, the maintenance crew was in good spirits. Considering the potential work ahead of them when they reached the Tennyson, Damien was happy to get their mood and confidence on the plus side.

Even with a few hours and some contention from Doctor Tanjea on his proposals, Damien felt he was ready with his directives for the crew. Truth be told, he wasn't entirely comfortable with them himself.

When the bulk of the crew had assembled in central mess, Victoria patched him into the ship announcement system for his presentation.

"My fellow Unity crewmates, I want to start by thanking you all for sticking with the rest of us through this adjustment period. We're coming on the last phase of assembling our final crew with the upcoming merger with the Tennyson. It's no secret we have a bit of a mystery on our hands with that ship. We haven't had any communication and she appears adrift. Our hope is the crew is fine and they're just having some problems with their systems. Let's just keep that in our minds as we pull up alongside our sister ship and prepare to board. We anticipate joining her within the next day. My request for you to join the boarding party will be coming to you shortly.

"We are on the precipice of a new chapter in humanity's quest for exploration and survival. Earth as we knew it is uninhabitable for probably thousands of years. As such, we've set our course for other possibilities in the cosmos. You and I will never see that brave new world. It will be the legacy of our grandchildren, great grandchildren or some generation beyond that to visit and colonize new destinations.

"We have only ourselves to start this new generation of explorers. As such, we're going to be doing things a bit differently. Our children will be a mix of everyone on board. It's the best way to provide a solid genetic baseline for future generations. In an effort to maximize potential and reduce birth defects, we have generated a system of matching pairs for a single birth. That system will be iterated for as long as each of us is fertile and can continue to contribute to the gene pool. There are only so many of us, so this is a purely scientific basis upon which we're making these selections. It isn't personal, it isn't salacious and it isn't romantic. As a people, we can't afford to cling to those concepts when it comes to childbirth and childrearing. We're literally a village, the last village of mankind and we'll have to join together even as we make sacrifices.

"This doesn't mean you can't pair up as a couple or whatever bond you feel is appropriate. It does mean that children will be created by selection, not romance. We're all going to raise this next generation together. All the children will be everyone's children. We can't afford to approach this any other way.

"As such, I've instructed all pairing selections to be public. There is no reason to keep it a secret. Get used to it. I'm not comfortable with it either, but I see the need to get over it. Reach outside my comfort zone. I only ask that you be respectful and caring when you're performing this duty. It's not how we'd like it to be. It's how it must be.

"Secrets don't help us as a society. Starting in two weeks, we will also make all medical records publicly available. If anyone has medical issues, it won't be a secret. It will also be accommodated where possible so those people can continue their contribution to our society. Until we receive additional crew from the Tennyson, there are only four hundred fifty-nine of us now. We are all we have. Let's be supportive and respectful and we will survive. We are the future of humanity. Thank you."

The murmurs started before he'd even finished, but he wasn't waiting around for discussion. He'd read every personnel file and he knew who the main objectors would likely be. Most of the personnel had a heavy scientific background. He wasn't expecting much resistance from them. The blue collar types were the ones he expected most of the resistance from. Anyone who had formed bonds with someone else on board might very easily get protective, defensive and problematic. On the other side, this was very much a burden on the female crew members. Some of them may indeed be very resistant to being directed to get pregnant and give birth especially with someone not of their own choosing. There were a small number of crew who had sexual identity concerns that would have to be navigated with some care, but he hoped there would be some understanding among them as well. Then, of course, there were those who didn't like being told what to do under any circumstances.

He was a few steps down the hall before he had his first surprise. Silvio Donner, his primary materials research scientist, fell into step beside him.

"Damien, I have some concerns," Silvio said.

"Really, Silvio?" Damien replied as he continued walking, his step even and unhurried.

"It's not typically something I advertise, but I am religious," Silvio stated.

"And?" Damien said. "Do you have a religious objection to our course forward?"

"God intended a man and a woman to be married and faithful to one another," Silvio started.

"Abraham, among others, had multiple wives in the Bible, Silvio. It's not like I haven't thought about this. But tell me, what of God wiping out nearly all of humanity? Seems to me there was a promise of some sort made that he wouldn't do that again." Damien continued his normal pace forward. Silvio seemed to stutter step a bit as he thought about his response as well as trying to maintain pace with Damien.

"It's not right," Silvio responded.

"Silvio, we're very much back at ground zero as a race. Be it like Adam and Eve or after the flood, there are only so many people to go around. If we don't do this with an eye to science, we'll suffer birth defects in a generation or two that may be insurmountable. We're already up against the unknown of conceiving and raising children in space. Sure, we have the rotation of the ship providing a semblance of gravity, but it's not exactly equivalent to Earth's and we're facing other unknowns like cosmic rays among other things. As a scientist, you must realize this is the only rational path forward."

They continued on in silence several hundred feet before they came to a fork.

"I'll have to think on this," Silvio said as he stopped. Damien turned to him and grabbed his shoulders gently.

"This is medical science we're talking about. We can't afford to not think two or three generations ahead with every decision we make. There aren't any do overs. This is it. Do the math. In the Bible, there were unconventional solutions to the number of breeding pairs available to humanity. I'd say our solution isn't anywhere near how controversial that would be to modern day society." Damien smiled.

"It seems wrong," Silvio said.

"I won't argue that," Damien replied. "But we'll have to get beyond our own sense of normality for the good of the human race. Look, none of us ever thought we'd be in this situation. We're doing the best we can with what we've been handed, okay?"

Silvio nodded and gave a grim smile. Damien patted him on the shoulder, gave him a wink and left Silvio standing there as he continued on his way.

Hours later, Damien couldn't believe how nervous he was about the appointment with Anna. After some fumbling and apologies, they eventually were able to get the deed done. He never thought it would be so difficult. Anna was attractive, but there was no doubt she wasn't into it and neither was he. The act was purely physical and even barely that. As he left their appointment, it weighed heavily on him that this situation was going to be more difficult on the crew than he'd ever imagined. He was at a loss how to make it easier. It defied societal norms they'd all grown up with. The relationship triggers were hard wired into their brains.

When he got to his quarters, he took a look at the chronometer on the wall and realized he'd been up for over eighteen hours. The rendezvous with the Tennyson was just a few hours away. He needed some rest. Maybe being well rested would benefit his next appointment with Anna.

When his alarm went off four hours later, he felt like his head had only just hit the pillow. He groaned as he sat up and felt the soreness that had overtaken his body.

"I'm not getting any younger," he whispered as he rubbed his eyes. He took a deep breath and got up. As he dressed, a knock on his door made him sigh.

"Enter," he announced. Victoria opened the door.

"Just wanted to make sure you were awake," she said.

Damien chuckled.

"And when did you sleep last?" Damien asked as he pulled on his shoes.

"I slept for a full eight while you were still up for eighteen hours straight," she replied as she leaned against the door jamb. He noticed her blonde hair was down and flowing around her shoulders. It was a good change.

"Well, I'm glad you can sleep so easily," Damien replied as he stood up.

"Whoever said it was easy?" she replied as she stepped out of the way.

"Well, we don't have much in our supplies that help with sleep," he said as he stepped out into the hallway. Victoria fell into step beside him.

"We've recovered a lot of vodka in the last twelve hours hidden all over the ship," she said with a smirk. "Couldn't resist a little nightcap myself to calm the nerves."

"You trust his brew?" Damien raised his eyebrows as he looked her direction.

"Definitely had it tested beforehand. Plus, since he used Delta supplies to make the illicit brew, I figure that makes it everyone's property," Victoria smiled. "Properly rationed, of course."

"Of course," Damien shook his head. "You know, Victoria, I think you'll make a wonderful Captain after all."

"Thank you," she replied. "But don't go off retiring just yet. We have a few things to tackle together first."

"You're very confident today," Damien replied.

"First coupling," she replied. "It wasn't half bad. He has a really cute ass too."

"I'm glad it went well for you."

"Could've been worse, could've been better, but under the

circumstances," she sighed. "It was a welcome change. Wouldn't have been something I'd have done on my own."

"I'm sorry if you felt used," Damien replied.

"It wasn't that," she frowned. "As someone on the command staff, developing a relationship with someone on board can appear as favoritism. Fraternization has always been looked down on. With this development, I can get a release from those concerns and maybe enjoy myself for once. No attachments, but an outlet for some frustration. Oh, and he enjoyed a bit of vodka as well."

Damien smiled. "At least it will go well for some," Damien turned serious again as they stepped onto the bridge. "How is Tennyson looking?"

"Dana," Victoria said to a woman manning a console a few feet away. "Could you bring us up to speed on the latest with the Tennyson?"

"Yes, sir," Dana Stillson replied. She flipped her long braided back hair from in front of her onto her back as she turned to face them. "We've matched Tennyson's rotation and speed. The drones found a cracked window in the command module large enough to vent atmosphere from within."

"From a collision?" Damien asked.

Dana shook her head.

"It appears to have come from within, but with rapid decompression, the origin of the damage is hard to pin down."

Damien nodded.

"Further evaluation of the entire vessel noted no exterior damage," Dana said. She punched a few buttons on her console and the main screen on the bridge lit up with a schematic of the Tennyson. "As far as we can tell, all the other systems would remain intact. There are several bulkheads in place that may have closed to seal off the rest of the ship, but with no way to get help from outside, they may have limited capabilities to repair the damage and rescue themselves.”

Damien walked to the schematic and pointed at several points along the side of the Tennyson.

“These are all egress points from which a spacewalk could’ve been initiated,” Damien turned to Dana. “Why wouldn’t they have utilized them and gotten things repaired?”

“Sabotage,” Anna’s voice stated from the bridge entrance. Everyone in the room turned to look at her.

“That’s a great guess, Doctor Callen,” Damien said hesitantly.

“It’s not a guess,” Anna replied. “Sabotage. I felt it an hour ago.”

“Felt it?” Victoria asked.

Anna looked down. She will her fingers to stop fidgeting.

“I evidently have latent psychic abilities that have only just surfaced,” she looked at Damien. “A result, I suspect, from activities I’d never engaged in before. It’s not just sabotage, I sense. There’s death, fear and anger as well. Primarily fear.”

“Are the people aboard the ones who committed the sabotage?” Damien asked.

“Captain,” Victoria began to object but Damien just held a hand up.

“We’re in completely new territory in more ways than one, Lieutenant. Any information we can get will be helpful.”

“I don’t think so,” Anna said. “But, I’ve only just begun to handle what’s going on. I can’t be certain.”

“Thank you, Doctor Callen. We’ll take every precaution. You might want to check in with Doctor Tanjea just to be sure everything is okay with you,” Damien nodded his head respectfully toward Anna. She smiled grimly and left.

“Captain,” Victoria said quietly. “It’s not scientific.”

"Not everything is understood as well as we'd like to think, Lieutenant. The universe has many surprises in store for us, I'm sure. We need to prepare for all contingencies we might face on boarding the Tennyson including a hostile reception."

"Well, I can't argue with that under any circumstances." Victoria nodded and turned to Dana. "Let's make sure the entire boarding party has access to this schematic."

"Even Mister Simon?" Dana asked.

"Especially Mister Simon. He's going to be in charge of the engineering party," Victoria said.

"Alan Simon?" Damien asked hesitantly.

"It's amazing what an alcoholic will agree to do if you promise him access to a few bottles of his stash that was confiscated." Victoria smiled.

"I'm going to pin those captain's bars on you myself," Damien murmured so that only Victoria could hear.

Victoria winked at him.

"Boarding party is suiting up. I'll be here waiting for your orders," Victoria nodded, all business once again.

Damien left the bridge.

In the ready room, Damien walked in to find the other ten members of his boarding party suiting up including Alan who looked at him and then shook his head. Damien chalked it up as an improvement that he didn't say anything disparaging. Twenty additional technicians assessed their health, suits and all the interconnecting systems assuring they'd survive their anticipated exposure to the cold vacuum of space.

An hour later, with comms checked and half a dozen members armed with non-lethal weapons as well as tools, the ship extended the connecting tunnel to the Tennyson. Magnetic clamps in place, they disembarked through the large airlock into the tunnel which was void of atmosphere. Alan and two other technicians attached the necessary clamps and pry bars to get the outer doors of the bridge airlock open. Even as they prepared to crack the shell of the other ship, Alan directed the other two technicians back. If there was still pressure inside the ship, it could blow a tool through one of their suits.

Alan ratcheted the mechanical system to open the door just a crack and was relived there was no burst of atmosphere forcing its way through. The airlock was indeed empty of any air pressure.

The two technicians came back to the door and they pried it the rest of the way open. The process was designed to go slowly to reduce the damage to the internal mechanisms of the airlock door. Once inside the outer airlock, they went through the same process on the inner airlock door to much the same effect. The bridge inside the ship was also empty of atmosphere.

The eleven crew crawled through and the tedious process of sealing the outer door began. While the three engineers worked on the airlock doors, Damien and the rest of the crew ventured throughout the bridge that was a mirror of Grayson and Orion's bridges. With the proper repairs, they'd have three redundant systems to get them through their long journey to an unknown destination.

"Captain," one of the other crew said over the comms. It was Eric Rodriguez, the operations manager from Delta. He'd been a fantastic addition to the crew, helping coordinate the increased resources and personnel. "We've got human corpses here."

Damien looked over and saw the ruptured remains near a science console. They'd been flash frozen in the vacuum of space. It was hard to tell if they'd been dead before the bridge had been compromised.

"Another over here by the breach," Suzanna Breyer said over

the comms. Damien made his way over and noted the scorch marks on the inside of the ship around the breach in the thick window.

"Fire and maybe an explosion," Damien said.

"There's nothing in this console that would have caused this much damage," Suzanna said. She would know. She was one of the original computer scientists on the design team for the bridge systems of these ships.

"Can this be repaired to where it's functional again or are we looking at a bridge full of spare parts?" Damien asked.

"This section is redundant even on board the Tennyson. You can safely seal up this breach, not access any of this equipment and the Tennyson would be fully operational. Assuming..." Suzanna trailed off as she disconnected the diagnostic equipment. She turned away from the console and walked the length of the bridge. She stopped at an unassuming pipe on the wall. Using a screwdriver, she removed a panel from the pipe and attached the diagnostic equipment to it. After a few seconds, she turned to Damien.

"There are no signals between here and the rest of the ship. This bridge is entirely cut off. It's still repairable, but curious. This is why we couldn't talk to the ship. There's no way for the communication array to reach the redundant systems behind the bulkheads."

"Couldn't they use the rear array?"

"Not if they couldn't get out to do a spacewalk," Suzanna said. "It's intentionally disconnected from interior systems to protect it in case of an overload. But it's not designed for a full system disconnect. There are redundant lines running along both sides of the bridge and they've been severed. The rear array has a line on the outside of the ship, but by design it wouldn't be damaged by the kind of systems failure we're seeing here."

"Doesn't seem like a very good backup," Damien said.

"It's not a backup, per se. The system is already designed with a backup which has been disabled. That damage combined with the disconnection of the redundant lines points to intentional sabotage by someone. Possibly that someone who is wedged beneath the command console," Suzanna pointed back toward the front of the bridge.

Damien walked forward and saw a body wedged under the front of the command console directly across from the damaged window. Char marks on the front of their suit suggested they'd been at the window and console when it exploded.

"Suzanna, if you were a saboteur, where would you pick on this bridge to breach the hull?" Damien asked.

"Probably a window at the front of the bridge where there was an unused redundant console I could hide an explosive charge in. But captain, that charge wasn't inside the console. It was detonated on the surface. Someone had to make that happen manually. It would've been noticed otherwise."

Damien looked at the console and again at the figure wedged under the console. He couldn't argue with the assessment. He walked back over to the other two bodies on the bridge. He examined the front of the bodies and then turned them over. One of them had a clear puncture wound in the fabric of their shirt. They'd been stabbed in the back. He was no expert on anatomy, but he figured the injury could've punctured the heart. Death or incapacitation would've been nearly instantaneous.

"Alan, the bridge is a relatively small area. What effect would it have on the rest of the atmosphere in the ship if we sealed the bridge and opened it to the rest of the pressurized ship, assuming the rest of the ship is pressurized?"

Alan stepped forward from inside the airlock.

"We've got the outer airlock door resealed. If the other

bulkheads aren't in place and it's just the one, that's a lot of pressure if it isn't slowly introduced. You could blow out the seal on the window and expose the entire ship to a leak."

Damien nodded. "Well, we better make extra sure our leaks are well sealed. I want to get through that bulkhead and see if there's any crew on here to save." Damien changed frequencies. "Lieutenant, get Doctor Tanjea on the line. I need to assess the danger of slight decompression on the other crew members."

"Of course. Just a moment, she's right here."

There was an audible click and then Doctor Tanjea got on the line. "Captain?"

"Doc, here's the situation. If everything goes according to plan, our sister ship's remaining crewmembers will experience a slight change in atmosphere. The bridge appears to be void of air pressure, but our plan is to seal it. I'm assuming the rest of the ship still has pressure. Will they be able to handle the slight change in pressure or do we need to take additional precautions?"

"There might be some discomfort in their aural canals similar to a drop in pressure from descending a couple hundred feet in altitude. But, it should be temporary and confined to their ears. There should be no other dangers as long as the pressure change is slight. Too much of a change could cause serious rupture of membranes like eyes, but they're generally well suited to slight changes. Just be careful and everything should be fine," Illyana's voice was calm and professional. "Have you contacted the survivors to prepare them?"

"We don't have communication as such," Damien replied. "They may not even realize we're here."

"If they're alive, they know something has changed," Doctor Tanjea replied. "When we connected our ships together, we increased the mass and slightly changed the gravitational properties of our combined ships. There was a little bit of shaking as well. You may not be able to hear anything in space, but inside a ship you can feel these changes and hear the grappling system connecting the ships when they contact the hull. If they're alive, they know someone has at least connected to the ship. Given the timeline of the communication loss... they may not know what happened to Earth. That's more of a concern than their physical well being."

"Yeah, if they've been able to maintain everything else, they have enough food and supplies to survive. If nothing else, they'll assume we're a rescue ship which, in a sense, we are."

Alan stepped up to him and tapped his helmet. "Sorry, Doc. Gotta go. We'll be in touch with our results. We have three dead, so prepare for up to the complement of the ship minus three for medical triage."

"Understood." Damien clicked over his comms. "What is it, Alan?"

"Well, if you're done flirting with the other ship, you'll be happy to know we've got the inner airlock secured and the instaseal is curing. I'm prepping the bulkhead for opening. Same as the outer airlock but with a greater likelihood of an atmospheric burst."

Damien nodded and yawned. "All right. Let's get this show on the road. Thank you," Damien smiled at Alan who just rolled his eyes and turned to walk toward the bulkhead. Damien shrugged. At least they weren't at fisticuffs.

The bulkhead procedure turned out to be less dramatic than anticipated because it was one of several they need to open. The air inside each sealed section lessened the change experienced by the whole.

After the first bulkhead, the telecommunications and engineering sections there were searched, but found to be empty except for four decomposing bodies. They'd been stabbed as well. They hadn't been exposed to the vacuum of space, but the temperature had been reduced in the section. While the reduced temperatures had slowed the decomposition, it was still clear they'd been dead for a long time.

The next bulkhead opened and the air pressure seemed to even out so there was barely a perception of a change.

"Readings?" Damien said over the comms as he glanced briefly at Maria Chang, the nurse they'd brought to handle casualties and immediate triage if necessary.

"Normal readings for a moderately maintained recirculation system. Breathable, but a bit stagnant," Maria replied glancing at the air sampler in her hand. "Slightly elevated CO_2, but it's breathable and no significant contaminants."

"Let's open up our suits, but keep the weapons handy. We don't know what to expect," Damien said.

It didn't take but a few steps for them to find the unexpected. As they rounded the corner and entered the mess area, a man with months long hair and beard growth dressed in shiny clothing stood up on a makeshift throne at the other side of the room. To either side of him, chained to the sides of the throne, two undernourished women groveled at the base of the throne. Their hair was a tangled mess and they were dirty as well. The chains connected to metal collars around their necks and bands around their wrists. They were otherwise naked.

The shiny dressed man pointed a shaft of wood topped with a long blade.

"You have entered the realm of Jebediah! You are not welcome! Leave at once!" He took two steps down and poked his stick at them threateningly.

"Wilbur?" Alan Simon said as he stepped forward. "What the hell are you doing?"

"Wilbur?" Damien asked.

"Wilbur Dribury. He's one of the Tennyson's cooks. We used to, uh, have a drink now and then."

"This is my domain! Leave now or suffer the consequences!" Wilbur took another two steps down the throne.

"Wilbur, knock it off! This is serious!" Alan shouted.

"I don't go by that name anymore! You've been warned!" The man leaped from the throne and charged them.

"Light him up," Damien said.

Alan shook his head, raised the stun gun and fired. It struck Wilbur and he staggered a bit but kept coming.

"Again," Damien said.

One of the other technicians raised another stun gun and fired. This brought Wilbur to his knees and he dropped the staff.

"Avenge me!" Wilbur shouted before he fell to the ground and shook with the voltage running through him.

The two women at either side of the throne raised their heads and looked up at the ceiling. The tiles that had been a solid mass had been broken up and Damien got a sinking feeling.

"We might have attackers overhead," he advised the crew before the technician who had shot Wilbur suddenly grabbed his neck and fell to the ground with a scream.

Damien caught a hint of movement near one of the tiles and fired his own stun gun. He missed the target, but the leads got tangled with the metal rafters and after a moment there was a scream and a single figure fell from the ceiling to the ground, dropping a small cylindrical weapon. The wiry assailant shakily got up to their feet and stumbled awkwardly trying to escape, but they were disoriented and slammed head first into one of the support poles. They went limp and fell to the floor.

"Sparrow!" Wilbur cried out. He tried to get up, but he was still disoriented by the stun charges.

"How about we restrain Wilbur and see if we can find out what's going on," Damien said.

Maria tended to the fallen technician. She turned to look at Damien and held out a small sliver of wood.

"Careful, this is what hit Jamal in the neck. Probably some kind of tranquilizer. His breathing and stats are stable, but I don't know what kind of long term effect this might have."

Damien carefully took the sliver and held it up.

"Better restrain that other assailant too," Damien said.

"We didn't exactly bring handcuffs," Alan grumbled.

"This isn't exactly the battle mission I signed up for either, Alan," Damien replied. He initiated comms with Unity.

"Unity, we have apprehended two individuals and are evaluating two more for injuries. Jamal has been injured by an apparent tranquilizer dart. We're looking for other survivors," Damien said. He walked over to the two naked women with Suzanna and Maria at his side.

As he approached, the two women shrank back in fear. He stopped. Maria put a hand on his arm.

"Maybe Suzanna and I should talk to them. They have likely been..." Maria trailed off and frowned.

"I understand," Damien said as he looked over at Wilbur lying on the ground. "See if they can tell us where the others are, what happened, anything that can get us answers and find the rest of the crew."

Maria nodded and went with Suzanna to the women.

Damien walked over to Wilbur lying on the ground.

"They're my property! You can't have them!" Wilbur shouted. The battered women cried out, fear still ruling their minds.

"Gag him," Damien grumbled to Alan who was helping the other technician hold Wilbur down.

"I'm the king!" Wilbur shouted before Alan shoved an oily rag in his mouth and tied it off around his unruly head of hair.

"You just lost your crown," Damien replied. He stood up and started to walk toward the other prisoner.

"Guess you've still got yours," Alan grumbled.

"What?" Damien said and turned around.

"You're telling the women what they should do, who they should be with. You're no better than Wilbur here."

Damien paused for a moment and frowned. "It's not the same thing," he said.

"Isn't it?" Alan replied.

"Huh, maybe it is," Damien said. "I think you've earned your drink." Damien turned around and took a deep breath. Was he wrong? He looked over at the women Suzanna and Maria helped as they wrapped shiny emergency blankets around them from the first aid kit.

Was mankind best left to chance and fate? Without free will, what were they trying to preserve?
He looked at the unconscious attacker and then back at Wilbur. "We're the shining future of humanity," he sighed.

AN INTERVIEW WITH LAUREN PATZER

When did you start writing and why?

I've been writing stories since before I could even handwrite properly. I remember typing things out on my grandparents IBM Selectric typewriter when I wasn't even in Kindergarten yet. Of course, the stories were likely unintelligible, but that didn't stop me then. Hopefully, it hasn't bled through to my current works.

I always felt I had something to say, stories to tell and bits of my subconscious that were screaming to be shared. I've answered the inexorable call of my psyche to share what is in my head.

Which authors or books influenced you the most as a writer?

Ray Bradbury, J.R.R Tolkien and Robert Heinlein were probably my earliest influences. Bradbury's ability to essential flow between the genres with his tales has probably influenced me the most in my own storytelling goals. I don't like being pigeonholed into a single genre. It makes marketing a challenge, but it keeps my storytelling consistent with my heart and soul.

Which authors or books had the biggest impact on you as a person?

It's really hard to narrow that down. There are so many different facets of stories and storytellers out there. The breadth of talent and perspectives keeps life interesting and that's reflected in the variety of tales and tellers out there. Honestly, the variety of people who've told their stories and the stories they've told has a bigger impact on me as a person than any single tale or teller. It's shown me that there are possibilities for all writers to share the tales burning within them and that someone out there will likely read and enjoy it. I think that really drives me more as a person and writer than anything else.

Which of your original twelve Prompt stories are you most pleased with?

'The Most Dangerous Thing' is probably one of my all time favorites. The fall of society with the unexpected twist at the end so nearly mirrors humanity's very real history. I feel it speaks more truth than any other story I've written even as it highlights so many lies.

Which of your original twelve Prompt stories did you find the most difficult to write?

Progression is without a doubt the toughest story. It's more emotional than anything else I've written. While it's not a territory I normally explore, I found it rewarding. It's hard to edit your own story when it brings tears to your eyes.

What book on writing do you recommend?

On Writing: A Memoir of the Craft by Stephen King is one of my favorites. It really gets to the heart of why you write as much as actually crafting the tale.

What advice would you give an unpublished writer?

I didn't truly start to grow as a writer until I joined a writing group and experienced critiques of my writing form other writers. I was a member of one for several years until I eventually reached the point where the critiquers were not giving me any worthwhile advice any longer. I had, in a sense, outgrown that stage. It's an important one, though.

When you create that first draft, it's important to do it without a lot of editing. Get the story down, get those element s on the page and empty that story from your mind so it isn't jumping ahead to other parts while you go into your editing. The importance of editing cannot be emphasized more and if you've never experienced critique of your work, can you truly approach it with the idea it can be improved? A writing group let's you know everything can be improved and that first draft is almost never in good enough shape to deliver as is. As your writing experience grows, perhaps the editing becomes less extensive and more of a nuts and bolts spelling and misplaced phrases or words kind of endeavor, but if you've never been critiqued (and never critiqued others), you hardly naturally have the skills for editing.

My first novel, while it went through several self-editing passes, suffered by not having a professional editor go through it. When you've reached the point of novelization, you need another set of eyes to look at what you've put down and honestly help you correct errors you simply can't see because you're too close to it. My first novels had editors that worked with me to correct my own faults. I learned so much from them, as much as I did my first writing group. My current editors are a bit more hands-off, expecting a fully editing final draft product, but I couldn't have gotten to the point of producing that without the layers of editing and critique I'd gotten over the last decade.

Do you have a "dream project" as a writer? What would it be?

I'd probably go with mysteries. I've always been fascinated by the works of Arthur Conan Doyle and Agatha Christie. I'd love to be able to craft a story that gets mystery readers snuggled up on a couch with a cup of hot tea or cocoa reading late into the night wanting to know who the killer is.

The original twelve Prompt stories were written in 2019. In 2020 we all experienced a global pandemic. Did the pandemic impact your writing? How?

I think it has impacted my writing negatively. I get inspiration and energy from others. If I'm not able to be out, socially interacting with others, I feel as if my creativity suffers somewhat. I've found myself watching more television than ever and it is simply because I'm not compelled or inspired to write as much. Some of that may be environmental—my writing computer is in the same room as the television for the family. I can't escape the electronic distraction often. I can't head to the library anymore or the local coffee shop, so getting away from family activities to do serious writing has suffered.

HIROMI COTA

THE GODS OF AMERICA ARE DEAD

Content Warning: Suicide

No shit.

Not a single iota of shit.

If you had a shit detector with millishit tolerances, it wouldn't make a sound.

The fuck were we talking about?

Right. Yeah. Columbia's dead. Columbia? The Spirit of America? Yeah, she's dead. That's not a metaphor. Well — it is, and it isn't; it's both. Both the demigod Columbia and the ideals that she represents are dead. She came into being somewhere around 1796, along with the first paintings of her. She was radiant, gorgeous, and powerful. Fucking capital P Powerful. She had to be.

Back then, the newly-styled Americans dreaming her up had to compete with the disrespect that the British wanted to hurl at the idea of America. And if that sounds like the job of an old softy, you're very much mistaken. Don't get me wrong, the idea of believing a new god into existence in the same land where there are already hundreds of them is pretty silly.

The former colonists could have saved so much fucking time if they'd just turned to Great Spirit or K'uk'ulkan instead of reinventing the wheel. That's America for you, though. Land of "If it wasn't made here, fuck it." American-made is a whole identity for a lot of folks, which might be why Americans killed Columbia. The Spirit of America wasn't actually American-made; she was made from bits and pieces of half-remembered lore from the Greeks and Romans.

I mean, let's be real here. Americans of the time weren't even American; they were Aniyunwiya, Powhattan, Virginian, or Massachusettsers or whatever the fuck the demonym for people from Massachusetts is. America didn't exist anywhere except on paper, so it's not really that big of a surprise that Columbia didn't survive into the era of modern Americans.

Anyway, Columbia's dead, and so's Uncle Sam. Yeah, no, you'd think he'd be around here somewhere. His face sure is. We all know him and his catchphrase. "I want you!" Shit's iconic. But when was the last time you saw him out in the wild? When did you really get the idea that the country was going to roll up its sleeves and put in some work alongside you? When did you last feel like your uncle was gonna give you a hand in tough times, or box the ears off someone who was coming for you? The years after 9/11, right?

Yeah. That wasn't universal.

Everyone was spoiling to fight after 9/11 and sensed Uncle Sam standing up. The problem is that a lot of Americans thought Uncle Sam was coming after them. And he was. Hell, he'd been coming after Brown and Black folks for a long time. That Black Lives Matter stuff outside your window? Nothing they're saying is new. Those are the echoes of protests from generations ago. Things've gotten better since then, but Uncle Sam never treated Black and Brown folks right. After the Twin Towers fell? Anyone even a little bit tan or fluent in another language was a target.

How'd this inequity kill Sammy-boy? Well, gods need belief to survive, and Uncle Sam had plenty of it at that point. Pissed off people believed that he would crush the enemies of the US. Scared people believed he'd crush them. That's faith enough. Fear's faith. Just ask Kali. No, don't. Nevermind. Forget I said anything. At any rate, with that much belief fueling him, you know he didn't starve. So, what the hell happened to him?

After US forces ground to a halt in Iraq and Afghanistan, they just sort of sat there, holding onto checkpoints and playing whack-a-mole with the few militants who popped their heads up, both sides killing civilians because they didn't trust anyone who didn't look like them. Operation Iraqi Freedom became OIF 1, then OIF 2 and 3. The generals kept talking about phases, but all anyone saw was literal lines in the sand being blown away by the desert wind. It wasn't the great military victory the hawks were spoiling for.

So, the blood-thirsty Americans stopped believing in ol' Sparklepants, leaving him almost entirely fueled by fear. You know what that's like? Being alone except for people who're deathly afraid of you? Can you imagine living knowing that you're the bad guy, that you're the boogieman that frightens children so much they cry themselves to sleep, not daring to peek out of their covers for fear that you'll get them? That's not what Uncle Sam was stood for, so he tied a rope around his neck and stopped standing.

Uncle Sam hung himself in the Alamo. It took a week for him to die.

In the vacuum, people stopped believing in gods and ideas and started putting their religious fervor in people. Any historian worth their salt can give you a long list of reasons why that's a terrible idea. Some believed in a Black man, others in the destruction of the same man. The one who'd stood behind Uncle Sam hoping to sacrifice blood for power were in the latter camp; they traded their anger of stateless terrorists for hatred of their neighbors.

Do you understand the power of hate? The worship power created by wanting to unmake someone? It's like a cloud made by boiling venom. Like all clouds, what they worshipped could look like anything. Sooner or later, they had no idea what they were doing, only that they liked worshipping and wanted to keep at it. So, they bowed down to whatever was in front of them. And they hated.

They hated. Haaate.

Science? They hated it. Hope? Hate. Equality? H A T E D

Next thing you know, deadly bits of the air in 2020 killed as many as a hundred 9/11s. Thanks for that, you fuckers. Your worship of the poison cloud fucked up everything. We still have hundreds of other gods here in the US, but with Columbia and Uncle Sam dead, the American gods are fading out. Which brings me to the next bit of bad news. You know that goddess with the scales and blindfold? Big-ass sword? Hangs out in front of courthouses?

Justice is on life support.

That sounds really dramatic and metaphorical, but it's not. The goddess Lady Justice has chemical pneumonia. Turns out getting gassed by the police every day for months is bad for everyone. She's still conscious and lucid for now. She's not even mad at the cops. They're her kids just as much as everyone who walks out of a courthouse is. She can't be mad at them, but she is disappointed.

One of her children in blue kills. Another of her kids holds up signs and spits in a blue kid's face. Tear gas flies. Blast balls detonate. A child in blue kills again. It's a bad fucking time for Lady Justice and her children. If she could get her blue kids to stop killing, there might be a chance to right the ship, but that's not going to happen as long as people keep bowing down to the Venom Cloud.

We can and should still believe in Justice even if we don't believe in the system that builds statues to her. Maybe even especially if we don't believe in the system. Without Justice, there's no America. That idea's baked into every protest.

No Justice.

No Peace.

When we stop believing in her, we stop believing that people have rights. We stop believing that society exists. And, for many marginalized folks, civil society's barely a whisper of a promise. If they lose that, if we take that away from them, they have nothing but the strength of their own arms keeping them safe. For many, that's practically a death sentence. If we don't fight for Justice, not only is there no reason to not burn it all down, there's actually several compelling reasons to slap the button marked "Vive la Révolution!" And that brings us to America's last god standing, the French immigrant: Lady Liberty.

Unlike all of the other American gods, she's doing just as fine as ever, relatively speaking. She stands on her pedestal, broken chains at her feet, and stares out at the Upper Bay. She's a symbol of freedom, a welcoming sight to anyone traveling to Manhattan by sea. And she's miserable.

Decades ago, she stood powerless as planes slammed into the World Trade Center behind her. In the months afterwards, she saw the Venom Cloud's rise to power. She watched it happen and did what she could to preserve civil liberties, but standing firm wasn't enough. It never is. She promised freedom, but the Poison Cloud offered patriotism, the ability to lash out at an unjust world. As the memories of boats headed past her to Ellis Island fade, she cries, mourning the echoes of an America that was less obsessed with power and control. Her tears fill the New York Harbor fifty feet deep.

And here we are, a present where the American-made gods are dead or nearly so. Sounds bleak, right? You're probably thinking that the Poison Cloud's won. But, that's not accurate. This isn't a battle between the gods. This is a battle between us and the gods. And we're winning; there's only one left, and we know how to fight hate.

We fight it with love, but not in the way that people usually think. You can't hug a Nazi so hard that they become something good. That's not the power of love, nor is it a realistic or fair scenario; victims of violence shouldn't need to forgive their abusers in order to live in peace. But we *can* raise everyone else up. Nazis are only bold when they have someone to stand on. When we take care of each, we're all the same height. And we outnumber the bullies. We'll never eradicate hate, but we can cover it in bubble wrap and smother its power.

Go help a soup kitchen. Defy curfew laws and food handling restrictions and give out sandwiches at a homeless encampment. Tell your crotchety relatives that Black lines matter. That trans lives matter. Donate to your friends who are struggling. Your donation doesn't need to be money to make a difference; sometimes kind words are all you can give and all anyone needs. Help each other. Stand up for each other's rights.

Four gods down.

One to go.

AN INTERVIEW WITH HIROMI COTA

When did you start writing and why?

I started writing very early in life, although I'm certain that if I looked back at any of my early stuff, I'd hate it. I won an award for poetry at some point in middle school. It got printed in the school paper, which was probably the first time my work got published. What I can remember of the poem is awful, and I hope it stays lost in the pre-widespread-internet era. I wrote tons of short stories, comics, and novellas as a teen. They got increasingly better, but I hope none of that stuff resurfaces, either.

I'm a big believer in the idea that you get better at writing by doing a lot of it, as opposed to agonizing over the minutiae. It's a messy process, but the end result is a stronger writer. I'm better *because* I wrote a lot of garbage. I can recognize the flaws in what I've created and can avoid those pitfalls in the future. Had I focused on getting everything right the first time, that single work would be strong, but *I* wouldn't.

Why I started writing is much simpler; I had ideas in my head that needed to come out. It physically bothers me to hold onto an idea for too long. (And this is true of most folks. Persistent thoughts are referred to as rumination, which is linked to a number of behavioral disorders. Many theraputic methods encourage getting unloading those thoughts.)

Some thoughts are fleeting and go away on their own, but others are more interesting and persistent. I have to externalize those ones, or it'll affect my mood. If I have a tune in my head, I'll sing or beatbox. If I have a story idea or a fun quip, I need to write it down. Some of these things are entertaining enough to me that I want to work them into a story for other people to read.

Which authors or books influenced you the most as a writer?

Oh, hell. That's a long list. At some point of my childhood, I was challenged to read as many books as possible and, for a long time, I'd just eat novels — at least one a week, sometimes more than one a day; it was ridiculous. All the big names in sci-fi and fantasy went into the woodchipper that was my brain back then: Isaac Asimov, Douglas Adams, Anne McCaffrey, Robert Heinlein, C. J. Cherryh, Terry Pratchett, Roger Zelazny, Stephen R. Donaldson, Ursula K. LeGuin, Frank Herbert, Orson Scott Card, the list just goes on forever.

And that doesn't even cover the wider world of books I got access to as an adult, like the works of Octavia Butler, N. K. Jemisin, and Jessica Hagedorn.

Trying to pick which influenced me the most is like picking which drop of water in the ocean is my favorite. So, instead of a direct answer, I'll cheat: Mary Shelley invented the genre of science fiction by writing *Frankenstein*, making her the most influential author to me.

Which authors or books had the biggest impact on you as a person?

Fuck.

I should have read all the questions before sitting down to answer them. Well, no one reads these because they want a formulaic answer; they read them to get a sense of who authors are, so you readers get to see me somehow paint myself out of this corner. You also get to learn that I have an above-average level of profanity. I was infantry for 8 years, and "swearing like a sailor" is not at all limited to the Navy.

At any rate, I'd say it's a toss-up between Douglas Adams,

Terry Pratchett, and Stephen R. Donaldson.

DNA ("Douglas Noel Adams" sometimes gets abbreviated to "DNA" among fans since "DNA" is shorter than "Douglas Noel Adams" or even the cover version of his name "Douglas Adams." So, I'm using "DNA" purely for brevity's sake) wrote a wide range of characters into his stories and made most of them likeable. Marvin, the paranoid android, has deep psychological disorders, which doesn't prevent him from being cool. As someone with chronic depression, that was reassuring to see.

Terry Pratchett wrote extensively about the inequities of society and life, crystalizing a lot of concepts for me. He made it clear that society is made stronger through diversity and through looking out for one another. A dog-eat-dog world is a dead end.

And Stephen R. Donaldson wrote a bunch of very well-written assholes. I did my best to not end up like them. I was definitely an asshole in my early 20s, but I'd like to think that I've become a much nicer person since then and that I've managed to avoid being as bad as Thomas Covenant or Angus. I mean, I've definitely been better than Angus; that's a ridiculously low bar.

Which of your original twelve Prompt stories are you most pleased with?

Oh, that's tough. I think January's "Inside the Blue Circle" is one of my strongest. A homeless, gender-fluid wizard couple that break time to see what'll happen? How can you not love that? On top of that, I got to play with typography to cleanly delineate between the genders as the characters shifted their moods.

The names @ and & were natural extensions of Alfred Bester's typographical experiments with showing telepathy in prose in his 1953 novel *The Demolished Man*. In that book, several characters have their names partially represented through symbols, like ¼maine instead of Quartermaine or Wyg& instead of Wygand. I took it two steps further by using symbols as the nuclei of the characters' names, which can then form the basis for gendered varients of their names. Thus, when @ feels femme, she's N@alie. When they feel masculine, he's M@. Special shout out to Professor Tom Foster who had me read *The Demolished Man* during my undergraduate work.

@ and & are such fun characters that I've been working on a

novella series for them to get into further mischief and break more rules. It's much further behind than I'd like, partially due to overloading myself with projects and partially due to the pandemic. They should come out the same year you read this, which isn't too bad of a wait.

Which of your original twelve Prompt stories did you find the most difficult to write?

May. Hands down.

My story for May wasn't originally "Be Fae! Do Crimes!" I was originally going to write something much darker and personal, about how the criminal justice system's thirst for closed cases and "good" statistics has a human cost that kills people and ruins lives. 2019 wasn't a big year for Black Lives Matter protests, but that didn't mean that police violence wasn't on my mind.

My original story took the subject of police violence seriously and was fucking heart breaking to write. I felt like I had to do right by the people directly harmed by police, and that's an impossible weight to carry. So, with a few days to go before my deadline, I took an entirely different approach to the same subject; I made it a power fantasy where this fae changeling got to do whatever they wanted, and the cops couldn't hurt them. The fae creature got to just live without having to worry about getting shot or clubbed or gassed, and who doesn't love the idea of being able to live without being hurt?

"Be Fae! Do Crimes!" was *way* easier to write than what I originally set out to do.

What book on writing do you recommend?

I've already hedged a lot and answered questions like this with, "There are a lot of books." So, of course I'm going to give a complex answer for this.

Read many books on writing. There's no one step, one-size-fits-all solution to being a better writer. If there were, there'd be no market for books on writing; we'd all buy the same book and be done with it.

We write different things and our brains work differently. I'm not even talking about neurotypical vs. neurodivergent writers, although that's certainly something to consider (and I suspect the professional writing community has a disproportionately large number of neurodivergent folks compared to the rest of the population; creatives are weird. We just are.)

If I process ideas differently than you do, it'll be a massive pain to get you to follow my writing process. I know this for a fact because I've been an adjunct English professor, a magazine editor, and a book developer. I've taught writing a bunch of different ways; it's not easy, and neither is learning how to write.

What works for one person may not work for someone else. So, avoid this problem entirely by not reading just one book on writing. Read a bunch of them. Take all the techniques and tips from them all and figure out what works for you. If you run across a tip that doesn't work for you, you don't have to put it in your toolkit.

And don't just read writing books for your genre. I get it. Books are expensive, and time is precious. But, read everything you can get your hands on. Make full use of your local library.

What advice would you give an unpublished writer?

Write garbage. **Write a lot of garbage.**

Acknowledge that your first few projects aren't going to be great. Give yourself the freedom to suck. And then write garbage. It won't be good stuff, but it'll be *your* words on a page. The more you write, the more you develop your voice and — hopefully — the more you recognize what you're good at and what you need to improve at.

Once you have a pile of words, you can fix what you don't like, you can find treasure to be used in a different project, or you can write something entirely new that's better than your first stab at it. You have options. But, write garbage first.

When you have something that you think is great, try pitching it to someone. You might get a rejection notice, but — look. There are a lot of authors out there who were still in their "write garbage" phase when they sold their first story by being in the right place at the right time. If you think you have a story worth reading, pitch it.

Do you have a "dream project" as a writer? What would it be?

It's probably no surprise that my initial instinct is to answer this with, "I have many dream projects." But, on reflection, I can actually narrow that down to a goal that's both abstract enough that I can share it and tangible enough that it can make sense to others.

I want to do what Terry Pratchett did; I want to develop a world rich with difference to allow a wide spectrum of tales to be told, critiquing society through the lens of humor. With a whole world in play, every aspect of our world is available for examination.

In the past, I've tended towards shorter work, which allows me to create worlds that readers only ever see a slice of. I work hard to make those worlds feel real and lived in, but I think it'd be satisfying for readers (and me) to stick around in a single world for a few years and get a real sense of it. These books would give folks frequent vacation in another world instead of a brief stopover like I've been doing.

The original twelve Prompt stories were written in 2019. In 2020 we all experienced a global pandemic. Did the pandemic impact your writing? How?

Uuuuuuugggggggggghhhhhhhhhhhhh (groan noises)

Yes. Yes, it did. In January 2020, I working on five roleplaying games, two plays, and three fiction series. I've had the shelve the fiction because it's so much harder for me to create worlds whole cloth than it is for me to write tens of thousands of worlds for a world that already exists. I also had to shelve the plays because we can't perform them anywhere. Getting the RPGs written was rough, but I did it.

Honestly, RPGs are pretty much the only thing that I've been able to write this year. The pandemic consumes a huge amount of mental energy because so many things are either impossible or ill-advised. On top of that, the news is a constant source of alarm because our soon-to-be-ex-president is consistently terrible. When presented with two options — each with their own pros and cons — he finds a third option that's even worse than the options that were on the table. As of this writing, 22 November 2020, we're at 256,000 COVID-19-related deaths in the US. And, that only covers the deaths directly related to the virus. It doesn't cover ancillary deaths caused by increased psychological and physical stress or from scarcity of medical treatment.

On top of that, both my spouse and roommate work from home now, which means that we each have to carve out our own space and time to work, which means we all mildly interfere with each other. And, we're well aware that this makes us lucky. Millions of folks have jobs that force them to stay out in public spaces and risk exposure to the virus.

It's a terrible year for everyone, but especially service workers.

Tip them. And keep tipping them after the pandemic is over. They deserve every penny.

AMBER

RAINEY

A KISS

She'd kissed me.

I was rooted to the spot, unable to move, the electrifying tingle still lingering on my lips from the brief pressure of hers touching them. My heart was pounding and I felt dizzy. It was a quick kiss, merely a peck, really, but it was the moment everything in my life changed. My brain was struggling to find the right actions to take but it was already too late. She'd disappeared into the crowd and I didn't even know her name. Something told me I'd waited my whole life for that moment. For her to come and wake me up.

I tried to shake myself out of my stupor, to pay attention to my well-wishers, and to celebrate with them. I tried to be grounded in the moment. I could worry and wonder about the kiss later. Perhaps it meant nothing to her, just a spur of the moment kind of action one takes when they aren't thinking. Perhaps she was just as excited as everyone around me. This was a momentous occasion and it was meant to be celebrated. I was supposed to be portraying elation, not utter shock.

My son grabbed my arm and it almost broke the spell. I looked up at him, staring down at me in confusion, and shook my head slightly. He'd gotten taller than me by the time he was twelve and now stood a good half-foot over me. He smiled a little half-smile that made his handsome face even more beautiful. It was his way of reassuring me, even if he didn't understand my consternation. I smiled back and then stared out at the people clamoring for my attention with glazed-over eyes. I still couldn't focus properly. Perhaps that was her aim, to throw me off balance, to make me make a fool of myself. No. A kiss like that could not have had any nefarious purpose. I had to stop and regain control of my thoughts. I wouldn't think of the kiss anymore. I had a duty to perform. I'd just achieved the culmination of my hopes and dreams and I should be reveling in my victory.

Patrick leaned down and whispered in my ear, "You okay, Mom?"

I nodded. He looked at me with skepticism but shrugged, turning to shake the hand of a man who'd stepped up to him, then throwing his arm around his wife. I had to get a grip. If not for my sake, then for the sake of my son and his family. I had a job to do and people were counting on me. I took a deep breath, pasted a smile on my face, and nodded to my campaign manager. She gave a thumbs up and headed to the podium on the dais. My son squeezed my shoulder and I patted his hand reassuringly. It was time to get back to business.

"Ladies and gentlemen, I have the distinct pleasure of introducing the next President of the United States. Please give a warm welcome to President-Elect Annica Charlton."

I smiled and waved as I went up to the podium. The cheering raised to a deafening level just before when the news had been announced on the big screen behind me. I was making history. I was the first female president ever elected to the office, the first atheist, and the first Libertarian. So many firsts. It was a huge achievement, one that I'd worked on for years... and yet the kiss still lingered.

My lips began tingling again from the memory. I'd get through my speech—it was prepared days ago and rehearsed ad nauseam so that I could say it in my sleep—and then I would celebrate with my supporters. The kiss would have to wait until I was alone.

AN INTERVIEW WITH AMBER RAINEY

When did you start writing and why?

I started writing when I was about ten years old. I wrote because it was the only way I could escape a less than stellar childhood. I was an avid reader and I loved escaping into books and novels but writing was my way of dealing with my childhood and the things I was not confident in telling any other person. I was very shy but always had a very active imagination. I am forever creating stories in my head and now that I get to tell them, it seems more are knocking around my brain than ever before so I have been trying to write them all out as quickly as possible. In writing, I can give myself confidence where I did not have it. I can make my characters be the people I wanted to be and that helped me a lot.

Which authors or books influenced you the most as a writer?

I don't feel like I am influenced as a writer much. I probably am and I don't recognize it. I am very cerebral when it comes to books, I experience them in my head when I am awake and dream about the characters when I am asleep. I try to solve their problems and I wish I could talk to them and make them understand what I see in them. It is the same for me with anything creative. I tend to process what I have read over and over again until my mind is satisfied with the outcome. I joined a group once to get constructive criticism on some stories I wrote but I ended up being more stressed and upset than if I just write what I want and edit it myself. I get very attached to my characters and they have lives outside of my stories so it is hard to see them impugned—for better or worse.

Which authors or books had the biggest impact on you as a person?

It is so hard to answer this question because I don't know if there are any that really haven't impacted me in some way. I read both fiction and non-fiction. I have to balance out the realities of the world with fictional worlds where the good guys always win. I absolutely adore books by Malcolm Gladwell because I agree with a lot of his conclusions and I am constantly recommending these books to people. I feel like his books really help people understand why humans interact with the world the way they do. Secondly, I have always been a person who has handled emergencies well and the book *The Unthinkable: Who Survives When Disaster Strikes - and Why* really gave me insight into why I am able to cope so well when others around me are running around like chickens with their heads cut off. As for fiction, I think there is only one book I have ever read that I didn't finish and I think I would start a war if I mentioned the name of the book because it is very much revered in the world of writing. I love good fiction. The biggest book that impacted me as a person was *The Grapes of Wrath*. I might be in the minority but I absolutely despised that book. I was forced to read it and do a book review on it in high school, which helped me the next year in literary criticism, but

I will never get back the time I spent reading one hundred pages describing dust. John Steinbeck was a good writer but *Of Mice and Men* is something I would recommend more, even with the very sad ending. I was reminded I never wanted to bore a reader with so much description that it became a chore to read.

Which of your original twelve Prompt stories are you most pleased with?

A *Different Holiday* was the story I was most pleased with for several reasons. First, I feel like it was my best story because I feel like I improved in my storytelling over the course of the year. Having a deadline of one story a month really pushed me to explore what it meant for me to be a writer and what kind of stories I wanted to tell. Second, I feel like my characters are braver than I am and I want that bravery in my real life. I am bisexual but have never come out to my family. My husband, son, and friends know but my actual brother and mother do not know. I feel a bit of sadness because the grandmother I was closest to never got to know all of the real me before she died. So, in that way, I was able to tell the story of someone who could be brave and live with those consequences even when it pained him to do so. Finally, I felt some relief that the whole project was successfully completed. I'd never written so much in one year for someone else's consumption. It gave me more confidence in myself as a writer.

Which of your original twelve Prompt stories did you find the most difficult to write?

The Last Broadcast was the most difficult to write. Last summer, our lives were completely upended. In the process of making a cross-country move, my husband's mother passed away. A week later, my grandmother and my rock passed away. She was the only person in my family that loved me for me in my formative years. We had several houses fall through and we were on a deadline because my father-in-law had Alzheimer's and was suddenly moving in with us. On top of that, we had to deal with our move and his move all within the same week and I ended up very sick. It was a completely hectic month. I feel like the story was me saying goodbye to my grandmother and trying to find peace in the chaos of my life. I cried several times and I stressed over deadlines. I had the story in my head but I couldn't get it to come out properly. I wasn't ready to say goodbye to her and I think that came across in my writing. I have since been able to write a story that I feel gives her a proper sendoff and it will be published next year.

What book on writing do you recommend?

Do y'all have some suggestions? Honestly, I have never read any books on writing. I have read books on other creative endeavors I do, like acting, but I am a very visual learner and a very visual person so reading about how to do something isn't very helpful to me. I can gather some reference points but I "learn on the job". I tend to write everything I am going to type out in my head before I ever sit in front of a computer. I have full novels and stories in my head that are not yet published because I have not taken the time to sit and actually commit them to a form someone can read. This process makes it look like I am turning in rough drafts when, in reality, I have gone through four or five drafts, at least, all in my head. I don't sleep a lot when I am actively writing a story and I could probably get a lot more if I would take the time to put what I have down on paper, but I feel like I am *living* with the characters if I keep them with me in my head.

What advice would you give an unpublished writer?

I will tell you what a very dear friend and mentor of mine once told me. *Never throw anything you write away!* I threw everything I ever wrote away from the time I was ten until 2014. There was so much potential thrown into the trash can or deleted that I will never get back. Even if no one had ever read any of that lost work, it could have helped me to see how far I have come. Another piece of advice—don't pay a press to publish your work. Vanity presses are not worth it and they don't really care about you as an author. Either find someone who believes in your work or self-publish and market yourself.   I am not great at the marketing part but if you are social media savvy you can really build a brand and get your name out there. Patience is key in this business. Finally, I would say don't write hoping you will make millions of dollars. The realities of how much an author makes might get you down, but if you have stories to tell, tell them. Don't let anyone tell you what you can do.

Do you have a "dream project" as a writer? What would it be?

Of course, I would love to write the next great American novel. I would love to write something that speaks to people the way books have always spoken to me. However, I have many passions and writing is a secondary passion for me so, for now, I just write the stories I want to tell and not worry about how they will be perceived by others. I am lucky to have friends that like the things I write and if none but a few ever read it, well then I will be happy knowing I was able to entertain those few people. My writing comes from who I am, who I was, and who I want to be and that is enough for me.

The original twelve Prompt stories were written in 2019. In 2020 we all experienced a global pandemic. Did the pandemic impact your writing? How?

Well, for one thing, it got me to get off my keister and finish editing my second novel. It took me several months of quarantine to talk myself into it but I was finally done doing absolutely everything else that would keep me from editing. It is very hard for me to do second round editing because I have to get back into a world and a mood to be able to find my character's voices again. I also worry that I am tapped out. It happens every single time but I still have stories swirling around and new ones cropping up, so I assume I haven't peaked in my writing career yet. I am very excited that the second novel is finished and it grew by so much that even I was amazed. I was also able to write another three stories for an anthology and one of those stories deals, somewhat, with the pandemic in a fictional world. I think it is a little too soon for the pandemic to completely affect my writing because I am still in the middle of it. I am still staying safe at home as much as possible and missing my old "normal" life. Do I think it will affect my stories? Absolutely, one day it will definitely affect them. Everything that has happened in my life affects my stories and I put a lot of me into some of the characters so I know that my quarantine life will stick in there somewhere. My stories are just starting to reflect things that happened to me four or five years ago so I assume in the next ten years or so, my stories will be affected by the pandemic.

MARSHALL MILLER

DEATH AND TAXES

ring out your dead. Bring out your dead."

The electronic recording of Mike Black's voice droned on as he maneuvered the electric corpse transport cart down the street. Mike started in the job yelling the phrase/request/command himself, then decided he needed to save his vocal cords. Thus, like the old ice cream trucks of old playing a jingle to attract customers, the broadcasted phrase, as well as an occasional refrain of AMAZING GRACE, helped to prod people to bring Mike the newly deceased.

Mike had been the Dead Man for a year now. The previous Dead Man became a 'customer' when he caught the New Death. That was about the same time the egghead scientists discovered about two percent of the population had a genetic immunity to the virus, the New Death. Testing showed that Mike Black had this odd set of genetic taggants and exposure to an early version of the New Death. Thus, a new immunity existed.

When first announced, some people resented those not affected by a virus. With a fifty percent mortality, if you caught it, the joke was that God flipped a coin. Heads you lived, tails you took it up the ass and died. That is if you were not going through puberty. During the teen years, the rush of hormones, up to about age 18, seemed to boost the immune system just enough to keep you from dying if you caught it. Injections of the hormones were used as a prophylactic. There were only so many injections around.

Of course, there there was the lucky five percent who survived, but the virus fried their brain. This group often became violent psychotics.

The very young died, the terrible teens lived, and the older folks died, some people's brains fried. Mike often laughed to himself as he could remember when everyone was screaming about the Covid-19, with a mortality rate of about five percent of the proven positive tests. Plus, most who died had pre-existing conditions or were over sixty-five. People in the U.S. screamed and pointed fingers at each other about who was killing who and ignored China and the Chinese government. And where did the New Death originate? That great petri dish known as China. And who once again sat on the information until people started dropping dead in the street? The Chinese Communist government.

Mike's father had said that two things stuck around: Death and taxes. He was one hundred percent right about death. Taxes were a hit and miss proposition with a collapsed worldwide economy.

Just over five years later and society in most parts of the world ground to a halt. People out of fear killed other people they thought were unfairly immune. Only the fact doctors could use Mike's blood as a prophylactic treatment through blood transfusions kept people from killing the Two Percenters in the U.S. That and the fact he could be a Dead Man, collect the dead, and not spread the disease. Thus, he had a new career.

Mike dressed in black and either wore a hood or the bird's head, Black Plague mask of the Middle Ages. He wanted there to be no question about who or what he was on the streets. He was the official Grim Reaper, now named the Dead Man, as he hauled off the dead.

This day Mike already had three corpses on the government provided electric cart. He worked alone except for one of the two ex-military working dogs. Today it was Ajax, a full-sized Belgian Shepherd. Dogs did not catch the New Virus, and they kept people in line. Sometimes people resented the fact that Mike piled the bodies on the open-air cart with just a tarp covering. However, what Mike did needed to be done quickly with easy cleanup. Having to disinfect a hearse took way too much time and effort. The dogs helped handle the brain-fried citizens also. The Dead Emergency Government, DEG, had seized most firearms the first year as people were shooting up what was left of civilization and would mob you to get your gun if given a chance. The dogs acted as a deterrent, along with matching throwing axes Mike carried. He also had an Arkansas Pigsticker Bowie knife on his belt. The Dead Man did not advertise the compact Glock 26 nine-millimeter concealed under his black tunic. Mike supposed he had one of the last boxes of ammunition for miles around.

Mike saw the Skull and Crossbones flag in front of the house as three teenage kids, ages thirteen to sixteen it looked, came out into the front yard. Mike maneuvered the cart towards the walk-in gate of the chain-link fence.

"Family member?" Mile asked in a subdued voice after turning off the recording.

"Yes, Mom and Dad," said a teenage girl just before she started bawling.

"You three wait here with Ajax. I'll bring them out."

"They're in the back, wrapped up."

"Thanks."

It made Mike's job more comfortable when there was a family who wrapped up the deceased. Sometimes, the rotting bodies sat for a month after the New Death claimed them. Mike then had to put on gloves and a gas mask to load them up while praying the body did not burst or break into pieces. Before the discovery of the Two Percent immunity, people dressed in Hazmat suits. In hot climates, it wasn't enjoyable.

Mike managed to maneuver the body cart to the side of the yard. He loaded the two bodies over the fence and onto the cart. Five bodies were not a heavy load.

Petting Ajax helped to calm the three kids. The dog was well socialized but could turn into a land shark if need be. Mike moved the cart back onto the street and handed each of the kids a chit. The policy was one per family, but Mike had ripped off the DEG Corpse Removal Office when no one was looking, so he had a crapload of the food box chits. A box of canned food for each teenager would keep them comfortable until they could find jobs or other family members for help. The regular monthly government dole no longer existed.

Mike continued on his route when a regular neighborhood contact approached. Mary Reilly kept track of who lived or died in exchange for occasional Salvage. If Mike had to take care of the body himself and there was no family around, he claimed Salvage. That meant Mike could grab anything the Dead Man wanted or felt the man needed, which he could also transport on the cart. When Mary helped, he gave most of the Salvage to her.

"Afternoon, Mary. Whatcha got for me?"

The once attractive but aged before her time blonde answered," Mrs. Hummaker at the end of the block. No one has seen her for a week."

Mike grunted and moved the cart to the house in question. He went up to the front door and pounded on the door and nearby windows. Five minutes later, Mike broke the front door down with a sledgehammer. He smelled death and put on a breathing mask to cut the stench. The woman was dead in the front room. She could have died from a heart attack but claiming her as a New Death victim was much more manageable, and no one questioned the Dead Man. Mike used bed blankets and sheets to wrap up the decaying corpse before dragging it out to the front door. The Dead Man then went through the house. Half an hour later, Mike gave the patient Mary a pickle jar full of coins, a gold wedding ring, and a can of beans all wrapped in a plastic bag.

"This should make it worth your while," said Mike.

"Thanks, Mike. You're a dreamboat. I'd kiss you but—"

"I know, the virus. See you next time."

Mike did not tell her that he had a wad of currency in his pocket and a small pistol stuck in his belt beneath his tunic. The owner of Mike's duplex home, Anson Baker, would help him dispose of the gun for a profit. Mike manhandled the body on to the growing pile of dead people and moved down the street. Some brave souls with Hazmat suits would strip the house within the next forty-eight hours.

The rest of the day was non-productive. As Mike made his way to the burn pit on the outskirts of town, a drunk citizen staggered up to him, yelling.

"You fucking ghoul, making a living off the death of others. Why don't you—"

Ajax sank his teeth into the man's ass. The drunk dropped his bottle of homebrew, screamed, then ran and fell into the roadside ditch. Mike laughed long and hard as Ajax growled and watched the man. The Dead Man moved the corpse cart towards the edge of town and the incinerator. The two armed military guards knew Mike and nodded as he passed with his load. He placed the bodies on the conveyer belt and stood by as the machine fed them into a massive incinerator. Open burn pits were used in some countries but not in the United States. People worried about infected ash.

An hour later and Mike was back at home. He stripped his clothes off and put them in a washing machine in the back yard shed.

A Dead Man's residence always had power. After Mike wiped Ajax down with disinfectant wipes and sprayed him with some flea and tick spray, the man stood up and let Anson Baker hose him down. Anson was Gay, so Mike always kidded him about getting a free show from the DEG employee's well-muscled body.

"Just because you straight guys are always leering at women does not mean we Gay men leer also," replied Anson

"Oh, horse shit, and throw me a towel."

The used towel went into the washer with the black clothes. The washer set on extra hot water soon sloshed the contents with disinfectant soap. Mike sat on the back patio with his landlord and friend and shared some beers.

"Yes, Mike, I can sell that pistol for a pretty penny. Which will keep us in food and drink."

"See, Anson. Renting to a Dead Man has its perks."

"I rented to you before DEG hired you, remember?"

"Yeah, after you checked out my tight ass from smashing concrete in condemned buildings."

"Don't project your fantasies onto me, young man."

They both laughed as the dogs Ajax and Bear looked on with bored expressions. They saw this every afternoon when Mike came home.

"Anything new, Anson?"

"Bear watched somebody crawling about in the brush out past the fence."

Mike grunted. He and Anson spent a week using surplus wooden pallets, strands of barbed wire intertwined with concertina wire to make the duplex a stockade. In this day and age, with little law enforcement, people took things because they could. Once a month, someone tested them. A perk of Salvage was Mike had a box of twelve gauge shells for Anson's pump shotgun. A "New Death" body just happened to have buckshot wounds, but who was counting?"

"Want me to take care of it?" Mike asked.

"Let's see if they try to get past the wire and test the dogs. We haven't had them that long."

"Or, Anson, we could see if that small pistol works before you sell it."

Anson shrugged his shoulders. "Okay."

The two housemates waited for a figure to move in the brush some twenty-five yards from the back stockade fence. Then Mike fired a shot from the thirty-two compact pistol. There was a cry of pain, followed by brush crushing and cracking sounds as a figure burst from the wooded area and ran straight towards the back fence.

"Great, Mister Brain Fried," said Anson as the wild-eyed and dirty figure ran into the barbed and concertina wire attached to the wooden stockade. The man screamed and cursed as he became even more entangled in the wire. Anson picked up a good-sized rock, one of many the two duplex residents kept for just such an occasion. He threw it and bounced it off the skull of the New Death survivor. The man's feet lost their grip on the dirt, and he fell full against the fencing, hanging from the wire stunned.

"I'll call the cops, see if they'll come for once," said Mike.

A half-hour later, a van with four Hazmat suited law enforcement officers arrived. Mike led them to the figure.

"Brainfried from the Virus," explained Mike.

"Someone called in a gunshot complaint, " said the officer with sergeant chevrons on his Hazmat suit.

"Someone must be hearing things."

"Yeah," replied the Sergent. "You two, grab the capture stick and drag Deadhead out of there."

The two officers used an enlarged capture pole like one used on dogs to grab the brain-damaged man by the neck. It took them a half hour to drag the man from the barbed wire and force him into the cage in the back of the van.

"You a Dead Man?" The Sergeant asked Mike.

"Yep. Six more corpses harvested today."

"Huh. Better you than me. See you later."

Anson and Mike returned to their chairs on the back patio.

"I have the blood transfer appointment tomorrow," said Anson.

"Glad I could arrange it."

"They say, Mike, blood like yours also works on the AIDS Virus. Your genetic makeup and your blood's reaction to various pathogens made it super special."

"You have AIDS? You never mentioned it."

"No, or I'd probably be dead by now. Treatment drugs are almost non-existent due to the New Death."

The men started on another beer as the Sun slipped behind the horizon. "Ain't this the life, Anson? All I need is a nice piece of ass."

They sat in a comfortable silence for a few more minutes; then, Mike noisily crushed the empty beer cans.

"Show off," said Anson. Mike looked at him.

"You're a good friend, Anson, in a world where most of my friends are dead or just gone."

"Flattery will not get me to make dinner. It's your turn."

"Shit. Well, hotdogs and beans again."

"Oh, God, no. Fine, I'll make dinner. You feed the dogs."

"Deal, friend."

The two men walked into the duplex and the end of another day of the New Normal.

Whatever that meant.

AN INTERVIEW WITH MARSHALL MILLER

When did you start writing, and why?

I became interested in Journalism in High School in the 1960s and joined the High School Newspaper, becoming the News Editor. I planned to become an Investigative Journalist/Reporter, derailed by a College Counselor, Mister Basnight, who said I had plenty of time to sign up for Communications/Journalism Classes. He was wrong as in 1970; EVERYONE suddenly wanted to go into writing and newscasting/film. I had an AFROTC Scholarship so as not to screw that up; I changed majors so I could finish in Four Years. The USAF originally wanted me to be a Pilot, but I wound up in Law Enforcement in the military instead due to changing requirements as the Viet Nam War wound down. Thus, I had Thirty Years in Law Enforcement, where I wrote many a Criminal Complaint and Report of Investigation. I retired in 2008 from federal service and began dabbling in writing on-line on various websites. After talking with a vanity press publisher, I started writing the War and Peace of Alien

Squid Invasion Novels. Blue Forge Press became interested in my work and republished my books, plus a bunch of other creations. In between, I and others created Kitsap Literary Artists and Writers to help creatives publish. We have a Public Access Television Interview Show on BKAT, Bremerton-Kitsap Access Television. The rest is history!

Which Authors or Books influenced you the most as a writer?

All the Golden and Silver Age Science Fiction and Fantasy Writers sich as Asimov, Heinlein, Howard, Lin Carter, Sprague DeCamp, Andre Norton, and Edgar Rice Burroughs influenced me. Later, so-called Military Sci-Fi writers like David Drake, John Ringo, and Eric Flint, who intertwined alternate histories and military action, led me to write what I call Adult Pulp Action Sci-Fi. Throw in Richard Matheson, I AM LEGEND as the first horrifying vampire book with a Sci-Fi twist, and you have stories with action that make you think! Of course, Ellison's DANGEROUS VISIONS and some New Wave from Britain by Aldriss and Moorcock showed me no subject was taboo, and you have Books I Like.

Which authors or books had the biggest impact on you as a person?

See the answer above. All the authors who influenced my writing had the biggest impact on me as a person; they made me THINK outside the box of my life. Science Fiction/Speculative Fiction creates new ways to look at cultures, people, genders, life, and deaths. Thus, you either allow yourself to grow, or you become stagnant.

Which of your original twelve Prompt stories are you most pleased with?

Campfire, as it allowed me to begin fleshing out a series that I initially planned as a series of movie scripts. It led to my *GameWorlds* stories, a short story collection from *Blue Forge Press* planned for publication in 2021.

Which of your original twelve Prompt stories did you find the most difficult to write?

I can't say anyone was more difficult in writing than any other. Once the prompt gives me the idea, I'm off to the races. Sometimes, the need to research culture, place, or thing slows things down as I want my stories to be believable even if I ask the reader to suspend reality as they know it. Every universe needs some rules. However, it is time constraints when day-to-day life intrudes, which causes the most problems, not the stories themselves. And of course, when your computer freezes. THAT is a problem.

What book on writing do you recommend?

I don't. Take some introductory writing courses in school to learn the basics, obtain some grammar books or a computer program like Grammarly or Hemingway, read the books you like to read and see if you can write in that style. Doing and experiencing is better than trying to learn from someone's book. Finding a good editor, you can work with one on one also helps.

What advice would you give an unpublished writer?

WRITE. THEN WRITE SOME MORE. Expect criticism from some and see if it is constructive or just someone being a Troll. I dislike Movie Critics as they seem to think they are supposed to be nasty and smarmy. Remember that H.P. Lovecraft and Edgar Allen Poe both died near broke, as did Van Gogh. If one person liked your story, you had some success. Never let people try to censor your ideas, dissuade you from expressing them. One person's pornography can be someone else's art.

Do you have a "dream project" as a writer? What would it be?

Turning *The Tschaaa Infestation* or *GameWorlds* into visual media would be a dream project. I would love to see my ideas and characters in film, television, or graphic novels.

The original twelve Prompt stories were written in 2019. In 2020 we all experienced a global pandemic. Did the pandemic impact your writing? How?

It added to the stress of day to day life. It also derailed plans to market my books and stories at various public venues. I enjoy face-to-face interactions with people who are interested in my books. I obtain a lot of ideas when I talk with people. It is so much more enjoyable to receive face-to-face feedback than to just communicate via the Internet.

ELIZA LOEB

ASH AND BONE

Most often times those who are emotionally unavailable carry themselves away with falling for fictional characters. Sometimes, even the writer falls for their characters or the characters of another person for good measure, so that they may avoid any pain or trespass from a stranger. In years such as 2020, it is just as hard and even as understandable to find ones self becoming emotionally attached to a character that cannot die or has died in a story. However, the thing about stories is that, that is all that they are. And when one is immersed in them, when one consumes the words, the thoughts and feelings that the writer conveys and the emotions that paint the landscapes and universe beneath the readers fingertips it allows an escape from reality. Even if it is just for a moment or hours or even a week. Sometimes it is needed.

I feel that many can agree that it has been an unprecedented year. And many children will vaguely know what birthday parties are like. Many adults and teenagers will never or vaguely understand the intimacy of a first date. Many are distant while others...not so much. The elections and the blatant disregard for human life have aged many like me. I have watched people I love succumb to illnesses because they could not afford medication and I have broken down and reached out for help. I have lost and fought for energy that I barely had.

Things will never go back to the way they used to be.

Honestly, as a human being, I don't want them to. I want things to move forward, for there to be extra precautions in terms of public health and safety rather than one leader after the other using fear as a means of controlling the masses. Preying on the gullible or narrow minded as a means of getting their way. As a writer, it is a great setting for a dystopian universe where a group of leaders do the same thing. There have been several thesis statements where many stories held some political backing and have even been brought up in creative writing and political discussion.

But that's the kicker.

When you already live in a dystopian society, where what used to be seen as fiction is now cause for a sick and twisted biography or chapter in a history textbook, what is the point in seeking dystopia between the pages?

My dear reader, are you looking for an escape? Would you rather some sort of alleviation or reprisal where the hero whisks the damsel away from their bindings or stops the villain? Are you looking for a villain with some troubled past that you can easily relate to who just wants to burn the world to little more than a pile of ash and bone?

If so, you have my empathy.

I have written characters like this and I have even gone as far as to sleep away half of the month of November just by writing a story that I could not find upon an old bookshelf in some hole in the wall of a used bookstore.

Even if the cat was the friendliest employee in the shop.

My point to writing this is, it's okay to find escape when the world is crumbling into nothing. It's okay to create your own escape and fall in love with fictional characters who you can trust will never hurt you. After this year, it's easy to say that an escape is perfectly rational.

AN INTERVIEW WITH ELIZA LOEB

When did you start writing and why?

I started writing when I was very young. My grandmother and I would practice my writing and paragraph accumulation by formulating short stories together. We would do this by writing one sentence, then two sentences and so on.

Which authors or books influenced you the most as a writer?

I would have to say Holly Black, Terry Pratchet and Niel Gaiman were major influences in my writing. Especially given that all three have impacted my view of urban fantasy and the use of psychology and how it can be applied to a story and it's characters. I have also grown up with a lot of mythology and classical influences in my life. But the three aforementioned are the ones that stood out most to me throughout my later adolescence.

Which authors or books had the biggest impact on you as a person?

I really couldn't answer that as there are several who have impacted me. I'm just the crabby little shut in who occasionally emerges from the abyss for some snacks and hot chocolate.

Which of your original twelve Prompt stories are you most pleased with?

I would have to say "The Escape" and "Call Me Kitten", specifically due to the fact that both deal with difficult topics pertaining to psychological trauma and politics in faulty medical systems. I'm not the type of writer who shies away from the gritty parts of life, in fact, I'm more the opposite.

Which of your original twelve Prompt stories did you find the most difficult to write?

The ones where it was me writing and delved into my psychological states. *Uphill Battle* was the first. But the one that stood out to me in particular was when I spoke about a young man who met a fairy in a meadow...that was after I had lost someone close to me.

What book on writing do you recommend?

There are many books on how to write and how not to write, and to ask me what books on writing would I recommend is like asking me how to make a family chicken soup. Everyone has a different style. No one is the same. So if you are going to write, know which audience it is that you want to cater to, know which genre you feel comfortable in and study the classics. Only refer to books on writing to sharpen your tools. Don't refer to them as a means of learning how to write an international novel.

What advice would you give an unpublished writer?

Take as much time honing and improving your skill as possible. It's okay to write fanfiction on a national platform, as some of the most well renowned classical writers of the Renaissance literally wrote fanfiction for funsies and munsies. Dante's Inferno and Paradise Lost are two of them.

Do you have a "dream project" as a writer? What would it be? Share what you feel comfortable sharing.

I have one for adults and one for Young Adults. And then there is the fanfiction that I keep posting because my creative blocks like to claw into me.

The original twelve Prompt stories were written in 2019. In 2020 we all experienced a global pandemic. Did the pandemic impact your writing? How?

The easiest way I can describe it is that I was pretty much watching anime and talking about my characters while taking notes these past six to eight months. The rest is not necessarily rated E for everyone or T for teen.

SHEILA
MENGERT

A VALEDICTION FORBIDDING MOURNING
An American Story for the Year 2021
Taking its Inspiration from a Poem by John Donne

John Donne wrote his poem, *A Valediction Forbidding Mourning* to one that he loved. He explains that love forbids morning because of its constancy. No journey is a final severance because its circle is confined by one point of a compass that remains forever fixed. Location of thoughts and desires demand a focus. In times of involuntary change a focus keeps us rooted in a sense of identity and attachment to places and to people. In the year 2020 I was exiled to the very place I had once longed to call my home, condemned to the very fate that I had long cherished as a dream of happiness. I first saw it coming home to Washington from California, a coastline so reminiscent of Stevenson's *Treasure Island* that I half expected to come upon the old Admiral Benbow Inn and see the old mariner Billy Bones who styled himself a Captain with his spyglass on the headland. I vowed then and there to return someday to walk the sands and explore the coves.

In subsequent years I visited this stretch of the central Oregon

Coast often but my home, my ports and vessels were located on Liberty Bay in the Puget Sound country of Western Washington. After years of living aboard I decided in 2019 that the time had come to enjoy the sea from the landward side instead of falling asleep each night to the roll of the inland waters with seals, otters, and gulls as my nearest neighbors. So it was that I broke up a chill and even snowy period of interlude and headed south where I remain even as I write these words.

Circumstances have made solitude a necessity. I was forced into what has amounted to a long retreat this year of 2020. I thought that we would have the virus under control by now but as I listened to the news tonight I discovered that yesterday America lost more Americans to the pandemic in than were lost in the 911 attacks. Who would have thought we would be in this position, certainly not the seafarer, now landlubber, who left Washington in late February. With each month I thought that America would get the virus under control and that I could return home to visit the life I had left behind. Instead the gap widened week by week so that now I find myself entertaining choices that I left behind in my twenties as equally possible to returning to a life in my sixties that in many ways has ceased to exist for me.

But I forbid mourning for it. Whatever the coming decade brings for all of us it will not be a return to the past. We know better now. We know now that the secure ground on which we once stood can be shaken by more than earthquakes. People can become overnight little more than vectors for disease. We know that a President can hang onto office like a South American dictator and that half of America would still follow him even into death by refusing to exercise basic health precautions. Those of us who are transgender know that another four years of Trumpism would only further deny our right to exist.

To find a form in formless experience is the lesson of a year spent here by the open sea. Sky, plunging foam, and sand alter with each day and the footprints along the shore are never the same. People form tableaux of friends and family while I have remained in solitude through the accidental confluence of time and place with a global pandemic. Only ones long schooled in solitude can endure such long separations. Yet my very experience as transgender has made me well acquainted with exile and emotional self-reliance. I draw my strength from sea and sky like the plants that find root somehow in the shifting sands and bear tiny purple flowers. These are my daily companions as I sit in the sand reading or lie in semi-slumber bathed in the sound of the breaking waves.

To the student of beginnings any story begins in *media res* or to take a more usual metaphor we merge with the traffic of history. But tonight such thoughts are far from me. A fog bank has moved in on the coast, a warm one and the winds are still after a two-day blow. I have become used to the moods out here on the edge of America where I walk each day virtually oblivious of the upheavals occurring across the nation. The air is moist tonight and still as though taking a break from all the recent tumult. Only the waves breaking further out than I have ever seen them before shows that big waves riding the summit of the high tides forecast two days ago have finally arrived in full force. They have been breaking all day at the foot of the cliffs where the big houses are planted, where the lights are just coming up now like little sentinels. Looking down on me from high-ceilinged living rooms the inhabitants must wonder who that lone figure might be, the one that always walks back along the beach each night carrying books.

I wear my winter shoes now. I gave up the ones with the holes in the soles finally just as I was getting used to the gravel burn on my feet from the road down to the beach, before the soft sand makes it feel as though my feet are nestled in the shoes that have been magically restored as they were when I bought them down in Newport three years ago. I could spend my days then in coffee bistros writing or maybe run up to the casino for the dinner buffet: smoked tri-tip roast, crepes, and all the Indian fry-bread I could eat. I am known there and they treat me like the transsexual princess that I still imagine myself to be. But then those activities and destinations are from memory. This year I only managed to catch the tail end of normal life in February and early March never imagining that I would still be here in December. I came down for just a short early visit to brush pine needles from the roof and be sure that the mice had not gotten in over the winter. Then suddenly the pandemic arrived, suddenly, brutally, remorselessly, not like this fog tonight, gentle and soothing but more like the great blade out of the *Pit and the Pendulum* swinging like a scythe of death over my head.

Everyone has a key bodily weakness and for me it is my lungs. I knew from the beginning that I could not afford to catch this virus. I thought back to when I once suffered from tuberculosis. It was 1980 then and I had gone down to California to live out my little version of the lives of Jack London or Robinson Jeffers. That summer I used to drive my Honda 360 over the coast range to Pescadero from the quiet little peninsula towns of Los Altos and Mountain View and head down to Carmel for the day. I recall that I had some of my poems printed up like bookmarks to be sold in the bookstores there.

One day in August I drove my motorbike back from Berkeley where I had gone to visit the campus and the next day I had a strange cough that just wouldn't go away. I had left my job and was house-sitting in San Francisco. I was flattered at first when I discovered weeks later that I had the same illness that had killed Katherine Mansfield and D.H. Lawrence. I guessed that I must be destined to be like them a writer after all. Soon after my diagnosis I said goodbye to California. I came home to Washington and was cured at the county's expense.   I would line up for testing and medications with the recently arrived Cambodian refugees, fresh from the killing fields of Pol Pot. I was still fresh from the romantic literary dreams nourished during my previous years in Michigan working in an industrial setting before I escaped to California. I dreamed then of the life of men like Jack Kerouac, Henry Miller, or the early John Steinbeck, a life spent around Big Sur or wandering about America and soaking up atmosphere for the big book that every author dreams about writing after the first years of struggle and neglect.

My recovery from tuberculosis gave me time to ponder my future and to travel. I drove 8000 miles the summer of 1981 crisscrossing the western states: mountains, valleys, and deserts before starting grad school at the University of Washington that fall. Everything was so intense then. Each decision was so pregnant with destiny and yet uncertain. I could have returned to Europe as I had planned to do in 1978 when I stood on a train platform in Luxembourg and said goodbye after six months spent studying abroad. Looking back now I realize how much I was living according to a prearranged drama bred of too much reading and an innate sense of the dramatic. It seemed natural in those days to think of my life through the long perceptive of dreams. Time seemed infinite then and there was always the possibility to correct course and start all over again. I forgot that American life can be brutal for those who miss early opportunities.

America tends to neglect its artists so that they often end up in places like Key West or Provincetown, somewhere on the edges of the continent that they are always trying to leave behind. The lucky ones make some money but then fortune shows its teeth and they often start that long slow road of self-destruction that their poverty had once kept at bay. Successful writers may end up like movie stars always hoping for one more big success to get them back on the bestseller lists.

Some seek to exploit their onetime celebrity status. They appear on the midnight talk-show circuit and try to say amusing things without a typewriter or computer screen in front of them. People look to writers as oracles to explain experience and capture in print the zeitgeist of the age. They don't see the lonely hours that writers spend alone with their thoughts and unsolved dilemmas that by a strange quirk of fate are not theirs alone. Writers write as long as they can. Many write the same book over and over again always looking for that magic formula of perfection that will ensure recognition and esteem. Others are one-book wonders who die young or go off into hiding to protect their sensibility from intrusion.

Some like me end up on a foggy night along the Oregon coast during a national pandemic. I climb the stairs up from the beach now and walk up through the trees along the path that I now know so well. It is enough that I will be warm tonight and that good food awaits me. When I sleep I will have the comfort of knowing that I am not stranded out there somewhere on the road or listening to the boom of tarps tied down to my deck to keep the rain at bay. Adventures are no longer sweet to me. I prefer warmth and comfort, to wake secure, and to hope that the virus will soon be the stuff of histories and the dimming memories of those who were fortunate enough to live through these days.

Where was I? Oh yes, I was speaking about the fog lying up along the coast tonight like a blanket in a chilly room. I walked up along the path not meeting anyone tonight. The beach was all mine, except for a few silent groups, separate and anonymous the way groups are now when social distancing is a must. I knew that dinner would be easy tonight, leek and potato soup with sausage and my favorite Greek seasoning. Maybe I will write a little before bedtime, maybe catch the evening news and hear the death count of the day.

Funny isn't it how the news of a thousand or more dead Americans has now become just routine, sort of like a 747 plane crash every day of the week. Now, nine months into the plague the gross death figure is like the Dow or the NASDAQ stock indexes, just one more figure to gage America a nation that lives by its indexes. How did all of this become so normal? The world that was lost in 2020 through the advent of the coronavirus and the resulting pandemic has been less a sudden inexplicable scourge and more of a revelation of what has been wrought by human expansion and invasion of the lands where indigenous peoples have lived for centuries yet survived the presence of these strange microbial agents. It is how we live in nature not nature itself that is the problem. We come to conquer subdue and decimate so should we surprised that nature reacts in kind? For every action there is a reaction. Our own seeming omnipotence has brought this disease forth as a great corrective to our pride. Was it always sleeping among us somewhere like a time-bomb ready to spring forth and decimate us whenever we brought together in a critical mass diverse species, in this case the bat and the scaly anteater so that a fortuitous interchange or chance mutation allowed the species barriers to fall? Perhaps the mechanism has a different trigger such as mass deforestation, single crop agriculture, or even too much carbon in the air. Maybe some inner memory was triggered and nature concluded that the dinosaurs had unaccountably returned or maybe we are just careless in the way that we stack crates filled with beasts in cages. In any case from some inauspicious beginning all else has followed. Now the economies of the earth tremble beneath a scourge as contagious and omni-present as its distant relative the common cold. All of the flaws of our interlaced civilizations are now made manifest like sea-wrack visible high on the shore tonight before a withdrawing tide.

All our debts to nature are becoming revealed now. They stand forth as evidence that we must perforce shut down or muffle the great engines of carbon-based commerce. All of our poor and homeless are now revealed as working families face eviction and the hobo-camps of yesterday no longer find their domain beyond the railroad tracks but rather in our city centers. We who live always in advance of ourselves are now brought up sharply like a runaway horse. The stern bit in our teeth causes us to arch our backs in rebellion at being constrained when we would love to run on ahead to our own destruction off of an ecological cliff.

All was going so well too. Who needs responsible government anyway? The reign of King Trump began with a tax-giveaway, not by raiding the piggy bank but by saddling the next generations with a trillion dollars of unnecessary debt. We pocketed our tax savings, spurned old alliances, and thought we were entitled to brag about our selfishness, the key American virtue. "Stop us if you can," we had shouted in our renewed greatness! And then suddenly a tiny globule with spiked proteins like an old World War II mine around a harbor drifted in among us ready to bump into our cells through our vagrant exhalations. The worst is that no one had heard of it before, this virus new to our species working at most a passing inconvenience to its former hosts but to us a plague never encountered before and to which we had no immunity as a species.

Coronavirus alone would have been sufficient to make the year of 2020 stressful but it coincided with the greatest social revolution since 1968. In order to remember that fateful pivot year in any detail it would be necessary to be born at the latest by 1960. A person born in 1960 would be sixty years old in 2020. People younger than sixty would then have no direct experience to draw from in order to process a period of national upheaval of the magnitude of 2020 when the confluence of pandemic, anti-racism protests, and a critical national election all happened to coincide. Coping mechanisms require some degree of prior exposure or they must be in a sense invented from scratch. This has been the real characteristic that will forever mark the year 2020 as historical in the same way that 1789, the year of the French Revolution marked its era. To young people it has been a shock that will be felt years later as their education process has been either altered in significant ways or at least deferred. The gap of a year in critical socialization skills alone may show up years later in one more addition to the Diagnostic and Statistical Manual of Mental Disorders.

Historical distortions create social tremors that reach to the furthest filaments of the social fabric just as a tsunami leaves the point where an earthquake occurs and radiates around the oceans of the world. These perambulations and perturbations are worse if they coincide with structural flaws. America, when the virus first struck, had been for four years engaged in a great social experiment of deregulation, corporate stimulus packages, and anti-environmental measures undertaken to boost profits in the fossil-fuel industry. Global warming was proclaimed to be a leftist Democratic hoax supported by a group of newly elected women in Congress known as the squad and ultimately backed by the deep state, meaning the professionals that ultimately make our complex government run. Putting a man in the White House whose idea of literature is a Twitter storm, one who conceived of the duties and responsibilities of his high office with the same enthusiasm and lack of comprehension as a kid in a candy shop maybe wasn't such a good idea after all.

The year 2016 brought on the equivalent of a leveraged buyout of America, a sell-off of key components for a quick profit, and the reorganization for resale to a smaller and more focused ownership group. In order to make this palatable Americans were promised that history could be reversed in order to "Make America Great Again." The whole transformation relied on old symbols while ignoring whatever real meaning they once had. Old emblems were dusted off, flags were waved, military air shows recalled World War II, and even tarnished Civil War memorials to long dead generals of the Confederacy erected during the period of reconstruction when virtual slavery was imposed once again by a defeated South that refused to acknowledge its defeat were suddenly emblems to be cherished.

Rhetoric from the KKK and from various Neo-Nazi fringe groups was suddenly respectable once again. Chanting at political rallies recalled the pageants once staged at Nurnberg when ecstatic Germans had wept to see the Fuhrer drive past in his Duisenberg with his palm raised to stir the people onwards to some imagined glory. Now of course "the master race" was inferred by simply being a white American and the great task was to build a fabled wall to proclaim forever that brown-skinned migrants had better stay south of the Rio Grande. The west that we had stolen from Mexico in 1848 was ours now and so it would remain forever!

Where did this new American sense of collective enthusiasm and hysteria come from? Was it merely an ad hoc Republican invention or the dream of a reality television mogul whose grasp of history was derived from the westerns that he may have watched as a kid on television? It may help to do a brief retrospective here to answer these questions.

In the 18th century a group of merchants, diplomats, and gentlemen planters motivated primarily by economic considerations and secondarily by certain romantic notions inspired by Locke, Montesquieu, Rousseau, and Paine decided on undertaking to form a new sort of government for the colonies in which they found themselves. The problem was to clothe what was a manifest act of rebellion with an aura of virtue and inevitability. Few innovators in political science or the actual governments of the earth presume to grasp power or to retain it without invoking God, historical necessity, or some other overriding principle to justify their rule. It is the part of the majority of the human race to then submit to these readings, explanations, or constructs and to avoid violence to their persons in the form of imprisonment or execution and the confiscation of their property through open disagreement or non-compliance with the promulgated laws of the particular jurisdiction. Governments begin in idealism and end in inequality and subjugation.

This group of associated gentlemen having decided to break with England first constituted the new government as a confederation of independent states but since these individually could not hope to long resist reacquisition by the jealous powers of Europe they decided for the good of themselves and their posterity "to form a more perfect union." In the smithy of a great Constitutional Convention they forged a Constitution inspired in part by the democratic structures of ancient Rome, a practice that was natural since a classical education of the times demanded a close scrutiny of the writings of the Greeks and the Romans. This Constitution has survived to the present day due to two factors: a handful of amendments occasionally supplemented as new needs arise and the imagination and sagacity of the judges who have managed to find various rights and principles within the bare structures of that very Constitution through applied legal reasoning. The end result has been the creation of the most armed and commercially successful empire that the world has known to date.

This brief prequel is meant to sum up in a few words a great amount of history and the lives of the many persons who have made this progress possible. The nation that exists today is a product of various interactions in war and in peace between that nascent nation and the other nations of the world. It takes enterprise and determination to migrate to a new country. American genius is not innate but borrowed from a citizenry made up of voluntary exiles. Immigration is not a threat but the very life blood of the nation.

The rest of our good fortune is due to possessing a moderate climate, many navigable ports on two oceans, and continental dominance in the Americas. However to the mind of many Americans ours is a story pregnant with inevitability and as such America is the favored child of fortune, the beloved of our Creator, and the natural legislator in world affairs. For these Americans long schooled in the catechism of their own greatness flattery is only our just due and it should be paid in both respect and in revenue by all of the other nations of the world.

So it was that when a man in 2016 managed by what many saw at the time as a refreshing honesty and bluntness to capture the Republican Party and its nomination to the Presidency their collective hearts rejoiced that the new President-to-be would not be a politician or even a creature of the laws but rather a magical embodiment of everything that they did not know about America but felt in their hearts with that intuitive sense of pride and entitlement that Americans of both major parties hold dear.

It had not escaped the notice of many average Americans that the promises held out to them in childhood were not being kept. Their houses were smaller than their parent's houses had been. They took shorter vacations, had a higher debt load, and were dependent upon a dwindling source to obtain the goods that made their consumption-oriented lives possible. The great producers of their clothes and in fact most of the items from pharmaceutical needs to automobiles were located elsewhere. The economy of the nation was seventy percent consumer driven which meant that most citizens simply recycle the same thin slice of all of the outstanding dollar supply among themselves at restaurants, hair salons, and gyms while the bulk of dollars goes to workers overseas or funnels upwards as profits to the one percent of high wage earners and corporate stockholders. The American pantry was in fact almost bare and Mother Hubbard was living in a shoe that was manufactured in China or India. All was looking lost until a serial playboy, one who was famous for being famous as well as a propensity for lavish real estate projects that often failed, presented himself as a disinterested Robin Hood figure who would rescue forgotten America.

Donald Trump didn't reach far for his model, perhaps recalling how far another raucous orator had managed to get by using the repeated word Deutschland and histrionic rhetoric to extinguish democracy in Germany; so why re-invent the wheel. His crudeness became forthrightness and ingenuousness and besides the bad-boy mystique is so charming to people who dare not speak out in their ordinary lives. Arbitrary rule is the hallmark of the paternalistic Christian family. Commanded obedience was a matter of recent memory or current experience for many blue-collar Americans. Even supposedly liberated women evidently found it charming to imagine that here was a man who confessed openly to wide-ranging heterosexual explorations as merely one more version of the ancient *droit de seigneur* of the lord of the manor.

So it was that in 2016 that staid body of electors defied the popular will and appointed to office a man who saw the Presidency as the place where he could see his fantasies of ultimate power not only fulfilled but fomented by supposedly conservative politicians. The essence of romanticism of course is not conservation but change, the pursuit of a vanished golden age. Imagine a Camelot Presidency without any pretence at intellectual depth; this is to grasp the essence of the "Make America Great Again" ethos. The dusty closet of a vanished patriotism yielded its old and tarnished memorials now appropriated as just part of the brand and logo of the new Commander in Chief. Every neural circuit from elementary school received a new burst of electricity and suddenly everyone was in the back seat of the old family Ford or Chevy and it was 1958 again!

Only it wasn't 1958 because time moves in only one direction. America had already passed its accidental zenith which was a by-product of our involvement in two world wars. The collapse of the European colonial empires and the terrible decimation of the Soviet Union by Nazi Germany had allowed America a free hand to exploit the early developments and the technical advancements that emerged from the war after 1945. Japan and South Korea were then virtual American colonies and China was still stuck in the 19th century with an agricultural economy and a surplus population. The tax structure of America in the 1950's and 1960's favored a vibrant middle-class and the babyboom generation grew up on toys and cartoons dreaming of endless opportunities. So secure were they in their superior position that Americans of that time developed a sort of evangelical capitalism in the form of The Peace Corps and the Alliance for Progress. The whole world might now aspire to be American!

Then suddenly the sixties decade was over. The costs of the war in Viet Nam and the expenditures of "the Great Society" resulted in inflation. Young people struggled to find their footing in an expanding world economy. The flower children became yuppies, the tide of universal liberation went the way of disco, and Ronald Reagan was elected President. The 1980's was a struggle between libertines and conservatives, the seeds of today's culture wars found their first rooting places and forged valuable alliances in government. The first Gulf War began over the fate of Kuwait and suddenly America began the long hemorrhage and transformation into the sole remaining superpower ready for a thirty year experiment at creating a new world order that was in reality only the same old order of rebellion and reaction that has always characterized human history.

Every year after the dawn of the new millennium has seemed alien to me, without a central theme. Time seems to have sped up and there is no guiding vision. Events simply happen in a random and unconnected way. As the dreams of my young adulthood have waned and the long twilight period has begun I hunger for the same security that from an entirely different mindset Republican voters thought that Donald Trump could give them. I on the other hand hope for no messianic figure. I take comfort in virtues when I find them. Maybe I never realized that I had been born into an age in decline; that the high point of culture was reached long before I was born. I find myself answering the questions first posed in my grandfather's generation. I have always been playing a catch-up game with history.

Life all seems so inevitable now, resistant to any plan or order. This great loss of direction at the macro level is replicated on the micro level, so that as I walk the beach each day reviewing my own minor place in these great events I wonder what remains to anchor my values and my perceptions. I wish I could begin all over again, although I realize that I cannot do so. My own flesh is part of that turning of cycles, those wheels within wheels. Can I be getting old after all? Is there a reason why the movie stars whose names and films I knew don't show up at each year's Academy Awards anymore? I am startled when the yearly collective obituary runs to see how many familiar names appear, knowing that film alone preserves them as they once were? As a member of a media-obsessed generation film stars were my pantheon of idols. I thought of them as intimate companions and role models, imagining that some of their glamour might become mine so that by stepping into the film I could leave behind the constraints that held me bound to a sex that didn't seem to really be mine.

My daily sense of self sifted through imaginary ideals. I found that I could slide through various characters like an FM radio dial always looking for a clear signal with no static interference, always looking for a confirmation of illustrious ideals that might have only existed in my mind. Now here I am marooned by coronavirus and forced to engage in solitude with what I have become and to look over the depository of my days and nights to see what endures and what might be dissolving away now day by day erased by the interminable waves of time.

I came down to the coast then before winter was over and by the end of March the state of Oregon was in lockdown. It came as such a surprise. I should have remembered 1982-1983 and the way that another virus was suddenly seemingly everywhere. The difference is that coronavirus is less focused on a particular community and it takes people from health to gasping for breath to death quickly whereas AIDS in the beginning might take two years from the first night sweats to the final skeletal end of its victims.

In those early days I knew drag queen friends in their twenties who turned from being delicate sylph-like creatures into the semblance of old ladies as their flesh melted away. I didn't think I would ever live through anything like that again. Doing the covid-19 numbers in real time was shocking at first but as the year has worn on the faces have disappeared and their stories with them. Maybe someday an encyclopedia will be assembled to remind us of just who these people were and how they were plucked out of life to make the bitter vintage of tears that is a pandemic. It is only now that we are seeing what exponential growth rates mean when translated into mobile morgues in city after city.

I decided early on in the pandemic that I would do whatever it took to stay healthy and not be a part of history. If nothing else I would hang on until the blessed day when I could watch Donald Trump be voted out of office. Every day I check out the conservative websites, some religious and some mainstream news. I told people in January that 2020 would be a stressful year. It would be a political confrontation of maxed-out dimensions, but never did I foresee what was about to descend upon us.   I had first heard about the coronavirus on the news blaring over my head from a big-screen television while I shoveled down yummy food at my favorite Chinese restaurant. Part of being a regular customer is possessing right of first possession. I guarded my usual table like a pit bull, me with my model-length red hair and fierce blood-red nails to give emphasis to my summary dismissal of anyone who tried to turn the channel over to Fox News from MSNBC. My first impression of what was soon to be known as covid-19 was that here was just another of those predictable flair-ups of weird viruses in China that blaze up like brushfires and are soon extinguished. If a few cruise ships were infected they would go into quarantine along some dock in California and the whole thing would soon be another false alarm.

I was wrong. By the time I got down to the coast there was already a case in some school in Oregon and two weeks later coronavirus was a real issue.   Suddenly my comfy routine in Washington had become an inaccessible memory. Platters of food fresh from the kitchen, big serving spoons, and nothing but mounds of shrimp and General Chou Chicken were now light years away. Days spent among crowded tables with everyone talking and eating were like a time from some former life spent in gastronomic paradise.

Yet even now, even this late into the pandemic, covid-19 denial is everywhere and mask-wearing is interpreted as the ultimate abdication of our right as Americans to demonstrate that we can muscle our way through this thing by holding it in contempt. The virus is spreading most readily in precisely those rural Republican-voting states where it was at first slow to arrive. Things can only get worse in the next three months. It isn't easy to keep screen-doors and windows open for ventilation in the midst of a Dakota winter. I find myself getting mad at the people who have deliberately avoided precautions out of supposed loyalty to Donald Trump. Next to the National Anthem and the Pledge of Allegiance nothing demonstrates rabid patriotism like ripping a mask from your face, just like the boys in 1917 when commanded to go over the top into steady machine gun fire, according to this invincible fantasy of pointless risk.

Now as December arrives I realize how I have kept putting off my return to Washington day by day and now month by month waiting for things to improve. I don't know what I will be returning to and as long as I stay here I can pretend that I have a life there that I can take up again just where I left it. The rhythm of a day is like an orchestral score but now whole pages are missing and the conductor's baton is broken.

When I walked down to the beach today I saw how the king tides have erased old landmarks and deposited new driftwood logs along the now familiar shore. Even the beach has been sculpted by the waves raised up by two successive gales with winds gusting to 60 MPH overnight. The beach is no longer flat but is broken by low hillocks of sand, littered by tangles of kelp uprooted by the great waves and flung onto the shore. Everything changes but then I have changed also in my months spent here, bereft as I have been from the mirroring influences of my usual home and community. Instead there is only this great gap between the routines of a life that I had established over twenty years and whatever remains of my life.

How shall I spend it? Is it too late to create something entirely new? Wandering makes no sense without the possibility of return to display our discoveries. All maps today terminate in a starting point and I begin to suspect that there is no land of promise to which I might escape the baying hounds of memory that pursue me. Why did

I ever allow so many indignities to be meted out? But then did I really have a choice at the time? I did whatever the day demanded in order to survive and I took comfort in the little details of daily living. Isn't it that way for everybody?

The surf rises and suddenly I find myself pinned up against the sea cliffs. The friendly ocean appears menacing and the need for escape suddenly imperative. I respect everything more now, all of the blind forces of creation. I am beginning to suspect that I play no permanent part in the panorama of events and that my observations are for this day only. The waves will soon cover my footprints and a day will come when it will be as if I had never been.

How long can my heart beat so that the world can explode with each day into sight and sound before me? The sunlight today works harder to warm the air. I have decided once again to remain where I have been safe, well-fed, and granted the freedom to read and to write but even more to meditate on what my life has been, the choices that I was forced to consider and to make because they ensured survival when anything more was too much to hope for. I looked for love in the wrong places and held on too long to relationships that would have never been started if I had comprehended the many options that I could never manage to believe were my due as a human being. Transgender persons often take on the coloration of the abuse that surrounds us. It is how we end up dying too soon and living in deprivation because we take the first hands stretched out to us for fear that otherwise we will remain alone, unprotected, and bereft of all human sympathy. We are thrilled by events that most people take for granted, pathetically savoring each morsel of recognition and acceptance, and who can blame us for that?

The shame is not ours. Those of us who recall the early days when we were not only obscure but virtually invisible need to remind the present generation that as bad as it can be now it was once far worse for us. The rainbow now reaches from horizon to horizon whereas it was once confined to a single prism of glass held up against the sun through a solitary windowpane to catch the light. We were in a state of stealth even from ourselves.

I came out early and paid the price for it but not as much as many others. I owe them some sort of elegy in everything I write because I am here and they are not. The early imperatives of gender become less insistent with age as various diva possibilities fade. Humanity ceases to be two separate oceans of appearance and perception. Each sex begins to resemble the other. The spark between opposing poles is less as the two electrodes come closer together. But for all of this our souls remain grounded even when fractured by a life of multiple gender representations.

The easy binary assumptions of the first writings on transsexual identity are less mandated now. We have less to fear from doctors who once held our fate in their hands. These were the people who spoke for us because we were denied a voice. In those days it paid to be selectively crazy because that was what we were expected to be. We can take our time now and reflect before making choices under pressure from immediate circumstances. We can be honest about our doubts and fears. We can tolerate ambiguities even in our most closely held convictions. We can claim the full spectrum of our humanity without being dictated to by words and symbols. To claim our full humanity means being something besides sexual fetish objects for those who would claim an automatic right to explore and to exploit us. Above all else we don't need to compete with each other for transgender door prizes along scales of "realness" and "passing." Our bodies are not ends in themselves but gateways to being able to fully experience this world that surrounds us. Life is not an audition, not even a performance, but the thing itself.

Every day now the numbers of the dead go up in an ever increasing spiral. In the beginning I prayed for them one at time, then in tens and twenties, and now in hundreds but still under the same basic phrases, "For those who will die this day and their afflicted loved ones and their patient and long-suffering caretakers, may their souls and all the souls of the faithful departed through the mercy of God rest in peace, Amen."

Now even those days of more focuses prayers are left behind as the daily death count crosses two thousand. I have finally lived long enough to live through one of history's great watersheds. Lives that just a short year ago were immune and filled with expectations have been cut off sharply and cleanly by an organism that no matter how long it had slumbered in an alien species had done us no harm. Along the wing-like membrane of a bat's widespread fingers it lived in the blood or traversed the lungs while below we could walk oblivious of what soared aloft over our heads. In any case a vast ocean separated us from its source and so whatever swift transfer made human infection possible would surely flare briefly before being extinguished. The rich variety of our individual pursuits would go on and we would live to fulfill our destinies. But now a great interruption had taken place and tears appeared in the fabric of our lives. People who could not be replaced left unaccountable holes where we had been accustomed to seeing them each day and had every expectation that they would be there tomorrow and again tomorrow.

I thought of all matters often as the sea days arced swiftly over my head and the waves beat their incessant rhythm to mark my solitude. I would wait it out no matter how long it took. From the hour of my awakening and the first news of the day on Democracy Now to the last hour when I would read until my concentration waned before drifting off to sleep I would hope for deliverance from the chaos of the country and the ravages of the virus. It would be hard to take up the strands of life again when the period of contagion has passed. Never before had it seemed so evident that we are flames from a common fire, sparks blown upward red and glowing against a clear sky on a summer night while the shore wind blows in from the sea to disperse them.

Ego ties us to our particular history so that we don't see that another's eyes are really identical with our own. Their pain or loneliness is identical to ours and ours to theirs. Individuation ignores how we are joined at the stem and at the root, nourished by a common force that some call the Holy Spirit. We are walled up behind our own eyes, imprisoned in a skull of bone while somewhere a ligature joins us to all other lives. A common pulse beats inside of us, a beat mirrored by the unceasing sea. We carry the same salt ocean in our blood and even our bodies are vehicles of metabolic transport so that hearts may replace hearts and lungs replace lungs. Those who receive organ donations do not say, "This part of me is not me." Are our brains any different? Can we transfuse identities? Is language only a brief signal like a lighthouse flashing outward to vessels that approach our shores? Did I come to the coast this year to find myself or to lose myself, to tear myself away from the comforting routine of the last twenty years, to return to a time of hopes that had not known disappointment, to regain an era of infinite belief? I wanted to find the freshness again, the icy thrill of new experience when everything was new. Perhaps I had thought too much, found sources of opposition everywhere. Maybe now I could grant a general amnesty to life and start over and do it right this time.

But death was close in 2020, closer than it had ever been before. People younger than me were dying and I was in a group that did not bear up well after a positive diagnosis. This thought plunged me back into separation. "I must survive because my life is not yet complete!" Others had done so much more in half the time. Their charity was a down-payment on eternity while I only leased my life in thirty day increments, always waiting for something definitive to emerge. Would another's virtues need to cover me as well? Could their surplus cancel out my debt that having lived so long I was just approaching … what? Was it a definitive formulation? Something culled from a thousand books sifted and set out once again in my own words? Is that enough for a life?

But then the sea is profligate and human life is profligate. The beach is a littered burial-ground of preliminary efforts, crabs half-grown, bundles of kelp, empty clam shells. I walk over them to my adopted place each day when the weather permits, set my books down and begin underlining and annotating. "Ah here is a passage worth a double star!" Life is a vast allegory, the poem copies nature, no rather enhances and transports it to another level of apprehension. Very good! "Look out there, a squall line has come up over the horizon moving towards me." Unsuspected it springs upon me, the first drops falling. "Close the book before the ink begins to run! I had better start back now the wind is already beginning to blow and the squall is closer now. Look where the rain shadows like a grey curtain make the south bay invisible."

So having read passages from Longinus or Horace or Plotinus I set out for home across the sands. I have read them as though we were engaged in some long debate and I could meet them later over a beer to thrash out a disputed point, but they are long dead these two thousand years and my comments, even made with such advantages, ones born of the resources of later commentaries, cannot eclipse the brilliance of the initial formulations. For Classical writers the Trojan War was yesterday but is it less so for me when set against the slow accretion of geological time that has worn rocks into sand?

There was another autumnal gale last night, so for today warnings went out for high surf and the possibility of sneaker waves that can wash ashore and pull the unsuspecting beachcomber out to sea. Sneaker waves are like miniature tsunamis. The water simply keeps on coming as though from an irresistible source of reserves. It is a function of the preceding waves interacting with the slope of the beach which might have been eroded in such a way that hills and valleys that were absent only yesterday provide new channels of flow and retreat today. This sea phenomenon might be taken as an analogy for our present political and cultural situation as the chaotic year of 2020 slips beneath the waters of history. The certainties of yesterday are caught up in the tidal flow of events such that entire industries are being transformed before our eyes. Job categories are not merely migrating; they are ceasing to exist. Old loyalties are being broken and new and perhaps equally transient alliances are forming. Perhaps only people like those of us who have managed to surf the waves of identity and the expressive modes that support identity can find within us the skills to adapt when the ground shifts beneath our feet. Only people who have embraced instant exile as the price of personal authenticity can know what losses of this magnitude entail for a culture.

Early transgender people were solitary gender samurai. Now we senior members are people who blossomed before the dawn and are now wilting away. Our testimony is almost embarrassing because our lives were once so restricted. Our early transitions or lack of them are reminders that surgical and hormonal resources were then in short supply and not readily available at that. I am surprised at the seeming fluidity of gender-change today and the widespread acceptance of a category of experience that was formerly confined to psychiatric journals and scummy talk-show formats. Opposition now requires at least a few sidelong glances before being verbalized. We are still victims of violence and even murder but gone are the days when such events were not even newsworthy because we were deemed expendable and deserved what we got. We have made progress and no doubt President Biden will reverse some of the last gasp persecutions of our people under the recent Trump regime.

I am tired though; weary of being a cultural icon to be exploited by conservative media as a sign of cultural malaise or even decadence. Once we are unmoored from our assigned gender we are too often reduced to being piquant manikins for sexual exploitation because of our very difference. We get swept into debates not of our choosing because most of us simply want to live. Some of us are able to make careers out of leveraging our life-experience, but to do so is a subset of the entertainment industry and yesterday's star is likely to be today's tabloid tragedy.

I avoided celebrity in my youth by seeking shelter in the bosom of a small town on a peninsula during the years when I might have found a wider channel for expression in New York or Los Angeles. People like me were rarities then and like anything rare, exploitable. I opted for quiet and convenience because these gave me a semblance of what life might have had in store for me had I not been transgender. Urban enclaves in contrast invited more extreme fates of fortune or of disaster. Suburban life in contrast leaves us in a state of suspended animation between true acceptance and mere toleration. I chose the latter because it had the advantage of any pastel existence, quiet harmony with the other furnishings. I was just colorful enough to draw notice but not sufficiently aggressive to pose a threat.

After the election most Americans heaved a sigh of relief but I was still uneasy. I keep thinking of Neville Chamberlain getting off of the plane from Germany proclaiming that "peace in our time" had been achieved. I took daily comfort as case after case raised by the Trump campaign was being thrown out of court for lack of evidence. The midnight talk show hosts were able to laugh at these feeble efforts to reverse an election but always I heard the echo of jackboots in the streets and recalled how unlikely that Nazi takeover had once appeared, the dull-witted street thugs who supported Hitler, the inchoate enthusiasm of the nameless masses bewitched by his passionate rhetoric. The very fact that Trump was making these outlandish claims with impunity should have been enough to awaken people to a clear and present danger. If nothing else this man was seeding the ground for four years of domestic terrorist acts committed by those supporters who took him literally. Almost half the country had voted for him even while the hospitals bulged at the seams with the desperately ill and the dying. Would all of this disappear on Inauguration Day in the midst of an economic recession that would require further stimulus to recover even after the vaccination program?

Meanwhile I had my own personal damage control with which to contend. I had lived in virtual solitude for ten months. My former life now seemed as distant as my earliest memories. Looking at the tumultuous seas with their rip tides and brutal undertows and over-falls I wondered if I had extracted all that I might have done from the pageant of living. I was raised in a faith that proclaims certainties. Was it time now to begin the long process of repentance and reparation for a life that had been ill-spent or to rally round my convictions and even my doubts? I would like to have accomplished more in my past, but in which direction do I bend my future efforts?

Maybe I would have done more harm than good had circumstances not kept me on a short leash. To exert force in any direction after all is to set other things in motion just as the gale last night has produced today's huge waves on the shore. To see all things in motion seems to me to be a more accurate description of what exists than fixed and enumerated categories. The universe appears to have its own spontaneity. The balance of forces is harmonious without being static. Even language loses meaning when the same sacred phrases are repeated again and again. The function of literature is to constantly renew our language with new metaphors.

Thought grows a hard carapace when it is not constantly deconstructed and reassembled. But there is a corresponding danger in this. The breeding ground of every heresy always begins with the phrase, "Yes, but what if…" But a static orthodoxy finally loses contact with its original referents. Formulaic phrases become meaningless, but prior to that they become hard granules that only circle back on themselves in endless replication. This is why rebellion ultimately has a constructive and preservative role. It forces a new articulation of what has always been believed so that it becomes fresh and new again.

Rebels are always a threat though. I would have done better in life to memorize the rules and figure out who was in charge. Instead I completed the assignments while secretly questioning the purpose of the whole thing. I like to think that every equation has a remainder so that there is always something more to do. When the virus passes who will I be and where will I go? The erosion wrought by the coronavirus, as unique and catastrophic as it has been, is a subset of the greater changes that are occurring all around us in the environment and even in our inner sense of ourselves. The dense weave of the decades creates a common culture around us. It tells us who we are and what resources are available to fill our needs and where we can expect to find them.

I carry within me an inner road map of the stores at the local mall where I customarily shop when I need anything beyond my basic needs. I expect to see the same sales persons when I go to the mall and the same grocery check-out staff when I return to doing my own grocery shopping. When we all come out of our burrows blinking in the sunlight of recovery and renewal it is probable that we will return to a changed world without our favorite restaurants or watering holes. I usually notice changes even after a short vacation so what about a year of absence? What will it entail?

The worst part is that I will probably not return as the same person that I was because changes are part of me as well. I no longer have the same expectations that I had. I see my life now with an unaccustomed objectivity as though I had left the stage and gone down into the audience seats. What had once been routine for me seems now a strand of tissue neatly clipped off and floating about at random in the aqueous gel of my vision. I am connected by only memory to my former pursuits like a familiar VHS movie stored away in a box and now without the mechanism to play it. I will need to transcribe everything to the self that is over a year older. The perpetual illusion of my own youthful relevance is denied daily in the mirror by my physical body so that a re-calibration, let alone a re-invention from scratch, seems impossible. Reflecting on this makes me feel that it would be just as well if I simply started over again somewhere else at chapter one although I can no longer echo the first chapter of David Copperfield entitled, "I am born." Instead, I echo the sentiments in the poem by Alfred Lord Tennyson entitled, *Tithonus,* that begins, "The woods decay, the woods decay and fall, the vapors weep their burthen to the ground."

The nation itself has grown unaccountably old in its semblance of democracy. It will have to struggle to its feet after the Trump attempt to impose authoritarian rule. The racial divide that exists has never been more urgent because its reality has been made more visible by the Black Lives Matter Movement. Conditions of long standing will need to be ameliorated during the Biden Presidency. Those who will have been rendered homeless or jobless will have to draw their lives about them and assess the damage.

The dead of course will not return. For them history will have ended with Donald Trump and his rallies where the disease was simply dismissed as a democratic meme. These will not rise with the dissemination of a vaccine. For them there will only be the panic as the sedative took hold and the intubation device invaded their body in order vainly to keep them alive when the efforts to draw an independent breath became too difficult. The sun of their memories will have set on a world dominated by the constant noise that Donald Trump's noxious presence visited on America with the intensity of a laser beam for five long years.

If I survive then I must count myself lucky. I will at least have a prospect of renewal and for that reason I forbid mourning. We dare not tarry long over all that we have lost as a nation. We must take our disgust and loathing and put it aside, although never forgetting that the forces that brought Donald Trump to power still exist among us, all the envy, the desperate desire for vicarious celebrity, the esteem relished on his discourtesy, and the contempt for science, for learning, and for culture. The greedy will find some new avatar and the poor having been betrayed will seek another savior as the raucous chants of the Trump rallies fade away.

The America that will emerge with a national debt approaching 25 trillion dollars will need to realize that we depend on the rest of the world for constant cash infusions to keep our national debt from collapsing in on itself like a building set for demolition. But still we must forbid mourning lest our tears never dry. It is at times like these that it helps in some ways to have been transgender, to be accustomed to disappointed hopes, and to the dissolution of dreams. Transgender exile breeds its own independence. Transgender people know what it is to leave a ballroom rented for the night, to go out under the streetlights of a winter rain, to climb the weary stairs to a shared apartment or a solitary studio, to set aside a rhinestone crown if there is one, to see the tired face in the bathroom mirror, and to see all the colors of make-up on a washrag or swirling down the drain of the sink. After that we simply go on as we have always done. We gather the spare elements of style or glamour from the rags of fortune. It is an old trick for us.

Our newly acquired status and recognition raises grounds for hope. It is a capital mistake however to use the exceptions to ignore what is true for the majority of us. Many struggles are still in front of us as a community. The current comparative visibility of transgender lives is as deceptive as our invisibility once was. When we were invisible we were presumed not to exist and now that we are more visible and receiving unprecedented attention and sympathetic understanding in some quarters it is assumed that everything is finally turning out alright for us. Instead what is often occurring is that the same cultural anxieties that once marginalized us is now leading to an assumption that we are more powerful than we are.

The myth of "gender ideology" proclaims that we are engaged in and able to accomplish the breakdown of the identities of straight people so that what is exceptional will become a new imperative; the fear that transgender identities will become the new norm for human sexuality. The same oppression in other words that was once visited on transgender persons will now, it is presumed, be turned against heterosexual and cis-gender people so that they can no longer live as they choose.

Whether this paranoid supposition is due to a bad conscience within the society that has often treated transgender people so badly or not, its effect is the same, to make of the victim the victimizer.

Then, to add spice to this deadly political concoction, religion is stirred into the brew. It is now proclaimed that the very essence of religion lies in the right to discriminate by selective designation of the ungodly and then making their lives untenable through refusal of service, lack of employment or housing, and by refusing to afford to us the social amenities that usually accompany our gender.

This backlash is justified by linking us in with other marginalized groups. The present national hysteria of faux-patriotism that depends more on symbols than upon substance makes us into strangers and aliens. The Trump administration made this process all too clear by denying transgender individuals the right to serve in the armed forces and by reversing protections that had enabled transgender students to claim the right to full participation in their childhood and adolescent years, those crucial formative years when we mature in our gender expression and are launched upon adult life.

The latent fascism of the Trump Presidency and the pandemic that it did so much to promote through its own policy failures has left havoc in its wake. The recently acquired place at the table for transgender people is a tenuous one. For all Americans the reconstruction of our economy on a more equitable basis will take years. It will take even longer to disassemble the acceptableness of systemic mendacity that has made Trumpism not only possible but has rendered his noxious conglomeration of assorted bigotries acceptable for roughly half of the American population.

Conservative religion has forged an iron-clad alliance with political intolerance and a monolithic image of American life that denies the racial and cultural diversity that have always been the source of American vitality. This has been combined with an apocalyptic view of history centered on the belief that a war in the Middle East by pressuring Iran will usher in a period of Christian millennial rule. This belief system that overrides sensible statecraft and diplomacy is based on an unquestioned belief that America has been chosen by providence to insure the end of the world through an alliance with Israel that will lead deterministically to a final confrontation. The withdrawal of American participation in multiple international treaties, from environmental preservation and from arms control agreements and the constant abuse of NATO and the United Nations while exalting an American go-it-alone strategy, all are hallmarks and confirmations of this fanatically religious, dangerous, and isolationist mentality. The fortunate victory of the Democratic Candidate Joe Biden in the recent Presidential campaign gives us four years at least to return some measure of sanity to our republic.

The active engagement of formerly isolated groups demanding justice will be required. They will enter the fray against formidable obstacles raised by entrenched interests bolstered by appeals to tradition, patriotism, and an assumed favor from God, the same sentiments that have inspired every Crusade, made possible every case of genocide, and accompanied most of the wars of humankind. The deaths caused by the pandemic should have united us around a common cause of survival. Instead these deaths have left America fractured with one half of the nation convinced that to fail to wear a mask in public and even to die as a result is a sign of proud refusal to accept facts. This folly is the supreme expression of the brand of American exceptionalism that Donald Trump and the party that has enabled him has made mainstream. Together they have managed to marshal a deadly mixture of pride and insolence into a collective force of paranoid suspicions and latent violence. It will not be easy to absorb the fluid bred of this toxic abscess back into our democracy, but we must do so if we are to survive as a nation willing to cooperate with the other nations of the world to face problems of a global nature and to surpass these immediate threats to our survival without pretending that even greater challenges do not remain.

As December 2020 arrives the virus count climbs ever higher with its attendant deaths. In my place of refuge I seek daily solace by the sea. We denizens of the coast have left last week's storms behind us now; the sun has returned. I see daily groups of children wading in the ocean surf and the usual dog-walkers are out on their usual promenade. Last night the full moon rose up just behind the trees huge and round as it always is when it is close to the horizon. I was listening on my phone to a podcast promoting a new book lamenting the current crisis in the Roman Catholic Church and the remissness of the majority of the Bishops of the United States willing to reduce or curtail the usual church services in obedience to the civil authorities. To me this sense of responsibility is only to be expected from mature people in light of the present crisis. To the extreme Trump-worshiping right wing Catholic conservative movement however failure to court a readily available prospect of unnecessary death is to miss a great chance for martyrdom.

There has been much talk of late in conservative Catholic circles that we don't talk enough about hell these days. The unstated presumptions are always that conservative theology can readily ascertain the sign posts of salvation, that where God is concerned correct ritual is more important than the saving of human lives, and that God's wrath requires constant appeasement. Listeners to conservative Catholic media are reminded daily that hell is the default destination of human beings, a reminder particularly apropos when uncertain death in the form of the virus might now strike at any time and that the pandemic is a direct visitation of God to punish us for our sins. All of this of course is reminiscent of the religious hysteria that greeted the Black Death of the 14th century.

All the while as I listened to this broadcast on my phone I could hear around me the waves breaking and watch the moon rising on the placid human groups wandering about on the sand and see the rose-gold light of the sun shimmering in the tide pools after sunset. These spoke of a larger conception of creation, one that made the grim pestilence seem very far away. Death amidst such splendor was unthinkable let alone one that would only serve to inaugurate us into greater suffering still.

I believe of course that there is a wide path that leads to destruction but it begins at a Trump rally and it leads ineluctably to Wall Street. I also know about the narrow path that leads to life. It is found in the hospital wards where nurses and doctors spend each day gallantly trying to save the lives of people, many of whom entertain the idea that the virus is a Democratic hoax and that if we would only stop testing so much as President Trump insists why then the virus would simply go away.

Last night after I came home from the beach beneath the moonlit trees I turned on my computer and went up on the Gutenberg Project site to look at the books of the great philosopher and historian Thomas Carlyle. I was not aware that he had also assembled a book of the writings of the great religions of the world. I picked a few passages at random to read and was startled anew by the way that every culture and nation has found a way to embody in a sacred text the poetry of our sense of wonder at all that is and to assign some sense of order to a creator. Surely the artist is greater than the canvas of this present world and surely life as it greets us each day wondrous and immense gives the lie to death.

The phenomenal display that greets us by the ocean may be the mere test sheet of some great moral exam but if contemplated in its own vastness and incomprehensibility it augurs something more. Adjuration has its place but to make of moral disputes and ritual observances the essence of religion and of worship seems to me at least to diminish whatever eternal realm exists. I think that we know smallness and constrictive conceptions when we see them. The great religions do not exist to close us up like an oyster on a few sternly grasped truths but to open us outward to a fuller conception of what with a little generosity and compassion we could become.

I am daily astonished at the sheer wonder of my fellow creatures. I am astonished to find how love can awaken traumatized shelter animals to renewed trust and to play. Even wild beasts are turned from lions into lambs by love and if Catholicism means anything at all, and I think it does, it means to love. I rejoice at the broader sense of God's actions and designs celebrated by Pope Francis in his new Encyclical, *Fratelli Tutti.* It speaks of a brotherhood of the human race that exists even prior to evangelization, not to diminish evangelization, but rather to honor what is already present in the longings and aspirations of a created order, one yearning and manifesting a divine order that is already present in all things.

This affirmation awakens confidence that the wide path to destruction is not what many Christians think it is. The wide path to destruction is to entertain a narrow and parochial ideology that sees the other as alien and as a stranger. It is a frozen mindset that builds walls simply to keep others out. It is the paltry selfishness that refuses truth whenever truth threatens to diminish personal power. It is the lie that when repeated often enough gains in credibility, at least for the gullible. It is all that has reduced America in four short years to our collective pride and isolation. It has all been a great seduction that has finally condemned us to be its minions under the short unhappy reign of Donald J. Trump leading us to deserve the pity of the rest of the civilized nations and to become in this disastrous year of 2020 the undisputed coronavirus capital of the world.

What are we to make of the multitude of narratives that make claims upon us? A totalizing narrative reduces everything to itself. Art by its very nature enhances or transforms initial impressions into meaningful communication by various means. This involves a process of discovery mingled with active response by the artist and the final transference by this medium to another human being who in a sense co-creates the now independent artistic object by willingly subjecting herself to its influence.

Music and drama actually add an additional intermediary in the form of played instruments or an orchestra and in the case of drama by stagecraft and acting. The two essential elements however in any artistic work if it is to fulfill its ultimate destiny are creation and communication. The creation may be spontaneous and perishable like a chalk drawing on pavement or an improvised theater piece. Permanence and the ability to replicate its influence or to recover its existence at will are all irrelevant. The manuscript to a great novel may even languish in a drawer or be burned and thus never fulfill its destiny. Franz Kafka instructed his friend Max Brod to destroy the manuscript of Kafka's unpublished work, *The Castle.*

In contrast to the partial articulations that are art we have in the realm of science the pursuit of a Unified Field Theory that will reconcile all forces and in religion we have various authoritative revelations that are understood to set universal norms for conduct and authorized ritual observances. We would like to believe that human experience would make it possible to make an authoritative yet still personal choice among the various contenders for universal explanations and meanings. The idea of cultural variance implies an unacceptable degree of relativity among totalizing narratives. The certainty of the prospect of death provides the universal solvent, the one experience that every human being must share, although the meanings attributed to it vary considerably.

Something deep within us though allows us to vibrate to the chord of another person's emotions. We all know hunger, loneliness, and fear. Our joys may vary with their specific objects but tragedy is the great welding universal that awakens sympathy within our deepest selves. Pestilence! How inappropriate is such a word to our sophisticated post-industrial world. Surely that is a word that only fits the middle ages. Who would imagine that so many could die today of an affliction that a year ago did not even exist among us? Where shall we seek a source to sustain us as we reconstruct a world so recently eclipsed?

My time runs short to absorb and adjust to the claims made upon me by my past and the challenge of an ill-informed future. The sun has returned though and once again I marvel that I have been allowed to spend my year of solitude here where each day the prospect of the great ocean makes small our conceptions. I have no telescope to scan distant galaxies. For me there is only the velvet drapery of the sky filled with stars and beneath their placid gaze the midnight blackness of the sea at night reaching outward infinitely but confined by the laws of perspective to a single line along the horizon. This is wonder enough for me. I impose few limits on eternity; not because it is my allotted task to decide which gates are narrow and which are wide, but because the sea itself spurns any effort at confinement. I imagine God as equally unconfined, willing to break in among us if given half a chance.

I believe that my entire life has been spent seeking to get at the basis of things. Religion begins with fundamental narratives of origin and purpose. In this sense every religion is linear and related to how we live in time. They involve aspiration and choice. Nirvana is conceived as a way to step out of time, to prevent the endless cycle of rebirth. Dharma is the continual stepping stone path to an ultimate cessation of personal existence and a merger into the ultimate reality. Even the goal of Christianity is that in the end God will be all in all. This sense of the totality unites religions while their mode of expression may be singular and unique in their doctrines and demands.

The great Western Religions with their Judaic base take eternity as a given so that we cannot having once been born manage to step out of existence because immortality is itself our doom. Death is simply that gateway to a final judgment, a great binary that will forever separate the human species into one of two alternative fates. In heaven there are said to be many mansions while in hell there is only one shared confinement of solitude deprived of love yet condemned to occupy a single crowded cell. Even the concept of forever as endless time vanishes into a present where the ideas of before and after become meaningless. I like to imagine that something of the innocence of creation is a parallel source showing metaphors of the nature of God somewhat comparable to the written texts that ground most religions. No religion may be judged from outside the perceptual categories that each religion terms essential. Religious thought creates its own fundamental categories of apprehension that guide all further thought and talk about them. This is why religious debates are seldom fruitful. Conversion is an organic and holistic process. In Christianity, properly understood, the gateway is love, a paradoxical and reciprocal relation where each cause is at the same time its own effect. The point of entry is such that after entry the door vanishes and one exists in a different way just as once one is at sea the land disappears and on every side there is only a single embracing horizon.

Winter! The sun scans now in a lower arc across the southern stretch of beach. Only the ambient temperature separates this sunny day from what I experienced over the past months of spring and summer. My ideas also follow a lower arc. I usually begin each year with definite goals and the unfounded certainty that my faculties will expand proportionately to achieve them. Ordinarily when autumn comes I gather the holidays about me like a comfort blanket. This year of course all subsequent life and plans are contingent to a successful vaccine. I seem to have been orbiting about this year awaiting a re-entry vehicle to carry me back to the earth I once knew. Everything I valued is now filtered by this year and the books I have read and the lines that I have written. My sense of solitude is now baked into me like a hard glaze over the mobile clay that has received it.

I came down to Oregon hoping for a reassessment of my life and a clearly charted final quadrant, the last twenty years of my human life. There is no longer room for partial gestures. Every narrative matters now, particularly if it flows from my pen. I received again today pictures, samples of an endless string of cameos each to be encased and laid aside in the box of memories of one who cannot be named. People and places move like a tinsel mobile over my head now; all are echoes in Plato's vast cave of appearances.

Yesterday a cousin asked me not to forward any more political articles because they threatened family unity. A news item on the same day said that one out of four doctors knew a colleague who had contemplated suicide because of what they have witnessed this year in treating patients for covid-19. When the new year of 2021 begins there will be no time for mourning; the exigencies of stamping out the last burning embers of the virus will demand all of our efforts as will the task of putting our lives back together again.

The ocean has provided me this year will all the metaphors for such a transformation. Each day as I walk through the graveyard of whatever the sea has thrown up with the last high tide I see how interlaced are life and death so that the two bleed into each other. I sit each day with my back against the rocks and my morning selection of reading material spread out before me. I like to read in the shadow of a beach house that casts its long morning shadow out over the beach. No one interrupts me there although I can watch the walkers, single or in small groups, walking dogs or playing in the surf. One day it might be a young woman doing cartwheels for her boyfriend and then running up to him for a hug of approval that she can still do what she did so well as a girl. On another day it might be two elderly women with notebooks who were measuring and recording the dead birds lying in the sand, more this year, no one knows why. Perhaps the fish are fewer or harder to catch.

Once a college group gathered for a group hug and no one was wearing masks. There are two or three surfers who tackle the waves each day expending fifteen minutes of effort and energy for a ten second ride in, but they think it is worth it. They disappear at times beneath the waves and I am anxious for a moment waiting for them to surface again. The sand that is smooth each morning is chopped up by successive feet in the course of the day. I like to watch the horizon for brief storm squalls that can move over the edge of my vision with surprising speed. Sometimes a fog bank moves in so thick that even the expensive homes along the shore disappear and people emerge like ghosts out of the misty distance.

I have a driftwood pile where in the spring of the year I would rest my head and doze in that semi-consciousness of wind and wave that is always hypnotic. The weeks and months have drifted by with the casual inconsequence of a place that always changes yet is always somehow the same. There was no place better to return to while the virus raged so I simply stayed where I was and now it is winter and I do not know how to return. A year separates me now from everything I knew at home and I am also somehow different. Perhaps it is because this very transiency is part of me now; perhaps because I have witnessed sunset after sunset this year, each unique and distinct, and each bearing that sense that it relinquishes its grip with reluctance on the brief hours of daylight where it had once reigned supreme.

Sometimes the sun vanishes in a distant fogbank so that the final diminution cannot be witnessed. But there are days when the sun sits on a knife-edge of horizon and sinks like a lemon bit by tiny bit. At the end there is only a ever diminishing disk that grows smaller and smaller until only a fractional spot remains forming a dome of light … going, going, and then there is only a solitary line although the sky is still as bright, as if the sun now set had never left to begin its long journey to the other side of the earth.

The night wind comes up then and I gage the distance for my long walk home before twilight should engulf all that I see and leave me in darkness with only the white line of the breakers to my left as a guide. If the light permits I may read for a little while longer or engage in those quiet thoughts that we save for life's twilight hours: regrets for past mistakes, wishes that we had made better choices, or mere reflections that life is infinitely precious because it can unveil sights like the sunset that I have just witnessed.

I get up at last, not yet creaky-boned, but still with an effort, and begin the slow walk back. The beach is empty now and the long promenade of my fellow hermits of the sea is over for the day. I marvel that such an expanse of space can be my sole possession without traffic-light or buildings to hem me in. I can think now beyond the horizon and imagine destinies that I have neither time nor energy to fulfill, although at one time I felt that the earth lay golden at my feet with infinite possibilities. Time once stretched out before me rich decade after decade simply waiting to be segmented and cached into neat files of memory so that in the end I could review it all and say that I had lived a perfect life, one filled with adventure, variety, and romance and only seasoned lightly by mistakes or foolish choices.

There were few thoughts then that things are as vulnerable as they are or that the great institutions that sustain us are like cobwebs in a gale. I felt the world then like a spinning top balanced along the edge of a precipice: would it spin forever or plunge over an abyss beyond repair? I recalled then the need to never stop affirming alluring possibilities so that a time would come when I would write a valediction forbidding mourning. Until then I could always sustain a sense of hope as I do now anticipating the coming day.

AN INTERVIEW WITH SHEILA MENGERT

When did you start writing and why?

The best answer to this question is less a referral back to one's first attempts at recording thoughts in a formal and artistic manner, which is what writers do, than to ask oneself first why one continues to write year after year, producing book after book? Part of the answer to this is that writing is motivated by a desire to embody fleeting thoughts and impressions that would otherwise be forgotten before bearing the fruit attendant upon further reflection. Sometimes it is to explore a single theme in depth or to surprise oneself by a felicitous creation that even exceeds the initial experience or conception that has later matured into full form and symmetry. Perhaps writing is an extension of the personality of the writer, an attempt to survive oblivion, or at least to grasp the fleeting moment by recording it before it vanishes forever. There is also a certain celebrity attending writers who dare to express what others have felt so as to recall to them those common elements that make us human.

The importance of the writer's social role has long been recognized. The power of the written word and the power of oratory were recognized by the early Greek and Roman philosophers. The law itself is embodied in written judicial opinions and these in turn to the processes of litigation where lawyers as skilled advocates pursue the goal of justice. To debase oratory with lies and demagoguery is therefore an offense not only against the body politic but to those ideals that make civilization even possible.

As a writer I have watched in dismay as these high humanist traditions have been recently debased so that the very thought processes of a nation have been compromised and diminished. Repeated terms of abuse derived ultimately from the techniques of absolutist rhetoric similar to those of the Stalin era in Russia led inevitably to the infamous Russian show trials of 1938. These same techniques have now been adapted to an American sensibility fanned into racist and xenophobic intensity by a single-minded President who would portray any critic of his policies as "enemies of the people" who should be beaten up or even tried for "treason."

The equation of a sitting President's personal interests with our most hallowed traditions is an example of the most brazen political effrontery that our country has ever seen. There are many subjects to which I would have rather devoted my attention than assessing the conditions that have surrounded all of us since 2016 but none have been more timely or urgent. There is a great tradition in literature for what might be called a literature of engagement. Early examples of this genre in America are *The Jungle* by Upton Sinclair, *The Octopus* by Frank Norris, *The Grapes of Wrath* by John Steinbeck, and *Darkness at Noon* by Arthur Koestler. In Europe this genre is represented by Jean-Paul Sartre's *The Roads to Freedom Trilogy* and Boris Pasternak's epic on Stalinist Russia, *Doctor Zhivago*.

These authors have been my inspiration during the years since

2016 as I looked on in horror while the unaccountable forces of American selfishness, racism, environmental exploitation, and centralized corporate rule found in the personality of Donald J. Trump their perfect spokesman and avatar. The anti-intellectualism, the repetition of verbal memes designed to seduce great masses of gullible or self-serving Americans, and the general breakdown of all civilized discourse was reminiscent of the processes that took hold in Germany in 1933. The following years led to the burning of books and the wholesale repudiation of arts and literature under Nazi rule.

My contribution to the Prompt Anthology of short stories is entitled, *Auguries of Desolation.* The thought that led me to this title was that no better descriptive phrase could be found for America in the year of 2020. At the start of the final month of this fateful year we are approaching 300,000 dead Americans from covid-19. Many businesses have closed their doors permanently and the unemployment figures and the sheer numbers of food-challenged Americans show a fundamental class and ownership gap that is unprecedented in the past seventy years.

When I settled upon this title there was also the danger that Donald J. Trump might possibly be re-elected for another four years to complete his destruction of our democratic Republic and the final liquidation of effective opposition to his goals and ambitions. As the weeks since the election have shown, this President clearly anticipated that his base alliance of racists, fanatical religionists, and well-armed malcontents would bestow upon him the twin benefits of a shelter against charges of criminal behavior and four more years to leverage his office for the benefit of his business interests. He has even spoken in terms hinting at setting up some sort of family dynasty that would undermine American democratic mechanisms and ideals that have traditionally deplored any semblance of monarchical rule.

The result of all of the above has been a virtual fissure that now divides our nation into two mutually opposed camps. It is difficult to imagine the extent of the paranoia extant in this country as we approach the year 2021 and a new Presidency to restore order and sanity. The destruction reaches far beyond the traditional opposition found in politics. Various religious broadcasting networks have often become mere political arms for right-wing conspiracy theories not the least of which has been that when masses of American voters turned out to evict from the White House our only Presidential advocate of absolutist rule that this was a case of "stealing the election" rather than a fair and healthy just-in-time withdrawal from a descent into a would-be dictatorship.

The stories that I wrote in 2019 seem to me now in retrospect to have been prophetic of the climate of belief and the erosion of character that will hopefully be confined to the present brief era of American autocratic experimentation that began in 2016. Each of the stories that I wrote last year is prophetic in character and hence an augury. These are stories of fragmented identities, haunting resentments, and aspirations for some vanished land of promise and sanguine expectations.

On a more general note, short stories, in my opinion, are at their best when they hit the reader like a freight train so that the memory of the reader recalls them when similar situations occur in her own life. Two examples of stories like this are *The Lottery* by Shirley Jackson and *The Swimmer* by John Cheever. The short story format is a meeting of character and situation resulting in an abrupt confrontation with reality or a change in position of a significant character. There is little time for a series of incidents such as the novel format affords to the writer. Instead, life comes down upon one swiftly and remorselessly creating an insight into the deeper nature of things as in *Araby*, the first story in James Joyce's book of intimate portraits entitled simply, *Dubliners*.

Prior then to answering this first question of what led me to write I would like to explain what I have been writing in this year of the great pestilence, the year 2020. The term twenty-twenty vision will ever after this year have a special meaning. It will be the year when the world was brought up short by a world-spanning emergency that suddenly made death something that could not be outsourced to underdeveloped countries.   Death from the coronavirus, while still revealing great fissures of inequality in our nation and the world, was just as likely to affect those who denied its very existence as for those who could not dodge its cruel scourge because they were essential workers on the front lines fulfilling our necessities.

When it is all over a final study of the victim categories needs to be made. The usual indicators of disaster have proven to be inadequate. The fact that the stock market and certain remote service marketers have actually increased in value and market share while so many people have died and so many small businesses have gone under has clearly revealed whose bread gets buttered in America and who must go hungry even while they may have sacrificed the most in this time of need for the general welfare. Ethical vacuums have emerged in surprising places. Many Christian denominations for instance have raised Donald J. Trump to a virtually idolatrous degree of adoration and accolades even as the country has spiraled downwards into division, chaos, and death.

Of course Americans have died in great numbers before in theaters of war but no President since Woodrow Wilson has presided over such extensive civilian deaths and casualties. It is the single greatest signature event of his spendthrift, corporate give-away Presidency and one that will always mark his tenure in office as among the darkest in our collective history. The relish with which various Christians have embraced his postures and his rambling cliché-ridden rhetoric has revealed a singular gap in both spiritual insight and basic decency so that the words "religious freedom" are in this year of 2020 virtually synonymous with a claimed right to infect others by refusing to wear masks, as if they were some sort of facial condom.

So it is that my writing this year has been largely confined to non-fictional critiques of various social structures and systems. The isolation mandated by the virus has made me aware that writers are always somewhat removed from positions to directly intervene in emergencies. Instead we serve the role of assimilation so that when the emergency has passed we can find some meaning in what has occurred and some hints about how better to respond next time. Thanks to the favorable outcome of the election of 2020 we may now look forward to something other than the shallow dictatorship that for a time appeared to be a real possibility.

I am influenced in my writing by a classical consciousness in conflict with a romantic temperament, by a Catholic faith in conflict with a free-thinking philosophy grounded in vitalism, the *élan vital* of the philosopher Henri Bergson. I hope for heaven while being one fully committed to the earth. I have been influenced and indeed have embodied those drives and feelings that are labeled transgender while refusing to entirely assimilate any fixed identity so as to keep an escape route handy should its use be necessary. Much of my writing in recent years but above all in this year of my enforced exile has been to dredge out the anger within me so that healing might be possible when the world again opens its doors to freedom of motion and human intercourse. Vitalism has tended to be denigrated as a mystical sense that life is an immaterial force that guides the mechanism of living matter but which in itself is unknowable except through its material manifestation in chemical processes. Science only recognizes what can be quantified.

The problem with vitalism is that it is both focused and

universal but cannot be measured or even defined in itself. Vitalism recognizes a principle of organic unity and coordination that appears to transcend the constituent elements of an organism. It manifests consent of the parts without debate or legislation for the good of the whole. Lacking this coordination the organism or the community perishes. Cooperation is far more the underlying rule of nature than competition is. This surrender of discretion is not coerced as though it was ever possible for the organ or tissue to exist independently. The proper subordination of function is the very essence of each layer of inquiry as the living embodiment of the order existing just below it.

A cell requires the existence of mitochondria and mitochondria require the mechanism of intra-cellular transport and oxidation reactions. These in turn require the chemical composition of complex carbon-based molecules. Each of these levels of existence is embodied by characteristics that are encoded in behavior but the plan itself operates as a guidance system. It may appear to emerge coincidentally with the character of its subordinate elements so that any teleological extension might appear to be merely a metaphoric description applied to the final product but it must always be recalled until the final state is arrived at over time. The finality and goal was not clearly ascertainable but only predictable from within a range of possibilities. An eye lens without a pupil and a retina for instance would be useless. We look in vain for fossil evidence of the great refuse-heap of failed organ systems. Each existing being is perfected to a specified if limited formula.

This vital guiding force is to my way of thinking a source of theological insight parallel to any revealed sacred text and I honor it as such because the very existence of that force shows the fructifying nature of God. Similarly, to act disparagingly towards creation and to our own complex totality is to reduce God's own vitality to a set of static concepts. In this sense everything is sacramental and the rites of worship are enacted daily simply so that when I wake the world awaits me in the form of the explosion of light over the sea. The life force that is within me beats in unison with that tide that within me has taken the form of blood. My eyes invite the cascading waves and my ear rejoices in the plunge and whisper of the tides.

So what kind of writer does that make me? I hesitate to call myself a Catholic writer because I do not wish to confuse my own pronouncements with official Church teachings and practice for fear of leading others astray. My relations with Catholicism therefore are aspirational rather than conclusive. I am on my way back after a long period of exile but just how that way back is to be expressed I cannot say at the present time. I only desire that it should be sincere and not a reflex bred solely by the present crisis and the shortening path ahead of me as I age. I had budgeted for more time than is available to a single human life. As a result I feel that I am just reaching a point for commitments that others often make in their young adult years. I consider everything that I have done and thought as one great prolegomenon to existing as a single human being with a single destiny rather than one who endlessly reviews all options without ever taking a fixed position.

Some would say that to be a Catholic and simultaneously transgender is an oxymoron because these identities are incompatible. Both however have their roots sunk deep within me so that I have never been able to surrender one to the other. My participation as a writer in the Prompt Anthology Project requires a measure of identification however so I announce myself as both one and the other because both appellations are true of me to an extent. The process of realization of either is long and hard and I have not concluded them yet.

Turning then to writing as an activity proceeding from whatever inner qualities I possess; the question of why writers write is rather like asking why we breathe: we do so in order to live, not that most of us can live by writing in the pecuniary sense of the word but because writing is the path of our own vital impulses and thus inseparable for us from living at all. Art in all of its forms allows the life force to escape and to embody itself in a form that others can share. But even in the solitude of composition for the author alone it has value because it grounds us in language that like the force of gravity holds us to the earth. Writers do not exist though in solitude. To write is also to love reading what others have written and in this sense all writing is part of a long conversation between generations. I feel as close to many authors as if they were my own personal possession, as though the communication could reach upward through the text to the author and he or she would smile knowing that I understand them.

I first started writing in the seventh grade inspired by the writings of Edgar Allen Poe and my first reading of Bram Stoker's *Dracula.* Had I been more prescient and realized that Americans never tire of vampires I might have continued in that early strain of sensibility and created my own version of *Salem's Lot* or the *Twilight Series* and perhaps made a fortune. As a writer one takes one's chances with the public pulse and to anticipate a trend requires a gift of prophesy or at least a fortunate synchronicity.

Now and again it happens and the usual course of events is reversed so that publishers are found chasing writers rather than the usual case of writers chasing publishers. As for the reading public or rather publics, for they are both varied and integral, the writer drifts by temperament usually in a certain direction and if lucky finds an audience. I suggest however that to anticipate an audience and to write for it deliberately is to forfeit a higher calling that was once called being faithful to one's muse. In this sense a writer writes to please her own sense of excellence and if the public or a sector of it approves then all is well and good but first in the old cliché the writer must be true to herself.

This answers the question why I began writing and why I continue to do so. I began writing for the same reason that so many authors do: to discover in the process what I think about things and to use the medium of words as an artist. To this day I find that it is only in the process of writing that I discover my thoughts. I do not entertain a well-wrought and pre-conceived idea except in the most shadowy form and I am open to surprises as I channel as it were the voices of my inner being into print. If I use characters I let them speak and simply take dictation. Perhaps this is due to the fact that I began as a poet and poets listen before they speak because their very speech is meant to be overheard later by others though it was first an interior melody heard and transcribed. In this sense the *Ode to a Nightingale* by John Keats and his *Ode on a Grecian Urn* are the quintessential expressions of the creative process.

Once started writing I never stopped, although there were long periods of study when I was in pursuit of a facility and a voice that although fertilized by the efforts of other writers would be mine alone. Each new author brought me closer to that goal but like a mirage the goal itself always seemed to require something more before I could satisfy myself that I possessed the perfect tools for my task. I finally realized that I had been in pursuit of a mirage or a will-of-the wisp. Each writing effort is a discrete and insular endeavor and the work produced is similarly the fruit of its composition and in this sense a product of accident rather than design. There is no perfect preparation for this task nor is it ever complete; it simply is. At last I stopped waiting to be ready to write and began writing and all else has followed in due course.

The unasked question is why do writers keep writing? Some might say that it is only habit. Others would say that writing is now second nature to the writer. It may be a desire for a perfect object that has hitherto eluded the artist or it may be simply to do as well as one has done before even if our capacities diminish with time. To do so may bring pleasure or it may bring pain. It may recall past ambitions only to see them disappointed once again. It may be simply one of life's inevitabilities that the rising of the sun each day that beckons us to return to the notebook or the keyboard and to dare again to reduce thought to words. In any case we do these things and in doing them often enough we find that we have become writers.

Moving from writing in general and reflecting specifically on the Prompt Anthology stories I would like to say something about writing from a transgender perspective. There is a natural assumption that the transgender experience is a univocal one when nothing could be further from the truth. Transgender people face similar issues and experience various levels of discrimination and oppression, but our ages and circumstances are such that radically different prospects and life courses emerge in front of us.

I lived my early transition years in a partially closeted suburbia rather than New York or San Francisco or Los Angeles. I also came up in an era where transgender existence was very dominated by the medical model and where any real communal structures existed more accessibly among the drag queen margins of gay society. Repercussions for being out were brutal, swift, and omni-present. Even movies depicted us as so freakish that our presence might trigger instant nausea if not violent assaults. Was it any wonder then that our lives were, if not nasty, brutish, and short, as Thomas Hobbes once said of human beings in a state of nature, they were at least marginal, risky, and solitary. We were pathetically grateful for simple tolerance and to be left alone. We were magnets for ridicule and the crudest possible references to our probable or supposed genitalia. So painful was this period that I write about it with difficulty so that only one of my stories deals at length with transgender characters.

Only one of my other books is entirely dedicated to transgender topics, *Transsexualism and its Discontents: A Political Profile.* Even the word, "transsexual," dates me because it traces its origins to 1966 and to Dr. Harry Benjamin who coined the term. As the tiny ripple of out transgender people has grown now to a wave through early diagnosis and treatment individuals find resources and degrees of enlightened response that were simply not present to early adult or mid-life transitioning trans-people of the 1980's and 1990's. All of which is to say that there is a sort of creaking of metaphorically speaking whalebone and crinolines in any memoir of that silent era.

Youth and beauty open many doors now that were not available to stars of the silent-era of transgender existence when we were often referred to with embarrassment at family get-togethers. Many of us watched as our prospective career prospects disappeared overnight when we began our transitions while the younger ones of us often survived by sex work and appeared all too predictably as victims of assault or even murder. These dreadful outcomes still continue today but they now at least merit some degree of investigation and prosecution.

As regards the aging transsexual, America has little reverence for dowagers unless they are colorful and well-heeled. A steamy memoir is unlikely to generate much heat if the author includes a more recent photograph that allows the reader to essay the damage that the years have wrought. We prefer that our close-ups should be artfully staged and dimly lighted. From the perspective granted by mature reflection on our lives a universal tone comes to predominate as we survey humanity and its many afflictions from the august if perilous position that age grants to us who have seen life from two opposed perspectives and can therefore provide extra depth beyond the usual proscenium wall. The mind is most expansive when the years in which to apply any wisdom gained have proportionately diminished. The powers once bestowed by charm, if we ever possessed them, now must rely upon persuasion alone and the naked power of connected words to draw a crowd and to achieve their effect.

All of which is to say that social and political recognition is the beginning for transgender people of the lives formerly denied to us. Instead a path from the cradle to the grave was dictated not so much by our biology but by the imposition of what is permissible for each gender in appearance, sexuality, and even how we are allowed to move. Imposed gender norms are an affected dance choreographed by an oppressive society that values focused violence in the male and automatic submission in the female. Each sex learns the tricks of the trade by selectively weeding out manners and behaviors that are deemed inappropriate to one's given gender. To be a gender rebel even if not dictated by profound Gender Dysphoria then is to make our own efforts at transition less extreme because the society itself is less rigid in its imposed definitions. If gender was not the political fulcrum that it is but rather a spectrum of identifications and behaviors then the systematic indoctrination that begins in childhood would not be necessary because each flower would bloom in its own time and season.

Education in America is largely dictated by the need to prepare young adults who are willing to take their assigned roles in our capitalist structure. The long lines on the freeways, the stifling office cubicles, the corporate hierarchies are the tribal norms of industrial capitalism. Gender constructed norms have shifted lately but not substantially changed. The violence that exists towards transgender people still exists because our very existence implies that these carefully wrought distinctions are not stable; but to shift them or to seek to call them into question or to supplant them, even by our tiny minority, is seen as open rebellion against religion, nature, and above all the economics of systemic repression that is necessary for an exploitive capitalist economy to grind up and expend the resources of the earth as quickly as possible so as to increase national wealth and power. This process ultimately leads to overconsumption by a few generations by imperiling the survival of future generations who will be starved to a degree that is a proportionate measure of our own self-indulgence. The trend in my present writing is to call out these processes that are leading to desolation so that they become more visible. Hopefully what I write will in some small measure turn the tide.

Which authors or books influenced you most as a writer?

Proceeding from the position that I take that writing is not a tangential activity to the writer but rather an extension of the thought processes of the writer combined with a commitment to develop her skills as a literary artist, I would to a degree conflate questions two and three by saying that development as a writer is simultaneously development of the writer as a person because she has found in literature a path to give testimony to the human community of truths and insights that proceed only through the discipline of literary creation.

If this seems to be an encomium that is not deserved when so few people actively attend to writers as sources of culture rather than other media figures I would point out that along with history, and philosophy, literary artists precede even science as the source of human knowledge in western culture from the age of Aristotle to our own. If the audience for serious literature has diminished because reading is a more demanding task than the passive enjoyment of other forms of media this is not a reflection upon the value of the literary artist but rather a comment on the way that reflection, creative silence, and critical thinking skills have diminished in the general body politic.

So in answer to this second question it would be easier to answer which authors or books have not influenced me than to specify a small selection of those that have done so. I point this out because I find something of value in every writer that I read but of course historically speaking I have had my favorites. I find that these favorites share a confessional attitude to existence and often write disguised autobiographies in their fiction. The closer that a writer remains to her key convictions the more authentic her testimony is likely to be. At the same time it is part of the imaginative faculty that it must be able to set out a hypothetical situation and then to allow the characters to speak for themselves without being mere puppets of the author the strings of which are visible and intrusive. The abiding final impression should be one of verisimilitude so that the imitation of life becomes not only life itself but life enhanced by the literary skill of the author.

The claims that I am making for authors are not to diminish the value of literature as a source of mere relaxation or entertainment. A skillful mystery or a novel of sentiment and romance is within its more limited sphere of equal value if it achieves what the author set out to do which is to please his audience from within the limits of the genre represented. Examples of these are science fiction, fantasy novels, and of course mysteries. I am very fond of Raymond Chandler for instance because of his ability to set a tone of weary discontent in his gritty stories and novels and I enjoy the thrills provided by H.P. Lovecraft and Algernon Blackwood the two greatest masters of the uncanny and the grotesque in the tradition of Edgar Allen Poe. I would also like to praise Shirley Jackson whose skill at setting a mood of anxiety and disconnection in her work shows an accuracy of judgment and a power of selection that makes her one of the greatest and most subtle writers of her era.

Having said all of this though I would like to list a few names here of writers of special importance, authors that I have used as personal models and as guides to good writing:

Thomas Wolfe, James Joyce, Virginia Woolf, William Faulkner, F. Scott Fitzgerald, John Steinbeck, Thomas Mann, Robert Musil, H.G. Wells, Thomas Browne, John Donne, Anton Chekov, Fyodor Dostoyevsky, Percy Shelley, William Wordsworth, Alfred Lord Tennyson, Thomas Carlyle, Matthew Arnold, Ernest Dowson, Robert Browning, William Butler Yeats, Robert Frost, Carl Sandburg, Amy Lowell, Georg Trakl, Tennessee Williams, Oscar Wilde, and William Inge.

The books that have most influenced me as a writer are:

Thomas Wolfe: *Look Homeward Angel; Of Time and the River*
James Joyce: *Ulysses; Portrait of the Artist as a Young Man; Finnegans Wake*
Herman Hesse: *Steppenwolf*
Romaine Rolland: *Jean-Christophe*
Boris Pasternak: *Dr. Zhivago*
Virginia Woolf: *To the Lighthouse; The Waves; The Years*
Arthur Conan Doyle: all of the Sherlock Holmes tales
Bram Stoker: *Dracula*
Sheridan Le Fanu: *Uncle Silas*
Charlotte Bronte: *Jane Eyre*
Emily Bronte: *Wuthering Heights*
Robert Burton: *The Anatomy of Melancholy*
Fyodor Dostoyevsky: *The Brothers Karamazov*
Herman Broch: *The Death of Virgil*
Herman Melville: *Moby Dick*

Shirley Jackson: *The Haunting of Hill House; We Have Always Lived in the Castle*

Algernon Blackwood: *Supernatural Tales and Ghost Stories*

Joanne Greenberg: *I Never Promised You a Rose Garden*

Daphne du Maurier: Rebecca

Thomas Browne: *Urn-Burial*

Lawrence Durrell: *The Alexandria Quartet*

Andrew Holleran: *Dancer from the Dance*

William Styron: *The Confessions of Nat Turner*

William Faulkner: *The Sound and the Fury; As I Lay Dying; Absalom, Absalom*

C.P. Snow: The *"Strangers and Brothers"* Series of Novels

Eugene O'Neill: *Long Day's Journey into Night; The Iceman Cometh*

Tennessee Williams: *A Streetcar Named Desire*

Elizabeth Bowen: Her Novels and Short Stories

Edith Wharton: Her Novels and Short Stories

Robert Browning: Complete Poetry

Anton Chekov: All of his plays and short stories

William Inge: All of his plays

P.G. Wodehouse: Anything that he ever wrote

Ingmar Bergman: All of his Films

Alfred Hitchcock: All of his Films

David Lean: All of his Films

Such a long list demands an explanation and it is not hard for me to explain why these works were my models: because they and particularly some of their works answered something within me that was crying out for an answer. These authors and works like the Book of Ecclesiastes in the Bible seemed to confirm my own primary intuitions about the nature of the human dilemma and at precisely the time when I read them. I wanted to write books in order to answer essential human questions though not merely because they explored questions of interest to me but because their style of expression matched my own sense that manner and substance are part of a larger whole in which there is no separation. How we tell the story is the story.

Writing, if it is considered to be an integral vocation whether published or unpublished, affects every aspect of a person's life because it is based upon a habit of critical reflection and expression. For a writer the books that are read are testaments to living and inseparable from her daily life. Writers live their books for the simple reason that the act of writing consumes massive amounts of time and energy that otherwise might be devoted to more mundane activities and pursuits. To the true writer any time spent reading, reflecting on, discussing, and absorbing them into one's own repertoire of verbal and narrative skills is not time wasted but rather the very substance of life. Writers feel in connection with the long chain of prior aspirants who as artists are so caught up in life that they assume the role of re-creators in artistic form of the world that encases them but does not imprison them. Writing is an act of superlative freedom, a primary human endeavor that serves both a personal and a social imperative. It is personal in that it roots the individual in an identity and a position toward existence and it is social in that it is an act of communication that is potentially available to others through the act of reading. The author and the reader are joined in a single act of cognition and feeling, a celebration of the primal character of humanity occurs and the world is thereby enriched by a new creation.

Who can say why a certain book can affect us so deeply? I suggest that there is a synchronicity between the book and the particular sensibility of a person particularly at times of crisis. Adolescence and young adulthood are one long series of crises and for this reason young people are subject to being swayed into extravagant enthusiasm by what they read. This was doubly true for me because as a transgender person I was often in search of role models to help me to navigate an essentially chameleon identity structure. I looked to literature for the community structure and affirmation that was lacking to me in my everyday life. I used the written word to channel feelings that received no mirroring voice from my culture. Trans-people were essentially invisible. Their struggles were not celebrated but instead rendered unacceptable and therefore invisible. Part of being invisible is being gifted with an objectivity that would be impossible to a person who manages to neatly fit as just another card in the gender deck.

To transcend categories is the definition of freedom, not that gender is a mere choice, but rather that outcasts are allowed to find alliances wherever they can find them. I chose the classic authors to be my friends and to attune my own search to the vocabulary and the rhythm of their poetry and prose. This is a process of internalization. The paths of literature are as progressive in insight as those of scientists; each generation of practitioners builds upon what has gone before.

Which authors or books had the biggest impact on you as a person?

This question brings to the fore the responsibility of the author and further raises the question of whether writing is a moral or on occasion an immoral act. The fact that books have often been censored by governments and that the Catholic Church at one time, in its desire to protect the faithful from books that would harm faith or morals, kept an Index of Forbidden Books that required a dispensation or very good reason to read, shows the importance afforded to the written word. Examples abound from Baruch Spinoza to James Joyce of writers whose works were confiscated by religious or by civil authorities.

There is also the question of the vulnerable reader: what one person may read with impunity may have a bad effect on a different temperament. Still, a general disclaimer may seem somewhat affected or absurd. This element of personal responsibility as a writer has often troubled me, particularly on the vexed question of gender conflict and the legitimacy of gender transition. The spectrum of human freedom until recently has been curtailed by what for most cultures is a divinely ordained binary that runs through the human species and radically conditions our available options in form and in affective alliances.

That the body itself transitions from youth to age does not surprise us, but that the very seed-ground of sex roles may appear to yield to inner feelings and convictions is more problematic and even threatening. I will say here that the task of the writer demands an objectivity that in the writer's private life and personal decisions may not be interchangeable. Complete consistency surrounding subjects of great importance may prove impossible if one is to write at all. The best that I can do is to insert a cautionary note and leave it to the reader to consult alternate resources before assuming an authority in me that I do not possess. My own impressionist character and the nature of writing in general is tangential and evanescent.

I realize the power of influence however. The two writers who have touched me most deeply and personally have been the novelist Thomas Wolfe and the poet Conrad Aiken. Each has probed the primary terror and anxiety that exist beneath the placid surface of life. Each wrestled in his own way with the dark forces of destruction that Melville embodied in Captain Ahab's great white whale, Moby Dick. Each knew the knife-edged pain of a loneliness that has assumed almost metaphysical dimensions within him.

In a similar way I enjoy the way that Virginia Woolf manages to capture the fleeting immediacy of perception in her work. I respect Malcolm Lowry and James Baldwin also because they reveal the underside of life, the treacherous abyss of feelings and alienation that lie in wait for the unfortunate and the unwary, the addictive side of existence. Andre Gide and Albert Camus probe the nature of human sympathy and the problematic requirement of making human choices in a universe without a consistent vision of faith and an underlying girding in morality existing apart from our own inner feelings and compulsions.

The erosion of faith in the course of the 18th century enlightenment period and in the 19th century, when the Bible was first submitted to formal criticism and textual analysis and when science bore down heavily on various former presumptions of literal truth in elements of scripture, was followed by the repeated wars and existential crises of the 20th century. Literature has mirrored this erosion and the resulting anxiety and discontents. Thomas Hardy suggests that we should face our demons by looking at them directly and fully. I am not sure however that we are always prepared for the aspect of the head of the Gorgon and innocence once lost is with difficulty regained and restored. Still, I love Hardy's poetry for their irony but I find his inveterate depressive stance cloying over time. The same is true of writers like the Comte de Lautreamont, Louis-Ferdinand Celine, Emil Cioran, and other representatives of what I call the dead-end school of literature. Franz Kafka might also be listed in this school if his works were less accurate descriptions of the true horror of the middle years of the 20th century.

Depressive literature can deaden the heart and oppress the spirits. For this reason I recommend that those with a tendency to anomie or melancholy should instead read the books of a sustained optimist like Thornton Wilder or P.G. Wodehouse. This is preferable to wallowing in dark representations and I especially recommend

Theophilus North and *Heaven's My Destination* as helpful anodynes to human disillusionment and despair. I also think that the two books: *Cannery Row* and its sequel *Sweet Thursday* are must reads for every student of humanity.

My favorite authors are not necessarily the best craftspeople with elaborate plots but rather authors who describe life as fundamentally vague and inconclusive. It is often complained of that Chekov wrote plays where nothing ever happens; the characters are simply trapped in untenable situations from which they cannot extricate themselves. I find such visions to be true to life where our triumphs are often small and uncelebrated. This is why I adore books like Virginia Woolf's *To the Lighthouse* or Andre Gide's *The Counterfeiters* or Joyce's *Ulysses.* The vision granted is implicit, interior, and private.

My most recent novel is called *Pacific End: Notes for a Novel.* It is a work that questions the value of a meta-narrative for our lives asserting instead that life is for the most part a sum total of inconsequential moments. History can seek out grand patterns (Spengler, Toynbee) but the average individual is caught up like Humphrey Chimpden Earwicker and Anna Livia Plurabelle in a bar in Bristol dreaming universal history as portrayed in Joyce's magnificent verbal tapestry, *Finnegans Wake.*

My undergraduate studies were in the literature and philosophy. My degree is called a B. A. In Humanities. As an undergraduate my every instinct led me to adopt an interdisciplinary approach to my own education because I am fundamentally resistant to indoctrination. I compulsively see the flaws in virtually every system. This tendency led me eventually to legal study the very essence of which is to see the interconnection of precedents, specific fact patterns, and the rationale that directs appellate decision making. Lawyers are dedicated to a type of reasoning that is multifactorial in nature – policy must meet practice, method must meet content, and all must be both expressible and persuasive in an atmosphere of diversity and even conflict of opinions.

This mode of thinking has always been in me both natural and yet demanding of further refinement. My education has been a single-minded pursuit of what I might term significant truths leading to a vital engagement with reality. The writers that I admire share this characteristic: they are alive with a sense of intimate connection so that in reading them the spirit rejoices as precision meets beauty in accuracy of expression. There is a sense that the shadows of Plato's cave have been banished before a sudden access of divine light streaking out like lightening if only for a moment into total illumination of an aspect of experience. This is what I look for in my own writing and what I demand from life. Walter Pater in the conclusion of his book on the renaissance referred to it as a "hard gem-like flame." To have experienced it is to know what he was talking about.

The critic Matthew Arnold said that the goal of great literature was "to see life fully and see it whole." By this he meant a comprehensive view combined with accuracy in details. This goal presumed in the author a diversity of experience and careful observation. I used to imagine that my limited experience might be barring me from deep knowledge and variety in characterization, but then I reflected on Emily Bronte who from a girlhood spent in the isolation of a parsonage located on the West Riding of Yorkshire in the tiny village of Haworth managed to imagine Heathcliff and Catherine Earnshaw and their tempestuous romance.

Writers are not mere transcribers of reality but rather transformers of reality. Everything is filtered through the writer's unique sensibility and then reduced to words and these in turn may elevate experience to undreamed of intensity and insight. Behind the books that have meant the most to me as a person has always been the personality of the writer. I have always dreamed that these people must be fascinating. I have been surprised though when listening to author interviews to discover that the writer is not coextensive with her works; she may exceed it or she may fall short of our expectations.

In a sense the work of art is always a thing in itself to be judged independently. Often the sensitive reader co-creates the book by mixing it with her own experience. Often there is an ideal time to read a book when we bring to the reading a throbbing expectation that it will tell us something that we desperately need to know. I read Thomas Wolfe for instance at that time of life when everything was still before me and I could feel the poignancy of his own infinite longing for experience. Similarly when I read Voltaire today I find his saturnine reflections on human life and folly mirrors my own gently humorous tolerance for human frailty.

I have always enjoyed the 1960's song by Melanie where she speaks of looking for a good book to live in. Many books have been like that for me. I read *Dr. Zhivago* in college and it made even Stalin's Russia warm with the love of Zhivago and Lara. Movies can do the same thing for me. I carry the movie out of theater with me and only come floating down to earth hours later. This is more than "the willing suspension of disbelief" it is permeability to impressions.

The films of Ingmar Bergman haunt me in a way that nothing else can. I have to be careful because this very sensitivity can make experience like the long screech of feedback to a microphone. I have found ways to select environments so as to avoid falling into vicariously induced moods by sheer proximity to a source that creates an answering resonance within me. This tendency to take on the hue and shape of what surrounds me means that I can absorb too easily what I admire and lose something of myself in the process. To combine sensitivity to influences with a gradually evolving sense of personal convictions is the task of the writer. It means that we are open to experience but still able to sustain a central core of ideas and values out of which our literary works proceed.

I should also mention here several non-fiction books that made a decisive change in my view of the world. The first of these was *Walden* by Henry David Thoreau and his economic essay, *Life without Principle.* I was also influenced by *The Greening of America* and less popular book *The Sorcerer of Bolinas Reef* by Charles Reich. These last two were early manifestos that argued for an economy based upon a vision free of corporate control and for more tolerance for homosexual persons respectively. The book that completed by radicalization was *America is Hard to Find* by the Jesuit priest and activist Daniel Berrigan. These books in turn led me to books by alienated minority figures like James Baldwin and Edmund White and to books displaying a general attitude of rebellion particularly *The Rebel* by Albert Camus.

I developed a great respect and love for union organizers and worker movements that now extends to my ideological support for more open immigration and refugee policies. I favor liberation theology and the Zapatista movement in Mexico. The common features in all of these are simple: recognition of the basic dignity of all people, a standard of living and education that make a decent income possible to support all of the human, plant, and animal life on earth, an end to oppressive systems that benefit the few over the many, and the wisdom that each culture has to offer. Above all else I oppose systems that rely on fear rather than upon affirmation and promise as the primary motivators for human progress and salvation. I oppose a theology that uses an apocalyptic vision of history to justify depleting and destroying the earth and by crowding other species into extinction.

My current interest in post-modernist social theories require a critical reading of key texts in our civilization in the light of current needs and diversity while still retaining respect and reverence for the Western literary canon and its perpetual relevance. I believe though that the course of world history will no longer be Eurocentric. The future of the planet and of human life will be largely determined by Asia, particularly China and India. I am fascinated by geo-politics because history is largely determined by geological constraints and by ethnic loyalties.

I believe in the goal of a global sense of equity between nations while being skeptical of the human capacity for general empathy and goodwill. Absolutist claims to truth invite persecution and wars between contending groups so that peace on earth is more likely to proceed from a balance of mistrust than by perfect mutual understanding. I believe that social progress is slow and subject to reversal and that only by combination in the cause of justice does any human progress exist at all.

For this reason I despise dictatorships and ideologies of conversion by force or by the selective application of economic privation. I believe that the twin forces of leisure and culture do more to advance the happiness of humankind than mere superfluity of goods and the indulgence of material wants. Above all else I value actual freedom which means the ability to turn aside from exterior forces whether economic, political, or ideational structures that indoctrinate us, steal our precious time, and reduce us to serving others not through love but by artificially created scarcity and necessity.

I believe further that education as it has been traditionally practiced has been training in attitudes of subservience rather than a liberating force driven by curiosity and the simple joy of expanded cultural and scientific awareness. Each quadrant of life has its special tasks and abilities and there is neither time nor substance to be wasted on vanity and mental or moral slavery.

Which of your original twelve Prompt stories are you most pleased with?

I don't really have a favorite because each short story is a world unto itself and therefore not to be compared with the others. Having said that however I will attempt to square the circle and say that *Triptych* and *Ligeia* are the most personal to me while *Love and Death* is the longest and best exploration of character. As in *Triptych* I was able in *Love and Death* to use characters drawn from the LGBT community. This allowed me a degree of sympathy and intimate understanding that made these pleasant stories for me to write.

I like *Triptych* because I am in a very real sense all three characters. I also like the image of a three-paneled work of art. To borrow metaphors from allied art forms fascinates me in the same way that Thomas Mann thought of *The Magic Mountain* as verbal music in both composition and style, a sort of paean to illness and its effects upon love. My story *Love and Death* draws from that trend in German literature that traces how we often love in others dissociated fragments of ourselves seeking to heal in them what we cannot face or heal within ourselves.

It is often said that a short story should leave behind its own distinctive flavor or impact so that the reader is haunted for a time as if by a dream. Prose is allowed a certain poetic flavor. The reader enters unaware of who she will meet and must gradually acclimatize herself to the ambience of the narrative and to the person or persons she will encounter there. This means that as in reading poetry it is often helpful to read a short story twice or even three times because with each successive reading various structural elements and foreshadowing events appear and the story emerges as an integral and involved structure.

Novels may be written, poems may be composed but short stories are sculpted. Each genre has its own proper techniques and alliances with other art forms whether graphic or musical. Some vibrate around a central theme while others are discursive in nature and some manage to transcend all categories and are true to some organizing insight that may be particular to that single work. Some evoke a long tradition while others are their own genus or species. The fun of being a writer is to write with an awareness of the tradition and the main exemplars of it while being simultaneously free to challenge the form and to extend its parameters. My own two models for excellent short story writing are Elizabeth Bowen and Flannery O'Connor although they are very different is style and choice of subject matter.

The relationship between character and situation in the short story is bilateral. The best short stories probe a situation through the lens of a central character or a dyad of opposing personalities. I have always loved the ancient Greek philosopher Heraclitus who felt that all of reality is based on change which is paradoxically the only constant. He might be called the father of dialectical thinking that finds truth to be a function of the tension between opposing forces. It is not essential that a short story go anywhere or that it have an obvious termination or to reach a solution as long as the existing relations of the situation in all of its parameters are explored so that the reader herself is raised to a higher level of comprehension.

Chekov understood that to explore states of quiet desperation and unresolved conflict may be the best mirror of the average condition of many people. American culture thrives on the illusion of progress and ultimate resolution, a particularly naïve proclivity in the face of the long history of the world. My intention in the Prompt collection was to explore the form of the short story genre by allowing a degree of freedom to my expression rather simply telling a story in an A to Z fashion. Instead my goal was revelation, to let the story tell itself in whatever guise it chose so that no two stories would be alike. The Prompt Anthology is unique in the openness and diversity of viewpoints and styles of expression represented as well as the diversity of the authors that it has brought together.

Which of your original twelve Prompt stories did you find most difficult to write?

If I write at all I find that the stories just come. What I mean by this is that the words are not pulled out of me but rather ride on their own internal impetus so that I am in a sense merely transcribing them in real time. I have something to say and I say it. I may entertain an initial idea but the actual writing is as immediate as speech. This part of writing is therefore easy for me but what is not easy is for me to decide to let the writing go out into the world because the response is not something that I can determine. I take seriously the Socratic oath that physicians take, although I am not a physician but a writer, "First of all do no harm." In order however to tell a story I am obliged to honor the integrity of the story and its own inner dynamic. This is particularly necessary when the intent of the story is to write of something disturbing or unpleasant or confrontational.

The very title of my contributions to this anthology when gathered together, *Auguries of Desolation,* is hardly an invitation to a genial reading experience.   They are rather an invitation to contemplate a year of anxiety that was prophetic of what was to come and has now arrived in the garb of the covid-19 pandemic that of course I could not have foreseen but rather felt along that delicate membrane of sensibility that writers often possess. Many cultures consider that transgender people display by their very marginality abilities that make them sensitive to collective influences in their environment. Whether that is actually true in a metaphysical sense is not for me to say. It would be flattering however if I might claim this to be true because it would mean that insight and feeling can produce a public augury to help us through dark times.

I do not approve of many of my characters or condone their actions or opinions. Some of them are nasty or misled in their thoughts and actions but as a result they are indicative of social forces in the difficult times that we are living through. Often their hopes may be vain although they may be the best response that they can muster from within their limited world view and experience of life.

This is also how I feel about specifically transgender topics. I know the price that is exacted by coming out as transgender and the price that I have paid for it and I still carry with me a sense that I forfeited a parallel life by the choices that I have made. On the other hand any suppositions that I might make about the course that such a parallel life might have taken is mere supposition just as it is supposition for me to imagine that if I had gone to New York rather than remaining in a small town in Washington I might have been part of the increasing visibility of transgender people in this comparatively open era of our collective existence. A final gloss on this topic of "what ifs" is supplied by the narratives that transgender people find layered upon them by various sources of disapprobation and condemnation. It is not easy to be an artifact of cultural anxiety and loathing.

There is much talk of the danger of what has been called "gender ideology" which would tend to destroy (according to those who find our very existence threatening) all differences between men and women, weaken or destroy the family, and turn humanity into a soup of various body parts interchangeable at will. My answer to these fears has always been that transgender people would not run the risks that we run if we found gender markers to be insignificant and changeable at a whim. The search for "realness" and the desire to find intimacy and family undergirds much of our lives even when we are rejected or exiled from our biological families.

The ready slot of gender conformity that is assumed to be simply waiting there for us to claim and take up simply ignores the fact that many transgender kids and adolescents spent every possible effort to assume a standard gender role in their growing-up years only to be rejected by their straight peers anyway for being somehow queer or different. Very few had the support and opportunity to live a gender role other than that assigned at birth. That our lives can so easily be co-opted to serve the collective agenda and allay the anxieties of larger societal groups whether religious or social or political ignores the fact of our individuality. We are painted as subversive to the same gender normative canons that never served us. The people who hate us most have never met us and realized that we are human just like them and need love, respect, and an opportunity to thrive.

The dilemma then for the transgender writer when she deals with transgender topics is to retain a neutral stance among whatever joint loyalties she may have from her past life. If she is overly sympathetic to her cause or her people she is said to be engaged in special pleading and if she is critical of her own community she is a traitor or a sell-out. This means that to take up such a thankless task is costly. It isn't fun for me to write too close to the bone and I am even surprised to find myself doing so here but since honesty is the primary purpose of writing at all I am doing so. I do not desire to promote the transgender experience or to get others to adopt it. I will say that to confront the fact that gender discomfort exists is the first act of acceptance that we owe each other and that to reduce the quality of life of transgender persons by ridicule or condemnation is a violation of our basic common humanity. I will now take a moment to focus on the specific question here by profiling a single story and the difficulty that writing it presented.

Bats was my most difficult story in many ways because in writing it I was feeling my way and asking myself what the short story is all about as a form and a genre. This story was an experiment in a free-flowing narrative modality as I sought to find a style and format for what I would have to say as the process of my contributions to the Prompt Anthology continued. As such this story is a bridge to the later stories, a blend of drama and exposition as I felt about for a voice and a format.

A careful reading of *Bats* will reveal that the central character is not at all clear about who she is and whether writing isn't some sort of witchcraft. Perhaps she is possessed after all. She believes that her inner anger can influence events. There is more than a touch of Shirley Jackson here; writers as sorcerers. They bend the world to their own conceptions and they invite us into haunted groves to discover ourselves. My general intent in each of the stories was to mirror the mood of a dark era in American history under the Trump Presidency by exploring characters that hover along the borders of dissolution in their pursuit of a stable identity and life-course.

As the first of my wounded and discontented characters Tiffany Amorth is in search of a stable identity and direction in life. She lives in an isolated home under the shadow of a father who sees the shadow side of her personality and cannot affirm her. He concludes in consequence that she is possessed by an evil spirit, a position that justifies the continuous low pressure rejection that he communicates to her. This rejection awakens great anger within her and that anger seeks an outlet in her writing. She comes to believe finally that she can write people's fates into her stories and in doing so she can make things happen in real life.

Her sense of vicarious power relieves her sense of victimhood and discharges the energy of her over-whelming anger that would otherwise be internalized against herself. The question raised therefore is whether this method of coping with her interior states is by its very operation a kind of witchcraft that invites whatever dark spirits may exist about us to take residence within us (a key way to look at the phenomenon of demonic possession). In the literature of exorcism a specific environmental entry point can provide a pre-condition for preternatural activity in a person's life.

There is a bleed-over effect between persons so that her father's inability to deal with his own emotions has made Tiffany a culture medium for his own repressed feelings. She feels that her trust expressed toward both her father and the world that surrounds her has been compromised and in her loneliness she has turned to the shadow realm for defense and companionship. She seeks power over others just as people have always had power over her and she processes her own sense of betrayal and insignificance by an assumed air of omnipotence. This raises the question as the story ends of whether Tiffany Amorth is in fact indeed possessed. In a paired story that follows *Bats* she resolves this tension as she dreams of escape to Denmark.

As I continued to write for this anthology I found that the writing came easier. Another function of the short story format is to explore the way that stories are like those Russian dolls that contain ever smaller versions of the same thing. Stories are like cascading levels of reality. We assemble our life-scripts from the remnants of those lives in the generations that have preceded us. Our memories can provide fixed anchors for later dysfunctional behaviors that are replicated generation after generation. This is one of the causes of mental illness as many psychologists have affirmed.

My approach to short story writing includes the improvisational. I believe that short stories are essay-like in that they attempt to portray essential aspects of life through transient events. There is neither time nor space to elaborate on character as it is formed over time. Instead what is revealed are those lightening-like moments of perception when what was already present is revealed or where a substantial change takes place due to an overwhelming alteration of experience. These were the moments that James Joyce referred to as "an epiphany" as exemplified in his first book, *Dubliners.* The later career of James Joyce is the story of his successive efforts to perfect a literary form before moving on to the next challenge. Only his play *Exiles* is flawed.

James Joyce ended his career with the seventeen year project of writing *Finnegans Wake,* a vast compendium of everything and everyone. HCE or Humphrey Chimpden Earwicker means "Here Comes Everybody." HCE is a universal figure of the human condition, flawed but noble even in defeat. His wife ALP or Anna Livia Plurabelle represents the feminine life-force that winds through time incarnating various versions of the human form in her children: Shem, Shawn, and Issy or Isabel, a younger version of herself. The subject of *Finnegans Wake* is the life process itself as it appears in history, in religion, and in all of the scrambled words of the world as they are brought together in a molten magma-like state under the hands of the great artificer who Icarus-like dares to soar above the human spectacle taking note of all things and writing them down in a single volume. If short stories are cameo presentations, *Finnegans Wake* is a panorama or pageant. The two forms stand at opposite ends of the literary rainbow.

Which book of writing do you recommend?

I believe that writing is best learned by a process of absorption. Just as in figure skating individual skills can be practiced but flow and rhythm are only attained by free-skating and letting the motion carry the skater on and into the jumps and spins. Style precedes substance and is often completely individual and almost innate. Most writers develop their own signature sound and style so that simply to hear a passage read is to recognize the author. Ideas are something else again; these require reflection and a critical sense. The good writer is always aware of her reader but not so as to become self-conscious and mannered.

A critical sense guides construction but far more it makes possible the smoothing process that occurs in the second or third drafts. Some writers require the skill of a sensitive editor who can provide a third dimension to the two dimensional text. Writers know best how a text should mean and sound but an editor if she is sufficiently skilled can reveal latent ambiguities that the author may have missed because her underlying idea has not been sufficiently embodied in the text as written. Good editors are rare. Maxwell Perkins edited Hemingway, Wolfe, and Fitzgerald each of whom had a unique style and a personality structure that did not suffer criticism gladly. Perkins knew this and took on the role of a literary midwife rather than a voice from above telling these great authors how to write; his role was to pare and trim not to constrict or to construct. A good marriage of author and editor is rare. Authors are a prickly lot; it is part of their charm. This is also why authors seldom get along when they appear together on talk shows; there is room for only one diva at a time onstage.

Ideas and themes are another matter still. When people say, "I would like to write but I don't know what to write about," they are displaying the aspect of writing that requires knowledge and experience. These are only acquired through much experience of life: careful observation, imaginative reconstruction, and reflection. A good dramatist also adds the faculty of dissociation that allows her to speak realistically from diverse characters; otherwise they would all sound the same. The appreciation of plot and story, careful timing of effects, adequate foreshadowing, and some degree of reconciliation at the end of the various strands of the story require a sense of construction and timing. This skill set may be the most difficult to acquire.

Not that every short story or novel should read with the neat probability of a television show with its carefully demarcated mini-climaxes before each commercial to sustain interest. A form that is too predictable is always boring. Good literature should be story-based but ultimately tied to life and life is nothing if it is not unpredictable. Stories emerge out of a general Weltanschauung or world-view. How does one acquire such a general sense of the way the world is?

The book, *Recovering Your Story*, by Arnold Weinstein is a good place to begin. There is a therapeutic value in reading great works of literature because they enable us to discover ourselves by seeing our own lives in the wider context of a civilization largely forged by literature. Writing requires that one take a stance towards what has already been written. Works of literature do not emerge from the head of Zeus fully grown. I believe that writing can only be learned through absorbing the works of other writers until they are part of us. Writing is not like following a recipe. The only exception to this is technical writing and perhaps writing non-fiction where topical development and clarity of expression are helpful, even essential. In fiction however the key is to master a genre through wide acquaintance with the masters in the field until they awaken an answering voice within us.

Having said this however I would recommend reading as much as you can about favored authors: their criticism, their biographies, their letters if published, and their autobiographies or journals. Writers write about writing and it pays to listen to them. Realize though that their witness is personal. Seldom do two writers agree about anything, so be prepared to take a position and run with it. A good starting point is *The Summing Up* by Somerset Maugham which describes his own evolution as a writer.

Most writers cannot adequately explain what they do; they may be as surprised at the dynamics of their own creations as their readers are. Good writers follow a craft tradition but in doing so they advance that very tradition by breaking prior norms. There is an oscillation between romanticism and classicism in most literary traditions. Northrop Frye for example has created an entire taxonomy of literary works. There is a motion within most literary works so that in the end there is a change of fortune in the main characters as they meet challenges. In the characters the standards of the community are either affirmed or called into question. In this sense literary works are social products the value of which is often disputed as Sir Philip Sidney discussed in his extended essay, *An Apology for Poetry.*

I confess that my critical preferences follow Edward Young in his *Conjectures on Original Composition* and Edgar Allen Poe's *The Poetic Principle.* I would also recommend the critical writings of Murray Krieger in a more modern vein. I am fond of 17th century prose and am never dismayed by the convoluted phrase. I think that the mindset and faculties of our present age are diminished by the bare declarative statement without texture or nuance and it is my hope that a better embroidered prose may soon supplant the present style of discourse with something displaying more meat and flavor. We will never realize what we have lost until we spend time with the baroque masters and attune our ear to their diction and rhythms. I agree with Thomas Mann that literature is like music. Good writers hear the words that they write and are never in advance of them. Thoughts form organically and are not the mere aftereffects of foregone conclusions. Writers are not puppets of some exterior master but seekers on voyages of discovery.

To read the published letters of great authors provides unparalleled access to the writer's mind and preoccupations. The collections of the journals and the letters of Virginia Woolf are a great place to start, and to finish since she is inexhaustible and encyclopedic in her scope of acquaintance and reflections on various writers. Writers tend to form *ad hoc* communities. These communities are not always friendly because writers read other writers in the same way that people engaged in the same sport follow the competition. The grounds for engagement may be critical reception, sales volume, or attention from a publisher. The end result though can be positive because technique is honed by encounter with difference. Writers both admire and distain other writers sometimes because of differences in their creative philosophy. It takes confidence to be a writer and to resist the pull of contradictory influences. To stand forth boldly as one's solitary self takes courage and sometimes bullheadedness. Posterity rewards persistence. Innovation in the arts as in so much else may be a lonely pursuit. Herman Melville's relatives thought that the poor man was mad. Each book that he wrote had proportionately smaller sales. Thomas Hardy gave up novels after the public response given to *Jude the Obscure.* Henry James reached a sort of peak in his refined and convoluted narrations with his novels, *The Golden Bowl* and *The Ambassadors.* Some writers' peak early and some are prevented from achieving their full promise by dying too young like Thomas Wolfe.

Then there are a tiny few like James Joyce whose genius is so great that he leaves his readership behind. I am a virtual apostle of his final achievement, *Finnegans Wake,* which is a virtual love letter to the human race. In it Joyce turned humor and even a rascally sense of the obscene into a history of the entire human race. Reading it is like learning to play a musical instrument; it takes time and repeated efforts. Joyce appreciated that on the other end of original sin there exists the drama of successive failures; even our saints are flawed. Complexity hides an overarching simplicity and the value of love. Joyce was more Catholic that he knew.

The value of criticism is not to judge and to degrade but rather to illuminate excellence so that we can better appreciate how the great writers manage to achieve their effects. Criticism exists to illuminate and to explicate in other terms what the writer achieves in the first instance by her text. This activity is similar to the study of the Jewish Talmud where each successive reading of the Mishnah results in greater depth and understanding, the Gemara. A Yeshiva school teaches a discipline of approach so that the Torah becomes a living rather than a dead historical text.

At its most basic level criticism is a guide book. So for what might be called a more accessible criticism I would suggest the writings of Alfred Kazin and of Malcolm Cowley. It is often helpful to filter our own personal responses to individual works through the sensibility of a sensitive spirit. For this same reason I recommend the book *Cultural Amnesia: Necessary Memories from History and the Arts* by Clive James, an Australian literary critic of immense scope and erudition. Another work that is of primary importance as a summary of world culture is by John Ralston Saul and entitled: *Voltaire's Bastards.* I also recommend the classic book *Mimesis: The Representation of Reality in Western Literature.* Finally, as a unique attempt at a synthesis of the western literary canon I recommend: Harold Bloom's *Genius: A Mosaic of One Hundred Exemplary Creative Minds.*

What advice would you give an unpublished writer?

I have already expounded on much of my philosophy of writing. The function of the writer is to write, the function of the editor is to edit, and the function of the publisher is to create a marketable product and to ensure distribution. Each plays a key role in mediating between the author and the reader. Each role has its proper boundaries. The writer comes first in point of origin but the temptation to never let go of the work and to realize that it is finished can prevent the actors and the director from staging a play and it can prevent an editor from eliminating ambiguities and the publisher from reducing the text to a saleable product. An overbearing influence by an editor can frustrate an author's desire to completely realize his or her vision while a good editor can help an author to fully realize his or her intent by clarifying key themes and by smoothing the edges of a text through careful trimming away of confusing or non-essential elements.

The publisher can provide encouragement at key moments when an author succumbs to self-doubt or exhaustion. At least in the past publishers were often an essential buffer between penurious or unstable writers and the folly of their own intemperate habits. Talent needs a home and appreciation as well as a market for our creations and the best publishers can provide these. Of course such delicate handling is often reserved for treasured authors and the young writer who brings such temperamental demands to the publisher will be disappointed.

The days of the family-owned publishing houses are no more. Book publishers were gobbled up by corporate conglomerates with a bottom-line mentality in most cases. Fortunately the advent of print-on-demand and smaller private niche publishing has given more voices a chance to be heard than in the old days. Good work will find a place and much of the run-around has been eliminated.

My overall advice then to writers is to do the writing job well because that is the task of the writer. Avoid publishers that are in the business of teaching writers how to write. Look for a publisher that spares the writer superfluous tasks but be prepared for a key truth: very few books have what may be called general appeal; writers have a target audience and all fiction is finally genre dominated. Decide who you want to reach and how and then trust your instincts and continue to write.

Many recent books have been written about self-promotion and marketing for budding authors. To say that they leave a nasty taste in the mouth is obvious because there are many items from detergents to toothpaste that are easier to sell than books. It is a sad fact but after high school and college fewer and fewer people read anything beyond a smattering of self-help books and predictable romances and thrillers.

On occasion a supposedly sexy read will vault a novel into the category of a must-read for those whose fantasy and visualization skills demand hypnotically suggestive passages. Certain other works slated to an age group of children or female adolescents will create cycles of books to fuel a micro-addiction to witches or vampires or what have you. There may be a central figure that one can identify with; many men once could imagine that there was a slumbering secret agent inside them and that they could alternate defeating improbable foes with nightly bedroom antics drawing on an endless supply of available females, fatal or otherwise.

Then there are various university presses on the other end of the publishing world that publish scholarly books that may sell a few thousand copies to the scholarly community that find such matters interesting or professionally required. There are few captive audiences anymore and to presume to gage the national or the international pulse with a breakthrough insight is unlikely to occur. The occasional bestseller does not alter this situation. All of which is to say that the writer must accept that the time spent writing, if exercised for expected pecuniary rewards, is time ill-spent. The good news is that this very fact frees the writer to create the best work that she can in order to live up to her own standard of excellence and then to begin the long and piece-meal search for those who can appreciate what she has done. It is here that publishers can help the solitary writer.

I hear much of book tours and book-signings but even these presume some degree of predictable author name recognition and a following have been achieved. Publicity tours demand larger publishing houses to finance them or available private funds and time. Small initial print runs have long since made an author's second book to be at least as critical as the first. The time allotted to achieve success in major bookstores is limited. To be listed on an online store is in many ways to be located somewhere as a drop in a vast ocean where a theoretical presence is in fact virtual invisibility.

Financed expeditions to find the author where she is lost in a jungle of towering trees are unlikely to exist. In the world of publishing as in so much else it is success that breeds further success. The public's memory is fickle and sustained loyalty even rarer. The net result is that authors often find themselves in the position of Norma Desmond waiting for Hollywood to call. Sustained labor can achieve results of course but time spent in other pursuits limits the time for writing and meanwhile one must still manage to exist.

Copyright grants protection that extends long past the shelf-life and appeal of most books. Look up any best-seller of two years ago and see whether a current edition is available. Printing on demand makes it possible of course for a trickle of life to be sustained in the desert and this has been the salvation of many writers. Micro-publishing allows for more freedom and intimacy to exist between an author and her readers. One can no longer repair to Cannes or Biarritz and send a novel off to New York every two years when funds are running scarce.

After these discouraging remarks however I would like to point out that quality never dies and I have personally been delighted to find a treasure of delights preserved by the Gutenberg Project of books long since in the public domain that exceed in quality and relevance most of what is published today to an avid readership hungry for trifles written by dullards who have no idea or concern for the general decline of literacy in America. As John Keats said, "A thing of beauty is a joy forever." So I urge all would-be authors to value their writing as they value themselves, not for celebrity but for that group of people who love them. There is no greater joy than to stand back from whatever one creates and to say, "There it is!"

Virginia Woolf solved many of these problems by creating with her husband Leonard Woolf the Hogarth Press. It was the Hogarth Press that published T.S. Eliot's great poem, *The Wasteland.* It was Sylvia Beach who published Joyce's magnificent and celebrated book, *Ulysses,* out of her Paris bookshop, Shakespeare and Company. Authors are in many ways a self-sustaining community. Now and again a publishing miracle will occur and entire schools of authors find a simultaneous voice. It is no accident that Shelley knew Byron, Wordsworth knew Coleridge, that the Sitwell brothers and sister were from a single family, or that the writers of the Beat Movement were all friends. Ezra Pound promoted James Joyce. Only Amy Lowell was a solitary apostolic voice as a poet, but then she had the money to do so. Above all then do not surrender hope for hope always finds a way.

Do you have a "dream project" as a writer? If so what would it be?

The copyright laws of the United States protect literary works for the lifetime of the author plus seventy years so it is natural that a writer for both artistic and commercial motives would hope that her books would be purchased and read for the full time allotted to her estate. After this period her works enter the public domain and may be reproduced without royalties to the author. I mention this because it is the hope of authors that their works will prove interesting and relevant so as to ensure a long period of readership. One of the dilemmas of the artist is that the more localized in time, place, or genre the book may be the more risk there is that changing times will diminish the appeal of that book except for those with antiquarian proclivities and tastes.

A classic work in contrast aspires to immortality or at least to a degree of longevity that exceeds the period in which it was first submitted to the public for approbation and recognition. Even many winners of the Nobel Prize for Literature are little read today. Some great works are discovered though at later dates and finally reach a readership that eluded them during the author's lifetime. Examples of this fate are Herman Melville, Franz Kafka, and F. Scott Fitzgerald. This observation is why I insist that writers must be true to their own vision and purposes, particularly if they aspire to lasting relevance. Many curious books have qualified as classics because in them is found something of perennial value while many celebrated works with great sales perish is short order as the public's fickle interest wanes.

The best creations like slow burning embers give off more heat than swiftly consumed kindling. The diminishing costs of reproduction and the Kindle revolution has made the concept of a beautiful leather-bound volume with gilt-edged pages seem somewhat absurd. Words today and phrases are of such brief duration and of so arbitrary a nature that the idea of long reflection and perennial relevance seems the height of vain aspiration. Even the speeches of key public figures scarcely stimulate recollection within a week of their puppet-like delivery since everyone knows that they were composed by teams of unacknowledged minions who will never appear for scrutiny by the public.

Literary history has its great names who have attempted encyclopedic assessments of human nature such as Shakespeare, Dickens, Balzac, and Joyce as well as writers who due to a single major work will be equally immortal such as Emily Bronte and Robert Musil. I say all of this as a prelude to explain that my dream project is to continue to reach that special group of readers who share my reverence for the classics. No one can directly intend to write a classic work and no fortune-teller can predict or even describe how or when anything will be considered to have reached that level of significance and appeal. Still for all of that I believe that certain writers believe that they are writing in the classical tradition, seeking to advance the long inquiry of art as it probes the human condition in its unfathomable complexity and variety. My dream project has been and continues to be to echo in some far off way the sound of a distant clarion from the writers, often long dead, who are for me living voices.

I do have another dream project however. Like many writers I would like to write specifically for films, not Hollywood blockbusters, which are usually farmed out to well known screen writers, but films that have the same expressionist sensitivity of the Ingmar Bergman films. To encounter his cinematic creations is to realize how European film-making differs from American films. The films of Bergman are both realistic and symbolic at the same time; they are films of moods and ideas that explore relationships. They take you inside the characters by the expressiveness of their highly talented cast members.

It is hard to pick a favorite, but I have always loved, *The Silence.* It explores the adult world from with a child's vision and point of view. The situation is only vaguely defined so that the elements cohere only by the fact that they are happening. There are few existing categories through which to interpret them and in this sense

Bergman mirrors the way that reality impinges upon us in ways that are often dreadful and beyond our ability to find easy answers. There is no easy three act structure to provide resolution and because of this we are often left bewildered and anxious because we realize that Bergman has touched us in the places of uncertainty that exist for all of us. The dialogue is often less important than the visual scenes that develop an intensity and a significance that is more suggestive than it is literal.

I would like to write dramas and films like that because they are at once character specific and universal. They leave an impression that remains long after we leave the theater. Motion and facial expressions are no longer utilitarian but true windows to the soul as in Berman's film, *Cries and Whispers* or the suggestive but indeterminate relations between the nurse and her female patient in *Persona*. Some people are frustrated with Bergman because they expect an easy answer to what is going on in his films. This misreads Bergman's intent. His films are more like impressionist paintings, the painting is less a representation than an object that must be approached from within itself. There is no handy guide to offer outer testimony so that any two people might be affected by his films in different ways. The attention that Bergman devotes to minute details is not linear but three-dimensional so that meaning radiates outward in multiple directions. This type of art teaches us how it is to be apprehended; we have to step up to the challenges that it presents and by doing so we enlarge our own sensibilities.

Did the pandemic impact your writing? If so, how did it do so?

Before dealing with my personal response to the pandemic I would like to take note of the utter improbability in the minds of most people, particularly in America, that any such visitation was even possible. I had long since thought through the probabilities of the

Cascadia Earthquake or even an eruption of Mount Rainer or perhaps a nuclear war with North Korea but like many Americans I trusted that the filter provided by the World Health Organization and the Centers for Disease Control would prevent any widespread plague of contagion in America. As the year 2020 progressed Americans began to divide around issues of freedom and the common good. The wearing of face masks became the insignia of the degree that Americans could be counted on to adhere to common-sense public health mandates. Long simmering resentments or suspicions of unwarranted government intrusion on private affairs and religious observances soon erupted into large scale resistance that has resulted in the exponential numbers of deaths and covid-19 cases of November/December 2020, as these lines are being written.

Loyalty to the President became identified with scorn for the virus and a displacement of its world-wide spread to its first country of manifestation, China. Donald Trump's trade war with China was now broadened to a general mistrust that mirrored the anti-Chinese sentiments of the late 19th century. The religiously motivated animosities of Americans began to shift towards a specific focus on Iran and China. The wall that had been in the process of construction along our southern border with Mexico had little effect on a virus. Instead of women and children from Honduras and Guatemala the virus arrived by air flights from Europe and from return flights from China to the U.S.A.

I wanted this year to get things off to a good and propitious start so I did not wait for May or June to head south to the Oregon coast. Within a week of my departure I was surprised to hear that my brother was the admitting physician for the patient identified at that time, February 29th 2020, as the first American to die from the virus. By then I was no longer in Washington. The pandemic began to take hold for me shortly after my arrival in Oregon. I left for the coast on impulse the weekend before Ash Wednesday. Two weeks later I just had time to visit a monastery for a short retreat and to pursue upon returning to the coast my usual activities of writing in coffee shops and haunting various buffets before the spread of the virus really became widespread and the state lockdown happened.

After that I simply adjusted to my present circumstances and I have remained here ever since. The county where I am situated has witnessed comparatively low virus spread to date. Here I have been able to do a great deal of reading and reflecting and to work on two new books: a sequel to my multi-volume, *The Confessions of Sherlock Holmes* and an extension of a book of political essays originally entitled *The Great Reset* that I first published in 2017.

The Sherlock Holmes sequel has been a multi-year project to understand the role of the individual in history in the light of the First World War. The book of essays explores current issues in American politics and also deals with various problematic issues in the Roman Catholic Church. These essays share in common a sense of helplessness and dissolution in two areas of life where many people seek guidance and stability, viz. in our political structures and in our religious institutions. When fundamental institutions seem not only divided in terms of policy but in the methodological norms that govern their procedures and essential underpinnings the result is a sense of confusion and anomie.

If there is one sense that human beings share in common at this critical juncture of history it is precisely this sense of things coming apart so that we are experiencing a simultaneous sense of crisis and of failure in critical institutional levels of support in our collective psychic infrastructure. Valid answers are not forthcoming because even their sources are perceived as biased by political factors, personal advantage, and even by epistemological collapse. This is more than a simple loss of trust because of a temporary set of aberrations. Instead, when I speak of epistemological collapse I am referring to a general sense that the truth function of a society is unattainable because the primary axioms and their corollaries are now in dispute.

It was precisely this problem that was explored in the writings of Michel Foucault. Like many post-modern thinkers Foucault was able to show that many of our social systems if not all of them rest upon a consensus that is social in origin and power related and not metaphysically grounded. As such these fundamental structures are subject to radical questioning and may collapse suddenly under stress. I believe that the coronavirus pandemic has nudged social institutions at all levels into a condition of recognizing their fundamental inadequacy under the present conditions of rapid change whether in politics, climate change, religion, or economics.

This was precisely what occurred at the time of the Black Death in the 14th century. Conceptions of reality can suffer their own earthquakes. The more fundamental and unquestioned these axioms and corollaries are the greater damage is inflicted on a sort of psychic scale, one that is exponential in nature. As we approach the most fundamental institutions and concepts the damage done and the disruption that occurs through their diminishing utility as coping mechanisms approaches the catastrophic. Under certain conditions whole civilizations can collapse.

It is my belief that the stories in the Prompt Anthology written last year as my contribution manifest a premonitory sense that something dreadful was coming. The clouds were gathering and each of the characters in my stories was dealing with changes that threatened their former precious but precarious sense of a stable existence and the ability to cope with new circumstances. Someone somewhere was presumed to be in charge, competent to the situation, and could guide us through the collective crisis and therefore deserved our loyalty and allegiance. He was not Donald J. Trump and his menagerie in residence at the White House.

As the year of 2020 draws to a close these assurances are ever more questionable. The very simultaneity of the corona crisis has made it a general human dilemma where life cannot go on as we have expected it would with only minor adjustments and accommodations as we sink deeper into the 21st century. The world is being asked to make swift and perhaps irreversible decisions that will affect the balance of world-trade, national sovereignties, fundamental rights, and basic individual security. The result is a potential for a degree of existential panic and violence as protests fill streets in nation after nation and as various oligarchs wonder if the systems that have ensured their economic primacy are about to collapse.

These are critical times, but the juncture of decisions is at hand. The biosphere has shown inordinate patience with our greed and folly; now is the time for a severe assessment followed by action on multiple fronts. From the bottom ascent in the only direction possible and I prefer to end on an upsweep, an optimistic and more salutary note. For these reasons I have chosen to copy the title of John Donne's famous poem, *A Valediction Forbidding Mourning*, as my final entry to the Prompt Project's last volume as a poetic farewell to a way of life and a degree of world consensus that is about to undergo unparalleled stress but perhaps finally to lead us all to a new assessment of what it means to be human and a better life.

CARRIE
AVERY
MORIARTY

A FRESH START

Chapter 1

Bryan

That's it?" I asked.

"That's all we need," Dr. Robinson said.

"And you'll get the results to me when?"

"Once we have the final results," she said, "you will be informed. It shouldn't take but a couple of days."

"I guess I'll go, then," I said.

"I know this is difficult," she offered. "I'm sorry."

"It's OK," I replied. "I just wish I had an answer as to why it was me who got this."

"That's completely understandable," she said. "In your post visit notes there are names of some counselors that help with processing this type of diagnosis. You should call and make an appointment with one of them. They can help you with ways to tell your family and friends, as well as coping mechanisms for you to handle the next steps in your treatment."

"Honestly," I replied, "I just want to take some time to myself."

"Just be sure you let someone know where you are," she said. "We often see people go into a depression when they get this kind of diagnosis. I want to be sure that you're safe, that you won't lose yourself."

"I'll escape," I said. "But it'll be into my work."

"That can be just as dangerous," she admonished. "Whether it's work or some other vice, you need to be sure that you take care of yourself."

"I will," I promised. "Thank you for taking such good care of me. I look forward to hearing from you when you have the results."

With that, I walked out the door, papers in hand with a list of professionals to take care of the mental side of a diagnosis of cancer. I told the doctor I wondered why it was me, but I already knew. I hadn't taken care of myself very much since Suzie died. She was my world, the center of my universe. I'd put off getting certain tests done.

Honestly, she was more than my wife, she was my everything, and when the drunk driver took her from me, I wanted to do nothing but hide from the world. Fortunately, my work could be done from anywhere. I wasn't tied to a place, just to her. Now that she was ripped from me, I had the ability to go anywhere. The only thing that tied me to this city was the fact that this was where she was laid to rest.

What an odd phrase that is, though. Like, they're not resting. They're just gone. No longer tied to the planet. Not stuck here with the rest of us making a mess of this place. She was free, and yet I was rooted. We'd never had kids, choosing to be child-free, so no reason to not go somewhere else. Somewhere that the memories didn't invade my every moment. A place where I could lose myself in a crowd that didn't know me.

The problem with that concept was that I would always be recognized by my fans. My line of work put me in a place where some people recognized me. And when one did, then a dozen more would find me. This was why we'd decided the small town in the middle of nowhere was the best place to live. But then that monster had stolen her from me, taken the only good thing about this place away.

Oh, sure, I had a nice house, nice car, all the trappings of a successful career. It was worthless, though, without the lighthouse that was my Suzie. She steered me away from the rocks along the shore of this minefield that was my mentality. Kept me safe and guided me into the safe harbor of her love. The tsunami that was the crash took that harbor and made it unsafe, cluttered with the broken pieces that were once perfect, and I had to find my own way in this world without her.

Cancer sucks, sure, but if she'd been here, it would have been bearable. I could have navigated the turbulent waters of this section of the river if she'd been there as the rudder to keep me on track, going the right direction. Now I was alone, adrift amidst a turbulent sea, lost without a guide, without anything to show me where to head, a place that could be safe in this storm that was my life.

Chapter 2

Anna

"Hi," I said. "My name is Anna."

"Hi, Anna," the group parroted.

It was almost exactly like you see on TV, the group dynamic. You say your name, what is going on with you, and everyone encourages you for your progress and comforts you with your mistakes. Didn't matter whether it was for an addiction or anything else, the group dynamic was nearly identical.

"I kinda feel lost right now," I continued. "I'd been doing really good with keeping my needs under control, but I had a big scare medically and I felt like I needed the crutch."

"What did you do?" one of the members asked.

"Called my sponsor," I replied. "I know how to do the work, it was just a struggle."

"You did the right thing," another member said.

Honestly, I didn't really want to hear their praise. I wanted to lock myself away from the world and read. Fall into a world that didn't have everything I was dealing with in it. I wanted to escape.

"Thanks." I said what was expected, followed the 'rules' of the group, then shut up and let someone else have their turn.

My addiction had put me in mandatory group therapy like this for a couple of years. I had to get my little book signed by the group leader to prove I was here every week. Not like I had much of anything else to do. Being financially independent without the need for a job had put me into the mess I found myself, but thankfully I didn't blow through the inheritance. I still had the money, so could afford not doing any real work.

Maybe that was the problem. Maybe I needed a job to keep me on track, to give me some sort of purpose in life rather than just existing.

By the time the group finished, I hadn't heard anything anyone else had said. Oh, I contributed, parroting the greeting, nodding and looking sympathetic, but I was a master at being present without really engaging. Learned that from my dad. He was there, just not interested in anything, even though it looked like he was. When he died, I was relieved. I know it sounds bad, but it is what it is. At least he was good for something, even if it wasn't an emotional attachment to his daughter.

As I walked home after group, I passed the town bookstore. There was a sign that said they were hiring. I hadn't held a job in all my life, simply did whatever I wanted and let daddy foot the bill. Unfortunately, that's what got me to where I am now, which was not a good place. I decided that I'd stop in the next morning and fill out an application.

The little town was good for me, away from the bright city lights and away from temptation on every corner. I wanted to figure out who I was, find the real me, and being away from everything I knew was exactly where I had wanted to start. I felt very fortunate to be able to get away from my hometown and find a place where I could recover and recoup, away from the press that had hounded me for so long. They'd probably find me again, eventually, but for now, I was an anonymous nobody in rural upstate New York.

That was another benefit of these groups. No one really knew who you were. I mean, if I were someone really famous, like an actor or something, then sure, they'd all know me. But I wasn't famous like that. I had a rich daddy, and the only reason people knew about my mess was because I was in the city. Once I moved out here, away from the skyscraper that was my family home, I became just another faceless person with a checkered past looking to start over. It was actually refreshing to go into a grocery store or a restaurant and not have someone whispering behind me about all the things they'd read in the weekly tabloid at the check stand.

I climbed the steps to my little cottage and keyed open the door. Closing it behind me, I leaned against it and sighed deeply. Shutting out the world hadn't been the best thing, but making friends was always hard for me. I eased off the door and moved to my bedroom, flicking the light on. Opening my closet, I looked through what I had brought with me when I came, noting that there wasn't much that could be considered business attire, but there were a couple of dresses that would be sufficient to pass muster in this little town and the corner bookstore.

Pulling out a blue patterned one, I laid it across the chair in the bedroom and inspected it to make sure there weren't any stains or anything on it. Finding it suitable, I then pulled out a pair of sensible low heels and set them under the chair. I pulled out everything else I'd need in the morning to look like the professional I knew I wasn't. That was one thing daddy's money had been good for, boarding school. Not only did I learn how to read and write, but also how to present myself as a professional. Of course, it's also where I found my love of sex, and learned that sometimes it could be better than even the best of drugs that the kids brought with them.

Oh, don't get me wrong. I tried most every drug brought into the school. I just found that sex gave me a better high without all of the downfalls that the others had. No one in my support group knew that sex was my addiction, though. They all assumed it was alcohol, just like them. I could play it off as that, and my attorney assured me that no one in the group would know what I used to cope, and that even though it wasn't technically a support group for this, it counted toward my court ordered rehab.

Feeling pretty good about myself, I hopped into the shower to get myself presentable for the next day. I didn't shower in the morning. Actually, I didn't really people in the morning, either. My day usually started at noon at the earliest, and ran until after midnight, pushing two in the morning most days. Tonight, I would brew myself a cup of tea and get to bed early. I wanted to look like I did mornings when I went to the bookstore to apply for the position. First impressions were always important.

Chapter 3

Bryan

You would really be open to doing a reading and signing in our little bookstore?" the gal behind the counter asked.

"I've been out of touch with my readers," I replied. "I want to reconnect with them. I think this would be just the thing to get me over my writer's block."

"I don't understand," she said.

"Reading tends to get my creative juices flowing," I explained. "When I'm stuck, like I am now, if I read something I've written, it tends to get things flowing again."

"That's really interesting," she said. "Let me check our calendar, but I'm sure I can get you in any time you would want."

"Whenever is convenient for you guys is probably fine with me," I replied.

I didn't want to tell her that I just needed something besides a doctor's appointment to get me out of my house. I needed to do something, anything, that wasn't stuck inside with my laptop and the four walls of my study, with no distractions from the loss of my wife, with nothing but my disease to keep me company. The door chimed and a young woman walked in. She was pretty, but she wasn't my Suzie.

"Tell you what," I said to the clerk. "I'll leave you my card and you can email me a time and day that will work. I see you have customers and I don't want to block your sales."

"Thank you," she said, taking my card.

"Have a nice day," the woman said as I passed her.

"You, too," I replied, then stepped into the sunshine.

I walked down the street and stepped into the pharmacy. I hated the meds that the doctor had given me, but I knew that I needed them to stay alive, so I picked up the prescription and walked back out. Next stop was the florist to pick up some forget-me-nots. The cheery blue with the bright yellow centers reminded me of my Suzie, how she would brighten any room she walked into. I paid for those and then continued on my way down the road. Crossing at the streetlight, I passed the grocery store and stepped in to grab a can of soda. Mellow Yellow was Suzie's favorite drink, even though she didn't have it often. I always tried to bring one when I stopped to see her. I never drank it, just left it there at her headstone for her. They were always gone when I came back, so I have no idea if the groundskeeper took them, some kids picked them up, or what exactly happened to them, but it made me feel better bringing it to her.

The gate was open and inviting, even though it was a place filled with death. Virtually anyone who was in there was grieving, whether it was new and fresh or just waves leftover from times before. Mine wasn't exactly new, but it wasn't long lived either. How had six months gone by without her? I wasn't sure I was going to make it through that first day, and yet here we were, six months down the road, and I was still upright, still working, and still living. The world didn't end when her life did, and somehow, I'd figured out how to continue on.

"Hey," I said, though I knew she wouldn't answer. "Brought you your soda. Found these pretty things, too."

I leaned the can against the headstone, then set the flowers into the built-in vase in the ground in front. Convenient that they offered those so folks could leave flowers. Once they had passed their time, they were disposed of without the family having to remember to do it.

"I talked to the Good Book," I said once I'd settled the flowers and sat next to her. "Offered to do a reading and signing. I know you'd want me to move forward, and it's hard, but I'm trying. Doctor said that she thinks it should be a quick surgery to remove the small tumor in my lung, then the chemo will find anything that remains. I've already started with some pills, but they're awful. They haven't scheduled the surgery, yet, though, so we're still waiting on that. I'm hoping I can get the signing in before I go under the knife."

I didn't want everything I talked to her to be bad, but she was my rock, and I needed her during this.

"I think you'd like Dr. Robinson," I continued. "She's a lot like you. No nonsense, but kind as well. She wants me to join a support group or something. You know me and crowds, though. I'm not very open in the best of times, so spilling my guts to a bunch of strangers is completely outside my idea of something good. Maybe I can find someone to talk to one-on-one. I mean, I can talk to you, but you aren't that good at giving advice lately."

I laughed. I couldn't help it. It was morbid and horrible, but she would have found it funny. The laugh caught in my throat as I realized that I was making jokes about her being gone. I didn't want to do that. Didn't want to make light of her not being here when I continued on with my miserable self.

"Thinking of starting a new series," I said. "You know that fantasy thing I was talking about? Wondered if I should make the lead female like you. Strong, yet kind. Brilliant, yet goofy. Absolutely perfect in every way."

I waited. Didn't know if I was waiting for her to answer or just sitting in silence in her company. Either way, it was calming for me. Being with her, even in this morbid way, grounded me. She was always my rock, my lighthouse in the crashing waves, the one guiding me back to the safe shore. God, I missed her. I wonder what she would have thought about me sitting next to her, regaling my day and my first world problems. She'd probably tell me to get over myself and spend some time in the cancer ward at a children's hospital where kids who were toddlers were stuck with all sorts of needles and tests and likely wouldn't even make it to double digits.

"Guess I better get on that fantasy," I said, getting up and brushing my pants. "Not going to write itself."

I paused. This would be the moment she'd tell me that I could do this, that whatever I wanted, it was within me to make it happen. It was as if I could hear her saying these things to me, but it was all in my head. Sniffing, I walked away, only looking back once. The walk home was solemn. All I ever wanted was to spend the rest of my life with her, and I couldn't do that. She was gone, and there was no getting her back.

My desk was dark, so I flicked on the desk lamp. Opening my laptop, the screen came on and it was her, right there, staring at me with that cheeky smile she would give me when she knew I needed to write. I reached out and touched the screen, only to have it flip to the log in state, her face blurring behind the box asking for the password. I entered it and got to work.

Chapter 4

Anna

"Have a nice day," I said to the man as he was walking out of the store.

"You, too," he replied and went on his way.

He was familiar to me, somehow, but I couldn't quite place him.

"How can I help you?" the gal behind the counter asked.

"I saw your sign in the window," I said, pointing that direction.

"Wondering whether you had an application."

"We don't," she replied. "But you could leave your resume."

"See," I began. "I don't really have one. I've kind of never had an actual job."

"Oh," the gal said. "Well…"

I could tell she wasn't sure what to do with that information.

"I've always had someone to support me," I offered. "My dad was wealthy and I didn't have a need to work. But now I find that I have time, and really want to do something worthwhile. I thought this would be a good place to start."

"I mean," the gal said.

"It's OK," I replied. "If you don't have a way for me to do an application, I'll see if I can come up with something for a resume and drop it off later. I just love books, so thought this would be the perfect place to have my first job."

"Hang on," she said, then picked up the phone and dialed.

"I'll just look around," I said and stepped away from the counter so she could have a private conversation with whoever it was she was calling.

Normally I read romance, but for some reason I'd been getting into the science fiction and fantasy realms for my reading. There was something perfect about a world where even the crazy creatures were just as messed up as us humans.

"Miss," the woman said after I'd been browsing the titles along the shelves.

"Yeah," I replied, turning towards her.

"Would you be willing to wait about half an hour for the owner to come in?"

"Sure," I said, a little confused.

"I told him that there was someone who was interested in the job," she continued. "He said he'd come in and have a conversation with you and see if it was a good fit."

"That would be great," I said. "In the meantime, who was that who walked out when I came in? I recognize him, but can't quite find the name."

"Oh," she said. "That was Bryan Walker. He's a local who is also an author. He was asking about coming in and doing a reading and signing."

"I knew he looked familiar," I said. "I love his work."

"Yeah," she said. "He's had a rough year. It'll be nice to see him getting back out again."

"What happened?" I asked.

"Oh," she said, obviously concerned by what she'd said. "It really isn't my place to gossip. Let's just say that he's had a rough go round and we're all hoping that good things come into his life really soon."

I simply shrugged. I knew what it was like to be talked about behind my back, and I certainly didn't want to do that about someone else. "I'll find something to read to pass the time," I said, and began perusing the bookshelves once again.

Perhaps she wasn't prepared for me to drop it like that because she kind of stood there waiting for me to ask more, then realized that I wasn't interested and went back to the counter. After just a few minutes, I found the first in the Officers of the Solstice series that Bryan Walker had written. Pulling it from the shelf, I walked to the counter and set it down, pulling out my wallet.

"You can just read this until Mr. Holmes comes in," she said.

"I actually lost my copy of this," I said. "I think I left it somewhere and would really like to have it anyway. It's really no bother."

"If you're sure," she said hesitantly.

"I am," I replied and pushed the book closer to her.

She punched some buttons on her keyboard and then gave me the total. I handed her my card and she stuck it in the little machine, then punched the total into it so that it would charge me. Once the machine started printing the receipt, she pulled my card out and handed it back to me. Pulling the receipt off the machine, she placed it on the countertop and handed me a pen. I signed the charge slip, then she stuck it into her register, printing out another receipt for me. I put it into the book to use as a bookmark and went to the window seat to read while I waited.

I was just getting to the good part of chapter three when the owner came over and said hello.

"I understand you are interested in the position," he said.

"Yes," I replied, placing the receipt in my book. "Unfortunately, I don't have any experience."

"Tell me this," he began, indicating that I should retake my seat. "What do you love about books?"

"Well," I said, thinking. "Honestly, they've always been my escape. Whether it was in school when I didn't want to do an assignment, or at family gatherings that were boring, I always found a place to hide within my books."

"I feel the same way," he replied. "But, what do you want to do in working here?"

"I've found myself without purpose," I explained. "I don't need to work, per se, but having something to do, in order to make a difference, would be nice."

"So, why don't you volunteer somewhere?"

"I feel like," I began, then paused. "Honestly, I don't think I'd be very good at it. If I didn't have a reason to go, I would probably just forget or decide not to show up."

"What makes you think you would if you had a job?"

"That's something I thought about, too," I said. "But I am very reliable when it is something that is expected of me. My father would roll over in his grave if he thought I was unreliable. And that's not something I could stomach. So, I would do my utmost to be responsible, prompt, and ready to do your bidding."

"You are refreshingly honest," he laughed.

"Yeah," I replied. "Sometimes that doesn't work in my favor."

"Today must be your lucky day," he said. "Let's get some paperwork out of the way and get you on the schedule to train."

"Really?"

I was shocked. He hired me without knowing anything about me. Without even doing any kind of background check or anything. Seriously just had a conversation and hired me.

"I believe that oftentimes the first impression is the best," he said. "My name is Bill. What's yours?"

"It's Anna," I replied, holding out my hand to shake.

"Good to meet you," he replied. "Hey, Mal."

"Yeah," the gal behind the counter called back.

"I'd like you to meet your new coworker, Anna," he said. "Anna, this is Malory. She's been with me for, what is it, ten years?"

"Something like that," Mal replied. "So, what shall we do first?"

"Let's get her information and get her the tax forms she has to fill out," he said, stepping behind the counter. "You go find them in the office. I have no idea where they are."

"I'll go print them out," she said. "You have a Social Security card?"

"Probably," I replied. "But not with me. I'll have to call my lawyer and have him get it to me."

"Your lawyer?"

Bill didn't look too pleased about me using that word.

"I had some trouble a while back," I explained. "Nothing

serious, I promise. I just have him on retainer, and he holds all of my important paperwork. It keeps me honest, and helps to keep me on track with everything. If you want, I can have him call you."

"Oh, no," he said. "When can you get the card? I know we can't have you start until we get that."

"I can ask him to bring it up tonight," I replied. "It shouldn't be too much of a hassle. He may even send someone from his office with it. Do you need anything else?"

"If you have a passport," Mal said. "That makes things super easy. I've got a list of what documents we need to verify you. I'll be right back."

"So," Bill said after Mal walked back to the office. "Your trouble. Anything I should be concerned about?"

"Absolutely not," I replied. "It was a while ago, and I'm in counseling and going to meetings to help me cope and keep me on track. It wasn't drugs or theft or anything like that, just a little bit too much time and not enough discipline that led me into some dark times."

"As long as I don't have to worry about the cash I keep on hand," he said.

He was still eyeing me pretty suspiciously, but I offered, "I have more money than anyone has a right to have. My dad was Michael Freeman."

"Oh," he said, his eyes growing large. "I guess you don't need to work."

"Yeah," I replied. "I don't have the same last name, just so you know. My dad wanted to make sure that I didn't have anyone causing me problems, so he gave me his mom's maiden name as my last name."

"What happened to your mom?"

"I never knew," I said. "He didn't talk about her. I think she died when I was young, but I couldn't say for sure."

"I don't remember him every being married," he said. "Although I don't know much about the what nots of the rich and famous, so he could have been married to the Queen of England for all I know."

"Now that," I laughed, "was not the case. For sure, he was not married to her."

"OK," Mal said as she came back up front. "Looks like I only need a passport if you've got one."

"I'll call my attorney and have him send it to me," I said.

"Perfect," she said. "I've got the form you need to fill out here, along with the tax form you need to do in order for us to take your taxes out of your check. I also have this form that we use to set up direct deposit."

"Wow," I said. "I didn't realize there was so much to do in order to work. I guess that's what I get for coming to this game a little later in life."

"It's not too bad," Mal said. "You can take the forms with you and bring them back tomorrow, or whenever you get your passport."

"I should have it tonight," I said. "I'll stop back in tomorrow morning with the passport and all the forms filled out. I'll have to ask him what I need to do on some of these, especially since I have no idea what I'm doing."

"Great," Bill said. "Once we get that and get everything verified, we'll get you set up with Mal to have her train you."

"Why do you need someone else?" I asked.

"I'm going back to school," Mal replied.

"And I'm too old to learn all this new stuff again," Bill added. "I actually have a couple of other employees."

"My brother is one of them," Mal said.

"Oh," I said. "I think I've only seen you here."

"Because I'm here the most," she said. "Sam is only here on weekends because he's in school still."

"My wife works here, too," Bill said.

"Yeah," Mal said. "You'll love Carol. She's a hoot."

"Looks like this is just the kind of family environment for me to get my feet wet, then," I said.

"We are like a family," Mal said.

"I look forward to joining the family, then," I said.

"See you in the morning," Mal replied as I walked out the door.

I pulled out my phone and hit the number for Lincoln.

"Hey," he said.

"I need my passport," I told him.

"You know you can't travel," he said.

"I'm getting a job," I said. "I need it to show proof of who I am."

"Why are you getting a job?"

"Link," I groused. "I need something to do. I can't just sit around and do nothing, it's what drove me to my craziness in the first place. I have to have a purpose."

"Where are you going to be working?"

I told him the name of the book store.

"You sure you want to do this?"

"I am absolutely sure," I said. "They are super nice, and it already feels like they're family. I need this."

"I'll have someone bring it to the cottage," he said.

"Thanks," I replied.

"And Anna," he continued.

"What?"

"Be careful," he said.

"Now you're sounding like dad," I said.

"Your dad was worried about you," he said. "I am, too."

"I'll be fine," I said. "When will it get here?"

"I'll have someone bring it to you tonight," he sighed.

"Thanks," I said, then hung up and walked home.

Chapter 5

Bryan

"Hello?"

"Is this Mr. Walker?"

"Who is asking?" I asked.

I didn't get many calls on my home office number, so just pretended to be my own secretary. Suzie would usually answer when this phone rang, but she couldn't do that anymore.

"My name is Bill Holmes," the man said. "I own The Good Book. My assistant, Mal, said he stopped in to see about doing a reading and signing in the store."

"Then I am who you're looking for," I said.

"Oh," he replied. "I'm sorry I didn't recognize your voice."

"No problem," I replied. "I never know who is calling on this line, so I just have to be sure. Would you be open to me doing a reading and signing?"

"Absolutely," he replied. "I just hired a new employee, and thought I'd have you work with her. Would that work for you?"

"So," I began. "Someone who's new to the store is going to be in charge of it?"

"Oh, no," he replied. "I'll have Mal set everything up, get the word out and such. She's much more knowledgeable on that front. I meant I'll have her here as your assistant while you're in the store. You know, help with anything you might need. When would be a good time for you to do the signing?”

“I’m pretty open, actually,” I said. “Once I get started on the next book, my time tends to get taken up by that. Right now, I’m in between books.”

Honestly, I had no idea when I would be starting the next book. I hadn’t written a word since Suzie left, and with the cancer diagnosis and impending treatment, I wasn’t sure when I’d feel like writing again.

“Honestly,” I offered. “The sooner the better. I do have some engagements coming in the next few months that will make it impossible for me to do it after, say, the middle of June. Could we set something up before then?”

“I’m sure Mal can make something happen,” he said. “Shall I have her call you? Or would it be better if she emailed you? I don’t do that sort of thing, but she’s on top if it.”

“Email might be better,” I suggested. “That way we have it written down and can refer back to it. I look forward to hearing from her.”

“We’ll be happy to have you in our store,” he said, then hung up.

“Well, Suzie,” I said, looking at her picture on my desk. “Looks like I’ll be getting out there again. Hope I don’t do something stupid.”

Pulling up my email, I shot a note to my agent letting her know that I was going to be doing a signing. She sent me a response almost right away, saying she was happy to see that I was getting out there again and asked what she could do to help. I told her I didn’t have any details, but once I did, I’d let her know.

I opened a new Word document, pulled one of the hard candies out of my dish, and began typing. It didn’t take long before a story started to form, words falling into place. My Suzie had always been my Muse, and I could feel her inspiring me to keep going.

Three hard candies later, I had over ten thousand words and a whole new world building in my document. I could feel the cramping in my hands, and my back was beginning to bark, so I got up and stretched, then decided to see what I could find in the kitchen.

Dr. Robinson told me that once I started with the chemo, my appetite would go away, so I had to be sure that I was stocking up on calories now, and making sure I had high calorie foods available. She said that my foods wouldn't taste the same, and that I may not be able to keep much down, especially at first. I was determined to have the best options available once that time came, because I knew I wouldn't have anyone to keep me on track.

Risotto and a glass of wine were on the menu. The doctor said once I started actively taking chemo, I would have to give up the wine. Once I was done, I could have it again, so I wanted to relish the fact that I could still enjoy it. I thought about turning on the television, but absolutely nothing interesting was on, so I found my way back to my office and plunked back down at the desk.

By the time I felt like I couldn't stay awake, I realized that I had more words down than I had written in one day, pushing twenty-five thousand. My neck was telling me that I had to stop, even though the ideas were still flowing. Instead of continuing, though, I listened to my body and headed off to find a hot shower.

The beating water against my back and neck were just what I needed, and it didn't take long to realize that it had been a very long day. After I'd toweled off, I threw on some lounge pants and climbed into bed. It was so very big, and so very empty, but my weary body kept the demons at bay and I quickly drifted off to sleep.

Chapter 6

Anna

True to his word, Link had one of the underlings in his firm drive all the way up to the cottage and drop off my passport. I have no idea who the kid was, but he was younger than me by a few years and I wasn't even sure if he'd been there when I was last in the office. I guess it didn't matter, though, because he just smiled and handed me the packet with my document inside. I thanked him, offered for him to come in for a drink, but he declined and left almost immediately. Link probably told him not to stay, which was fine. It was already late when he got to the cottage, so I didn't mind that he didn't stick around for long.

I have no idea how I was able to fall asleep so quickly, but knowing I wanted to be at the bookstore first thing in the morning helped to press that issue. I had just three more dresses that would qualify as "work attire" in my closet, so I had laid one out and decided that a shopping trip would be needed after I stopped at my new job.

"Good morning," Mal said as I walked through the door.

"Hi," I replied. "I brought my passport and filled out all the paperwork."

Handing the documents to her, I waited as she perused them.

"Perfect," she said. "I just need to make a copy of the passport and add it to the paperwork. Did Bill tell you when you should come in?"

"He didn't," I replied. "At least I don't remember him telling me."

"Don't worry about it," she said. "Are you good to come in tomorrow morning before we open? I can show you around the store, give you a crash course on the computer system and how to do charges and such."

"I think I can do that," I replied. "By the way. What's the dress code for the store?"

"Honestly," she replied. "As long as you look somewhat professional and aren't wearing anything with vulgarity or conceived rudeness, you should be good."

"Dresses?"

"If you want," she said. "But, look at me. I haven't worn a dress in I can't even remember how long. If you are more comfortable in dresses, sure. But if you want to wear jeans or slacks, that's good, too."

"I have the dress I wore yesterday," I explained. "This one, and a couple more. Other than that, I think all my jeans are those trendy torn ones. And don't get me started on my shirt collection. I think they would likely all fall into that inappropriate category. I planned on going shopping today to get some things, so should I go with some plain or patterned shirts for now?"

"You honestly don't have to buy anything special," she said.

"It's no problem," I replied. "It's daddy's money that he couldn't take with him. Besides, I figure with a new job, I should do something new with my wardrobe."

"I mean," she began. "If you want to."

"I do," I replied.

"I am working with Bryan Walker," she said. "Working to get him a date to come in and do a signing and reading. Would you be interested in being the point person for him while he's here?"

"Sure," I replied. "What exactly would I need to do?"

"Basically, you'd just be his assistant," she said. "Get him water, keep the readers back, help with autographs and such. Typical stuff."

"You say typical," I laughed, "but you have to remember I haven't done anything like this before."

"That's right," she replied. "I forgot you are getting your first job. Well," she stuck her hand out. "Let me be the first to congratulate you."

I took her hand and shook it, smiling.

"So," she said. "Tomorrow morning. Be here at, say, eight?"

"I think I can do that," I replied.

"Perfect," she said. "See you then."

"With bells on," I replied.

I was much lighter in my step than I had been in a long time. This new adventure was just what I needed to get me out of whatever funk I'd been in. I'd called an Uber to come to the store and pick me up to take me shopping. While this little town had a shop, it wasn't quite my style. I directed the driver to the larger town just a few miles away, paid him, then went into the first of many shops to get a whole new wardrobe for my new job.

By two I was starving and had probably spent a small fortune on clothes. They were cute, country, and comfortable, and I couldn't be happier with my selection. I found a small teriyaki shop that looked to be one of those mom and pop places, where it was family run and obviously a labor of love. The menu was full of all my favorite things, but I opted for a chicken bowl. They had a cooler with canned and bottled sodas and the like, and I pulled out a naked juice to add to my order.

When she rang it up, I handed my card and she did the whole charging thing. I tipped the bill, exactly what the cost was, I added that much as a tip. The woman behind the counter tried to tell me it was too much, but I simply pulled out a hundred-dollar bill and shoved it into the tip jar she had on the counter as well. Her smile was pure joy, and I felt even better about my decision.

There were only a handful of tables in the lobby area, as this was more of a take-out place, but I didn't have anywhere to go, so I sat in the corner, my purchases piled on the end of the table, and waited for her to bring out my food. It didn't take long and she brought me my bowl, but also brought out an order of pot stickers.

"I didn't order these," I said.

"I know," she replied. "On the house."

It was obvious that she was grateful for my tip, and wanted to show her appreciation by giving something in return. I didn't begrudge her, and took the offering, thanking her profusely. Once I'd finished my late lunch, I gathered up my bags and ordered up another Uber to get me home. I had a lot of unpacking to do, and I wanted to be sure to be on time the next morning.

Chapter 7

Bryan

The email said I could pick my day and they would make it work, so I looked at my ever-busy calendar, sarcasm implied, and picked a Saturday about three weeks out. That would give everyone involved plenty of time to get the word out. Mal, the person who was coordinating the signing, told me I should come in a couple of days before and meet the person who would be my helper. Said it would be good for the two of us to chat and get to know each other better so we could work seamlessly. It wasn't a big deal for me to pop in, so I set it up for a week ahead of time.

The two weeks flew by, and I walked into the store on the Saturday before my "event" was set to take place. My publisher had been all over social media, getting the word out that I would be making an appearance. It would be the first one since the accident, and I was a little apprehensive that I may get mourners wanting to bring Suzie up. They all saw what happened, the fans knew that I'd lost her, and that I had been devastated, but I hadn't had any interaction since then.

There were signs up in the window, and a stack of fliers on the counter, all touting that the resident author would be in the store and signing autographs and reading from the most recent book that was out. I hadn't told them what I was going to be reading from, and honestly still hadn't decided, but it was good PR to say it was from my most recent piece.

"Good morning, Mr. Walker," the gal behind the desk said. She was the same one I had given my card to the last time I was in.

"Good morning," I replied. "I'm not sure who I'm supposed to meet with."

"That would be Anna," the woman said. "I'm Mal," she continued, sticking her hand out for me to shake.

I took the offering and replied, "Good to meet you."

"Officially," she added.

"True," I said. "We have met before."

"I'll be right back with Anna," she said, and stepped from behind the counter and walked to a different section of the store.

"Mr. Walker," the woman, who I presumed was Anna, said.

"Please," I corrected. "Just call me Bryan. You must be Anna."

"I am," she replied. "I've always been a fan of your work. It got me through some really tough times. It will be my pleasure to work with you on your big day."

"I look forward to it," I said. "Not sure what all we need to talk about, but shall we?"

"Yes," she said, turning and walking toward a set of chairs near the window.

Following, I realized this was the woman who was in the store when I was here a couple of weeks ago.

"So," she said, after we'd sat down. "Do you have any preference as to how you want to be set up?"

"What would you suggest?" I asked.

"There are a couple of ways we can do this," she offered. "We could set up a table for you to have a stack of your most recent books on, then you could read from behind it. Or we can set up a chair that you can read from, and we can put a smaller table next to it. I'll be there to help run the sales and such, unless you have someone who usually does that for you."

"I think if we did a chair that I could read from," I suggested. "Then, a smaller table next to it would be fine. Do you have copies of the book that we'll sell?"

"We did do an order to get a few extra copies," she said. "But you are welcome to bring your own stock and we can sell those first."

"I'm sure what you have will be fine," I said. "I'll have my publisher send a box so I've got extra if you run out, but we should sell from your stock, first. My goal is to bring in business for the store."

She made some notes on the tablet she'd brought with her, then asked, "We assumed you'd be reading from your most recent book. Is that right?

"I actually thought I'd read a little of the project I'm currently working on," I said. "If you guys don't mind. It's been one of those healing things I've used, and I'd really like to share it."

"That sounds wonderful." She sounded genuinely enthused.

"Great," I said. "Do you need anything else today?"

"I don't think so," she replied, then looked at her tablet. "Let me just go check with Mal and see if she has any other question or needs anything else before I let you get back to your writing."

She got up and went back up to the counter to chat with the woman behind it. Something about Anna was tickling the back of my memory, but I couldn't put my finger on it. It was like I'd met her before, but not really.

"Mal said that she didn't think she needed anything else," Anna said as she came back. "But if there's anything you think of between now and Saturday, please reach out."

She handed me a card from the store and smiled.

"It was really nice to meet you," she said.

"I feel like we've met before," I replied. "Maybe in passing?"

"Well," she said. "I did see you when you were in a couple of weeks ago."

"I think I remember that," I replied. "But it feels like I met you before that. Like we knew each other a few years ago or something."

"I don't believe I've ever met you," she said. "Being that you're one of my favorite authors, I would definitely remember meeting you."

Her smile was big, and she seemed honest.

"Maybe you just remind me of someone," I offered.

"I've been told I have a familiar face," she laughed.

"That could be it," I replied. "At any rate, it was very nice to officially meet you. And I look forward to working with you in about a week."

"It truly was my pleasure," she replied. "I can't wait to hear some of your new piece, too. I love it when authors I love come out with something new."

"This is very different from what I've written in the past," I said. "You may hate it."

"I highly doubt that," she said.

"I hope you like it," I said. "I guess I'll see you in a week."

"See you then," she replied.

I walked out the door and headed home. I had more writing to do, and was hoping that I could get close to the half way point in this new book. It was going remarkably fast, considering I hadn't flexed my writing muscles in months. Maybe it was the thought of not getting the chance to finish it that was pushing me. I had an appointment on Monday to get my port put in for the chemo, and then I'd start the Monday after that. The timing for this reading was perfect, in that it would give me a good idea as to how the new project would be accepted.

I found myself at the cemetery, though I don't remember planning to come here.

"Sorry," I said when I stepped up to her resting place. "I didn't know I was coming, so I didn't bring any flowers."

She wouldn't have minded, though, and I knew it. She never liked me getting all mushy with sentimentality, so why should I try to do it now? No, she was just as happy to get a dandelion from the yard than a bouquet of roses. I didn't have either of them, though.

"I really think this new book is going to be well received," I said. "I'm doing a signing next weekend and I'll read the first chapter and see what folks think. You would have been able to tell me, but I can't ask you now."

I sat in silence for a bit, then said, "I wish I could hold you. Just one more time. Maybe then I'd be fine with letting you go."

It was a lie, though, because one more minute would lead me to wanting another hour, then another day, and before I knew it, I'd want a century, because even that wouldn't be enough time to spend with my Suzie.

"My cave awaits," I said as I stood. "This book isn't going to write itself. I'll stop by after the reading and let you know how it went."

The walk home was uneventful, and by the time I started back in on the project, it was nearly noon. Suzie would have brought me lunch, but I settled for a cheese sandwich and dove back in.

Chapter 8

Anna

"You did really well," Mal said after Bryan left.

"Thanks," I replied. "Do you think he could tell I was nervous? I mean, I didn't stutter or anything, but I was shaking in my boots."

"I couldn't tell you were nervous," she replied. "And I knew you would be. This is your first big thing. You did really well."

"I asked all the right questions, right?"

"Absolutely," she replied with a smile. "You even thought of some things I wouldn't have thought to ask."

"Like what?"

"About sales and such," she said. "Usually we don't even think to ask that type of thing. I guess even I can learn new things."

"What I asked was OK, though, right?"

"You were perfect," she said. "Now, let's get the rest of those books unboxed so we're ready for next Saturday."

The rest of the day was spent unboxing the books we'd purchased for the event, along with shelving the other stock we had that came in. They'd asked if I could come in on Friday night after the store closed to help get everything set up. It was completely optional, they said, but I felt like it would be the right thing to do. Besides, what was I going to be doing on a Friday night?

I'd had two more group meetings since I got the job, and people were very helpful in telling me that they could see a change in my demeaner since I started. Even the early mornings, at least for me, were becoming easier. The week flew by, and before I knew it, Bill, Mal, and I were setting up for the event. Mal said they'd had a lot of feedback on their social media posts about it, and she was hopeful that this meant that we would see a good turnout.

The store usually opened at ten, but they'd put up special hours for this day to be sure that everything would go off without a hitch, so I'd been asked to show up at eight instead of my usual nine start time. When I walked toward the store, I could see that there were several people sitting in their cars in front of the shop. As I keyed my way in, someone asked when we would be open. I told them the store was opening early, but not until nine.

"Do you always have this kind of turn out for events?" I asked Mal when I came in.

"This is the first signing we've done in about a year," she replied. "Mr. Walker usually brings in a few, but it's mostly just folks from town. Looks like his absence in the writing community has brought in people from farther out."

"I saw a plate from Vermont, and another one from New Hampshire," I said. "I didn't know this would be such a big deal."

"When it comes to authors," Mal said. "You never know what you'll get. Some come with a whole bunch of awesome fans who are polite and wait in line. Others have crazy fans that will cause damage to the store. We've learned who to trust and who to keep at arm's length."

"I guess it's the same with any celebrity," I mused. "I'm just glad no one knows I'm here. That could make things a lot more complicated."

"We would make it work," she replied.

"Bryan said he'd be here in about fifteen minutes," Bill said as he came up front from the office. "I told him to come to the back door so we don't have any issues."

I turned to look up front, and even though it was still almost an hour before we were set to open, some of the people had gotten out of their cars and were now forming a line outside the shop. I could see some of them holding cups with the coffee shop next door's logo on them, so at least there was a boon to other businesses on the street, too.

The phone rang and Bill picked it up.

"Thanks for calling the Good Book," he said. "We've got your next adventure. How can I help you find it?"

We didn't usually answer the phone before we opened or after hours, but today was a special day.

"I'll send Anna back," he said, looking at me.

I headed to the office hung my purse on the hook in there, then went to the back door. I was pretty sure that Bryan was here, so wasn't surprised to see him when I opened the back door.

"Hey, there," he said. "I've got one box of books in the trunk, but I think we'll leave them there until we need them if that's all right with you."

"I'm sure that'll be fine," I replied, holding the door so he could come in.

"I saw there was already a line," he said once I closed the door.

"People came in from out of state," I replied. "I think it will be a good turn out."

"Let's just hope they don't hate my new book," he replied.

"I hardly think that'll happen," I said. "I've loved everything I've read by you, and I'm pretty sure you wouldn't be as successful as you are if you didn't write well."

"You'd be surprised at how fickle readers are," he laughed.

"This way," I said, heading back to the front of the store. "I've got everything set up how we discussed, but wanted you to check and make sure you didn't want to make any changes."

"Wow," he said as we came out from behind a shelf. "They really are coming in droves. I hope you've got enough room for everyone."

"We can make it work," Bill said. "Even if we have to do shifts."

"You guys are great," Bryan replied.

"We really appreciate the business you're going to bring in," Bill said. "It's always nice to have you in the store."

"I feel like it's my home away from home," he said.

We walked over to the set up and he said everything looked great.

"Maybe I should pre-sign a few of the books," he suggested. "Keep me from getting a cramp later on."

"Did you bring more?" Bill asked when he came to check on us.

"There's a box in my trunk," he said. "If we feel like we need it, I can give you my keys and you can get it."

"I can do that," I said.

"You'll be too busy here," Bill replied. "Between Mal and I, I think we'll make it just fine."

"Should I call Brodie in?" Mal asked.

"You know," Bill said, looking out the window. "Might not be a bad idea. Certainly wouldn't hurt."

"I'll give him a call," she said, and went off to do that.

"You've got about five minutes until I was going to open the doors," Bill said.

Bryan looked around and said, "I think we're good. What do you think, Anna?"

"If you're ready," I replied, "then so am I."

"Let's get this party started," Bill said, then went to open the door.

After a few hours, there were still people in the store wanting books or to talk to Bryan. He'd been gracious and considerate, giving of his time to most anyone who asked the questions. I watched him, making sure that he wasn't getting burned out, but he seemed to be in his element. By two, I wasn't sure whether he could take any more.

"I know you are all here to talk to Mr. Walker," I said. "But let's give him a few minutes to collect himself. You will still get time to talk to him," I continued, "and he will continue to sign your books, but I think we should give him a minute to recharge. You all good with that?"

The chorus of "Sure" and "Okay" were unanimous, and Bryan thanked me as he made his way to the back room. I don't know how he did it, just sitting there reading, then answering questions, signing books, and letting folks get their pictures with him.

"Does anyone have any other shopping they want to do before he comes back?" I asked, and the people began to look around the rest of the shop.

"You are a natural," Mal said once there was less of a crowd in the area.

"Really?"

"Yeah," she said. Dad said we've made more in sales today than we usually do in a month or more during the summer. Fall and winter are our busiest seasons, so having this boost in sales in June is just what we needed."

"I'm glad I could help," I replied.

"Me, too," she said. "Did you notice the way he looked at you?"

"What do you mean?" I asked.

"He lost his wife about six months ago," she said. "Horrible car accident. Everyone in town heard about it. I was actually surprised when he came into the shop that day. He's been pretty much a hermit since the accident."

"That's awful," I replied.

"He was looking at you like he did when Suzie was alive," she said.

"That just isn't good," I said, knowing exactly what she was implying.

"Hey," she said. "I'm not telling you to go after him. I'm just saying that if you were interested, he might be receptive to a dinner or something."

"I'm not in a good place for a relationship," I replied. "I'm still trying to find myself."

It was the excuse I'd been using for a couple of years, ever since the incident in my own life. The one that landed me in this little town where no one knew me.

"I'm not pushing," she said, holding her hands up. "Just saying."

"I'd appreciate it if you kept those observations to yourself," I said. "Nothing personal, but it's a sore subject for me."

"Hey," Bryan said as he came back. "You okay?"

"Yeah," I said. "Why?"

"Just look like someone who ate something sour."

Mal had walked off quickly, so must have seen him coming. The fact that she got all these thoughts running through my head, then abandoned me, was a little frustrating.

"Yeah," I said. "No, I'm fine. Just observing all the fans you have. How do you deal with being famous?"

"I'm not that famous," he replied.

"I beg to differ," I said, indicating the many readers still in the store waiting for their chance with him.

"Okay," he said. "Maybe I do have a significant fan base."

"I'd say that's putting it mildly," I laughed.

Before more could be said, some fans started back our way and we were left without being able to talk further. The more time I spent with him, though, the more I realized that Mal may be on to something. I noticed he'd watch me as I talked to customers, but then look away if I turned toward him. It was probably all in my imagination, though.

Chapter 9

Bryan

The day went better than I expected, and by the time the store was ready to close down, they were having to turn people away because they had sold out of every copy of every book I'd ever written, along with the few I'd brought with me.

"I think they missed you," Mal said as she locked the door.

"Apparently," I replied. "It was a much better turn out than I expected."

"Like I said," Mal reiterated. "I think they missed you."

"Anna," I said, turning to the woman who had been by my side throughout the day. "What do you think?"

"I agree with Mal," she said.

"I meant about my new book," I said.

"Oh," she looked surprised. "I'm not sure where you're going to go with it," she finally said. "I mean, it's a good start, but there are so many things that could happen. Is what you read everything you've got done?"

"Not by a long shot," I replied. "This was just the first chapter. There are twenty more at home."

"Wow," she said. "How long did it take you to write that all? I guess that's a stupid question, isn't it?"

"Not stupid at all," I replied as I folded my iPad up. "I started on it in the middle of May. I usually can get a full book done, first draft wise, in about a month, sometimes less."

"That's fast," she said. "I had no idea what the timeline was for writing. So, when you finish the, what did you call it? The first draft, what happens after that?"

"Tell you what," I said. "Why don't you finish up here, then we can grab a bite for dinner, my treat, and we can talk all about it."

"I mean," she stumbled over the words.

"It would really be great to have a friend to have a conversation with," I said. "I get tired of my imaginary friends sometimes."

"Never thought about them being imaginary friends," she laughed. "But I guess it makes sense."

"Any dietary restrictions?" I asked.

"Nope," she replied.

"What sounds good?"

"So," she began, then said, "never mind."

"No," I replied. "What is it?"

"Well," she hesitated again, chewing her bottom lip. "There's this little mom and pop teriyaki place up in Watertown that I went to a couple of weeks ago. It was super good, and the folks there were really nice. That's probably too far to go, though."

"Maybe for tonight," I said. "But we could take a trip up there another time, if you're interested."

I'm not sure what had come over me, but I felt like there was a connection between us. Something other than what I had with Suzie. Nothing could replace her, but I also know she wouldn't want me to remain lonely.

"There's Joe's Café just down the block," I suggested. "It's not very fancy…"

"I certainly don't need fancy," she laughed.

"If you're good with it," I said, leaving the question unasked.

"Sounds great," she replied.

"Why don't you two go ahead," Bill said. "Both of you worked your tails off today, and I think that a nice quiet evening out is the perfect reward."

"You sure you don't need me to help put things back?" she asked.

"Mal and Brodie have it covered," he said. "You two go enjoy the evening."

"If you're sure," she asked, clearly hesitant.

"I am," he replied. "You've both worked hard today, and I can't thank you enough, Bryan, for agreeing to come in."

"It was truly my pleasure," I replied. "Made me feel like I was back in the swing."

"Look forward to next time," the shop owner said, reaching his hand out to shake.

I took it, then thanked him again, and ushered Anna toward the back where my car was parked.

"Do we need to drive?" she asked.

"No," I replied. "I just wanted to drop this in the trunk."

I popped the trunk open with my key, then dropped the iPad into my bag there and shut it.

"Shall we?"

I offered her my arm and she slipped her hand into the crook of my elbow. We set out toward the sidewalk and moved to the front of the buildings along the street. She was quiet, so I wasn't sure what was on her mind, but didn't want to speak until we were a little more alone. It only took a couple of minutes to get to Joe's, and we stepped inside to see that the place was pretty full.

"Two?" the hostess asked.

"Yes," I replied. "In a booth toward the back, if you have it."

"Let me see," she said, looking at her map on the podium. "I've got this one," she said, pointing it out on the map.

"What do you think?" I asked Anna.

"Sure," she replied, and was subdued.

"This way," the hostess said as she grabbed a couple of menus and silverware and walked toward the back of the dining area.

We followed along and once we were seated, she let us know our waitress would be by to ask for drink orders and to let us know what the specials were.

"So," I began, but our waitress showed up with a couple of glasses of water and asked, "Can I get you something to start with?"

"I'm good with water," Anna said.

"Same," I offered.

She told us the specials, and then left us to peruse the menus.

"You were saying?" she asked once the waitress was gone.

"Oh," I replied, having lost my train of thought. "I wanted to see what you thought of the story."

"It was really a good chapter," she said. "I just don't know where you'll go."

"I should have kept my iPad," I said, kicking myself for the oversight. "It has the whole manuscript of what I've got so far. I'd love for you to read it and tell me what you think."

"That seems like it would be a little invasive," she replied. "Like reading your diary or something. I would feel like I was snooping by reading it early."

"Tell me what your favorite book of mine is," I said.

"I really like the first one in the Officers of Solstice series," she replied. "I had to get another copy because I lost the one I had."

"So," I said. "You liked that whole series? Or just the first one?"

"Oh, no," she replied. "I loved the whole series. It's just been a few years since I read it and I didn't know where my copy was, so just picked up another one a few weeks ago. Thinking I need to pick up the rest of them, too.”

“I probably have copies,” I said.

“It’s no problem,” she said. “I like supporting the bookstore.”

“Don’t they pay you?”

“Yeah,” she replied. “And I could take a discount on the books I buy, but I have plenty of money and don’t work because of that, so I always pay full price.”

“I don’t know anyone who would pay full price if they didn’t have to,” I said.

“Have you decided?” the waitress asked, and I realized that we hadn’t even taken the time to look at the menu.

“Can I get a chicken Caesar salad?” she asked.

“That sounds good,” I remarked. “I’d like the same.”

“Dinner size or side size?”

“Dinner size for me,” I said.

“Me, too,” she offered.

“Great,” the waitress said. “I’ll bring them out shortly.”

Once she was gone, I asked, “How long have you worked at the bookstore?”

“I just started a few weeks ago,” she said. “I needed something to keep me busy.”

“Do you like it?”

“I love it,” she said. “I mean, what’s not to love? I get to spend the day around books, helping others find just the right story for them, and watch them fall in love with that story. It’s super fun to have someone come back and tell me they loved the book I suggested.”

“Sounds like you’ve found the right fit for yourself,” I said.

“I really think I have,” she replied, and the smile on her face told me everything I needed to know about that subject.

“Here you go,” the waitress said as she set two salads onto

the table. "Cracked pepper?"

"No thanks," Anna said.

"None for me, either," I said.

"Enjoy," the waitress said, then went off to help other patrons.

"Salute," I said.

"Slainte," she replied.

We began our meal in companionable silence and I thought up how to ask her to read the rest of my story and tell me what she thought. From everything I'd learned about her today, she seemed like the perfect person to give me honest feedback on my work. I needed someone to do that for me, someone to fill that void Suzie left. I wasn't ready to replace my wife, but there were some things I needed help with. This was one area that I felt Anna could help.

Chapter 10

Anna

Dinner was nice, and not at all what I expected. We talked about his work, how he hadn't had anyone to read his work since his wife died, which, that was a horrible thing to learn. He was actually doing pretty good considering it'd only been half a year since she'd died. I don't know if I'd have been that put together if I'd lost my life partner. Then again, I hadn't found anyone who I wanted to be a life partner, so I guess I couldn't say for sure.

He told me she had been the one to read his work as he was writing it, give him feedback, ask him questions, keep him honest. When he asked if I would be willing to do that for him, I was a little uncomfortable. I mean, we'd just met, basically, and he didn't know me from Adam. Why he thought I would be good at it was beyond me.

But, the more we talked, the more open I became to the idea.

I mean, it wasn't like it was dating, it was a work thing. He said he'd pay me to be his beta reader, whatever that was, but I'd declined the money. If he was going to allow me the privilege of reading his work before it was released, that was payment enough.

The walk back to the car was nice, and we exchanged phone numbers and he said he'd be in touch about getting me the manuscript he had. He offered to drive me home, since I didn't have a car, but I told him I preferred to walk. Felt like he had done enough for me today.

By the time I was in my cottage, I could feel the day catching up to me. It had been taxing, mentally, and I was prepared for that. The physical exhaustion, and sore muscles, were something that I wasn't ready for. I started the water in my tub, letting it fill with warmth and the aroma of lavender from the bath bomb I'd dropped in. Undressing, I was glad I had not been scheduled for the next day, and planned to sleep in and just spend the whole day in pajamas reading.

Soaking in the warm water, I let it wash away everything that was on my mind, relaxing and letting it all go. By the time the water began to cool, I was ready to climb into bed and sleep, and I did just that. No alarm, no lights, just the warmth of the bath and the crisp, cool feel of the sheets.

When I woke, I stretched and felt things pop, but nothing uncomfortably. It was sunny this morning, and I looked forward to a hot cup of coffee to begin my day. After taking care of my morning routine in the bathroom, I turned the pot on in the kitchen and grabbed my phone.

Thanks for dinner. Send me your email address and I'll send you this manuscript.

The text was surprising, in that I hadn't expected to get one. Sure, we got along well, and the conversation was nice, but I hadn't really expected him to follow through with a text, especially so soon.

I responded and sent him my email. Then followed it up with another text.

I am not very responsive on emails, though, just so you know. I'll try to read it quickly so you don't have to wait for me.

Pouring my coffee, I pulled out my chocolate creamer from the cupboard and poured some in. I liked mochas, and this was nearly as good, but without the milk to add more calories than I needed. My phone pinged again, then once more.

No rush on the reading. Do it at your leisure. I really look forward to hearing what you think so far, and whether you have any ideas on where you think it will go. Enjoy.

Not only was the text there, but I saw there was an email as well. I went to the table with my coffee and opened my laptop, powering it up and signing in. When everything was booted up, I opened my email and found the one he'd sent. Attached was a PDF that I opened. Just as he'd said, the whole thing was there. I started and realized when I'd reached the end of the document that I'd shut out the entire world. Looking down at the time in the corner of my screen, I realized I'd been sitting there for three hours. I hadn't even taken a drink of my coffee, I was so engrossed in the story.

I hit reply on the email it came in and responded.

I read the whole thing. I didn't intend to, but I got so into it that it couldn't stop. It's wonderful, interesting, and I have a few questions.

I added my questions about the plot points that didn't make sense to me, then thought better of it and decided to just send the first part. I didn't want to make him uncomfortable or make him answer a bunch of questions from some random stranger, so just sent it off with the note that I liked it.

Taking my cup, I stuck it in the microwave and pressed the quick start to let it heat back up. It wouldn't be the best cup of coffee, but I'd had worse. I pulled some bread out of the bread box and stuck a couple of pieces into the toaster, then pulled out some jam and a spoon and set them on the table. The microwave buzzed, and just as I took my first sip the toast popped. I buttered the toast and took it with my cup to the table. There was an email from Bryan and I opened it up.

I'd love to know your questions. Was anything confusing? Did it flow well? These are all things that will make my story better.

Seems like he really did want to know what I thought, so I typed up all my questions, and the few things that I absolutely loved, and sent it off. I was like a school girl with her first crush, waiting for a response to my text. But that couldn't be it. There was an attraction between us, sure, but it was more business than personal. I had to believe that, because if I thought it was personal, then it might lead to sex, and I couldn't let that happen. At least not for quite a while.

Chapter 11

Bryan

It had been three months since I first really met Anna, and in that time, we had grown closer and closer. She hadn't seen me since the signing in the store, all our communication had been either via text, email, or the occasional phone call. I hadn't wanted her to know about the cancer, but she called me and I couldn't hide the fact that I was sick any longer.

"It's cancer," I said.

"Oh, no," she said, and the sadness was clear in her voice. "How long have you known?"

"I found out a couple of months ago," I replied. "I'm taking some meds, and surgery is scheduled for next week."

"Do you have someone to take care of you when you come home?"

"Dr. Robinson didn't think I would need anyone," I lied.

The doctor had said it would be best if I could find someone who could stay with me while I was recovering from the surgery. There would be lifting restrictions and things that I wouldn't be able to do for myself. But I didn't want to put that burden on anyone, so I just figured I'd struggle my way through.

"You should probably have someone with you," she said. "I mean, I can stay, if you want."

The offer was hesitant, but genuine.

"Are you sure?" I asked, though I wasn't sure why I was asking. Was this something I was willing to do? Could I allow this woman into my home, into my life, in such an intimate way?

"I'm sure I can take time off from the bookstore," she said.

"Oh," I began, but she interrupted.

"No," she was firm. "I'll call Mal right now and tell her that I am going to be staying with a friend who is recovering from surgery, that it was unexpected, and to make sure that it would be all right. I'll call you right back."

She disconnected before I could even get a word out. She was a force, that was for sure. I wondered if she'd let them know it was me that she would be staying with. If she did, would I be OK with that? I had to think about it, and finally came to the decision that if they found out, I would live with it.

I turned back to my laptop, trying to figure out where I was in the story when the phone rang again. I answered it without looking.

"Hello," I said.

"Mr. Walker," the woman on the other end said. "I am Penny from Dr. Robinson's office. I wanted to get your pre-op check in taken care of if you have time."

"Sure," I said.

It only took about five minutes to answer all of her questions and get my testing set up for tomorrow morning. There were a few things they had to do before I could have surgery, just to make sure I'd survive, I guess. They were non-invasive, save the blood draw, but that was negligible. By the time I was off with her I had lost my train of thought again and headed to the kitchen to see if I could find something that I could eat on the restrictive diet they'd given me.

Cheese sandwich in hand, I sat back down at my computer and saw that I'd missed a call from Anna. She left a voicemail, so I pushed the play button to listen.

Hey, it's me. I talked to Mal and she said it was fine to take as much time as I needed to help my friend. I didn't tell her it was you, wasn't sure if you wanted that info out. I also had to check in with my lawyer to make sure this was something that was allowed. Don't

That was unexpected. I knew she said she didn't have to work, but wasn't sure exactly why she didn't. Now that I knew she had a lawyer, things might be different. How do you ask that question? I mean, do you just come out and ask? Or is there some sort of finesse that is required when asking about the reasoning behind someone having an attorney on retainer? I guess there was only one way I was going to find out, so I picked up the phone and called her back.

"Hello," she answered.

"Hey," I said. "It's Bryan."

"You get my message?"

"Yeah," I said. "I gotta ask…"

"Let's talk about it in person," she said. "It's kind of a long and complicated story. Do you mind if I come over?"

"Why don't I come and get you," I suggested.

"I'll just call an Uber," she said.

"No need for that," I replied.

"It's fine," she said. "I just need the address."

I gave her my address and she said she'd text me when she left so I'd know when to expect her. The town was small enough that she could have walked it, but it was still big enough to make that walk take longer than was practical. I got the text just a few minutes later, and she said she should be here shortly. I finished my sandwich and took the plate into the kitchen just as I heard a car pull up. I opened the door before she had a chance to knock.

"Oh," she said, hand raised.

"Sorry," I replied, opening it wide for her to come in. "I heard the car, so thought I'd open before you got her."

"That driver was a bit off," she said stepping past me. "Most drivers I get are great, but this guy seemed, I don't know, just off."

"This is why I wanted to come get you," I said. "Then you wouldn't have to deal with strange drivers."

"It's fine," she waved the comment off. "I took self defense classes when I was in school, and have kept up with online videos to stay sharp. I think I should be able to take care of myself."

"Didn't think you couldn't," I replied, leading the way to my study. "Just looking out for a friend is all."

"I appreciate it," she said. "Wow!"

Her eyes were wide when we stepped into my office. She took in the space, the bookshelves lined with my own books, but also books of friends, as well as my resource materials.

"I don't think I've seen this many books in one place since I left home," she said. "Even then, though, they weren't this organized and neat. This is amazing."

"Yeah," I replied with a smile. "I am pretty proud of my library. It took a lot of work to get where I am, so I like to show it off if possible."

We sat, me behind the desk and her in a chair in front of it.

"Feels like I'm in a doctor's office," she said.

"Suzie always said she felt like she'd been sent to the principle's office when she sat there," I said. "Something about it feeling like she was in trouble."

"I never went to the principle's office," I said. "Occupational hazard of having a father who pays a large sum of money to the school."

"Money can change things," I replied.

"You probably want to know why I have a lawyer," she said. It wasn't a question, so I just nodded and allowed her to continue. "I got into some trouble when I was a freshman in college," she continued. "Well, the troubled behavior started before that, but I was always under daddy's roof until I went away to college. Even when I was at boarding school, he was still very active in my life.

"Anyway," she continued, and I could tell she was a bit nervous. "I was caught in a fraternity overnight after a party. I didn't get drunk, didn't do drugs, just wanted to stay with all the boys. By that, I mean I wanted to sleep with them. I know it's a horrible thing, but it was my vice. The one thing I could do that daddy couldn't control. That is, until the dean found out and let my dad know what was up. That was when he decided that I needed some consequences for my actions."

"Was anything you did illegal?"

"Technically, no," she replied. "I mean, staying overnight was against the school rules, as well as against the fraternity's policy, but according to law, no."

"So, then, what was the lawyer for?"

"There was a boy who was at the frat party that got into some really bad something," she said. "Not really sure what it was, but he got hurt, and ended up spilling the beans about my round robin meetings with the boys. The cops thought I was drunk under age and there were some issues of some of the boys there being under the legal limit and drinking. The cops thought it was rape, even though I told them I was there willingly. It was a big deal and my father was worried that I'd end up in real trouble if I kept on going the way I was, so he decided to send me to a rehab place."

"I thought you said you weren't doing drugs," I said.

"It's not that type of rehab," she offered. "Let's just say it was more a convent than an actual rehab facility. Daddy thought it would keep my mind off boys and give me a little more focus on my studies."

"Did it work?"

"Not exactly," she replied. "It kept me away from boys, but my mind still went there."

"Why are you telling me this?" I asked.

"Because I want to be up front with you," she said. "If I'm going to spend time in your home, taking care of you, I need you to know what my struggles are. I wouldn't feel right if you didn't know my history. That's why I wanted to check with my attorney, see if he could see any downside to me staying with you."

"What did he tell you?"

"To do exactly what I'm doing," she said. "Make sure you were aware of my faults and were comfortable with me staying. I'm not planning on trying anything. Won't accost you in your sleep or anything."

"Thanks," I said, a little taken aback. "I guess I appreciate your honesty."

"Kinda awkward, huh?"

"Just a little," I said.

"So," she continued. "Now that we have that ridiculousness out of the way, let's talk logistics."

Just like that, she swung the conversation back to something that we both knew had to happen. My need for someone to stay with me, and her need to help without the extra stuff. Honestly, it wasn't as awkward as I thought it would be.

I told her the day of the surgery, when I would be at the hospital, and when I'd be coming home. She'd told me she didn't have a license, but could definitely offer an Uber or whatever I needed, and would be willing to ride along with me to ensure my safety. All in all, it was a very productive afternoon, and left me feeling like we had this under control.

"Have you written more?" she asked when all the business and logistics were taken care of.

"Unfortunately, no," I replied. "Though, I hadn't expected to."

"Why not?"

"My brain's been fuzzy lately," I explained. "I think that with all the stress leading up to the surgery, it's shut the creative side down and has gone into focus on recovery."

"That's good," she said. "I mean, it sucks that you aren't writing, but at least you're looking beyond the surgery."

"I guess you're right," I agreed. "Hadn't looked at it that way. Just focused on the fact that the words weren't coming."

"They will," she said. "You said this happened after Suzie died, too, right?"

"It did," I replied.

"So," she offered. "Seems to me, when you're in the middle of it, the words stop. But once you're on the other side and on the road to recovery, they come back."

"I definitely need someone like you in my life," I said.

"Really?"

"You are encouraging," I explained. "You know just what to say to push me further, yet comfort me where I am. I appreciate that."

"Glad to be of service," she said. "So, you want me to ride with you to the hospital on Monday?"

"You don't have to do that," I said.

"It's no trouble at all," she replied. "Might make you laugh before you go under the knife. That would be a good thing, right?"

"It would," I said.

"Great," she replied. "What time should I be here?"

We worked times and then she was off, back to her cottage. I booted up the computer and realized that I wanted to write. It had been a while since that feeling came over me, so I set out to do just that.

Chapter 12

Anna

Helping Bryan after his surgery was exactly what I'd really been looking for. I mean, the bookstore job was great, and it got me out there and working, but caring for him, in his home, making his meals and making sure he was comfortable. Getting him to his appointments after the surgery. All of it was what I felt I was meant to do. You always hear about people finding their calling, and that's what this felt like.

I would be lying if I said I wasn't attracted to him. But it was more than anything I'd ever felt towards any other boy. No, Bryan was a man, and he treated me as an equal. Not once was there anything that was outside of the bounds of a normal friendship, and I really appreciated that about him.

"What's for dinner?" he asked.

"Chicken alfredo," I replied. "Unless you want something different."

"That's perfect," he replied.

It had been six weeks since his surgery, and while he didn't really need my help much, the chemo was taking its toll on him and my being here was just as much an emotional help as the physical one had been when he first came home after surgery.

"You see the doctor tomorrow, right?" I asked.

"Yep," he said. "Hoping she'll let me do some lifting."

"You don't need to do that," I argued. "That's what I'm here for."

"But I don't want to continue to take advantage of you," he said.

"I could leave any time I wanted," I countered. "I'm not a

prisoner. Besides, I really like taking care of you. I feel like it's given me a better purpose for my life."

"Really?"

"Really," I replied.

"I thought that's what the bookstore was supposed to do," he said.

"It did," I replied. "It led me to you."

He looked at me then, and I could see the wheels turning in his head.

"What?" I finally asked after I couldn't take it any longer.

"That whole 'you complete me' phrase is running through my head," he said.

"Okay," I said, drawing the word out.

"Not like that," he corrected. "Well, not exactly."

"Hang on," I said, sitting down. This was definitely not a conversation to be had while standing. "OK," I continued. "What are you thinking?"

We'd spent a lot of time together, and we'd learned how to communicate with each other really well. One thing we knew was that we had to process thoughts, sometimes out loud, and eventually we'd get to where we were going. Not once had one of these conversations complicated our relationship as friends, but that one phrase made me nervous.

"Suzie," he began. "She was my everything. We met in college when she showed me up at a reading. I was never the best author in our relationship, and I knew it. But she never wanted to put her work out there where people could criticize it. Our writing relationship was symbiotic, in that she'd read what I wrote and tell me how it could be better. You do the same thing, which is remarkable. To find someone who fills that role in my life once was a miracle. The fact that I found two people who have the same..."

He stopped, unsure of himself. "I get it," I said, letting him off the hook for trying to find the right word. That was one of the things that was so hard to watch with him. Between the surgery and the chemo, his brain wasn't working like it used to, and finding words to express his feelings would frustrate him to no end. As long as I understood the gist of what he was getting at, he let it go.

"Anyway," he continued. "The fact that you have the same eye for detail within the written word is beyond amazing. I know it might sound weird, but would you be interested in actually working for me in that capacity?"

"Like, as your proofreader or something?"

"To begin with, yeah," he said. "I like you, Anna. You are growing on me, and not in a bad way. Spending time with you has been a privilege and I would miss you if you left. Do you think you could see yourself working with me on my projects?"

"Aren't I doing that now?"

"Not in any official capacity," he replied.

"Does it have to be official?" I asked.

"Someone has to be paid for this," he said.

"I don't need the money," I reiterated.

"It's not about that," he continued. "I like you, and you are helping me in ways much bigger than just reading my work. You cook, you clean, you change my bandages. All of those things are easily hired out for. The thing is, you keep me company. You listen to my complaints, then help me get over myself and move on. These last six weeks would have been miserable if you weren't here."

"Anyone could have done that," I argued.

"No," he said. "Because what you've done couldn't be paid for as a service. There isn't enough money in the world to pay for what you've done for me. You brought me out of my funk and inspired me to continue writing."

"You were already doing that," I countered. "I didn't do anything."

"Can you just stop," he said. "I'm trying to compliment you, trying to let you know that you have value in just being yourself. It's something I want around me for a while."

"Just friends, though, right?"

Having borne my soul for him before we started on this journey, I needed to make sure that he knew I wasn't going to go there with him. I couldn't fall into that cycle again.

"Business associates and friends," he said. "What do you say?"

It was a curious thing, this feeling I had. Like I was embarking on becoming an adult. I mean, I was an adult, had been for a decade, but I had never really grown up.

"I can do that," I replied.

He smiled, and it was a beautiful thing. Yeah, I could do this.

AN INTERVIEW WITH
CARRIE AVERY MORIARTY

When did you start writing and why?

I have always been a storyteller, from before I can remember. I told stories and spoke a different language (not an Earth bound language) when I was about 3. Could be from the shock I received by sticking a bobby pin into an outlet, but maybe not. I was convinced I was from Mars. It's pretty fascinating looking back on it. Storytelling has been my outlet for most of my life. I wrote some short stories in gradeschool (found those recently, boy was that fun). I also created plays and the like with a neighbor that we would either act out with puppets or record on his home video camera (long ago, big and bulky, definitely not as easy as it is today). My first published short story was in 2014 in an anthology that I applied to get into. From there, I've written several under this pen name. I have also branched out to write some stories under a separate pen name as well.

Which authors or books influenced you the most as a writer?

That's like asking someone who their favorite child is. I began reading at a very young age, and was reading chapter books by kindergarten. I think the early books I read had a great impact on me, as they showed me that there were worlds out there that I could explore if I just allowed my imagination to be free. As I've grown older, I have found that many authors draw me in. I think currently, the authors that give me the most inspiration are those who I know personally. I see the "ugly" side of being an author, the work that goes into it and the theft that takes place from unscrupulous publishers and others. But, I also see the joy that readers get from meeting someone they admire. It's amazing the work ethic that many authors have, and to watch them craft a story from nothing, then create the world it resides in, and watch as others fall in love with their characters and want more, has really been an inspiration for me. I have a close friend who is an author and she has pushed me to go outside my comfort zone and work to create a name for myself with both pen names. I'm very inspired to see where my career goes with respect to writing.

Which authors or books had the biggest impact on you as a person?

Honestly, there are a lot of books that I see that can push a person to be better in what they do and who they are. Really, though, the authors that inspire me are the ones who continue to push through, even when they get critisized and put down. The ones who take nothing for granted and keep pushing, simply because they have stories within themselves that the world needs to hear. Authors who struggle with getting their projects done within deadlines and with many other things going on in their lives, those are the ones I look to in order to keep me inspired to keep on pushing forward.

Which of your original twelve Prompt stories are you most pleased with?

Again, which child is my favorite? I think that March was a fun one to write. I had just found out that I was going to become a grandmother for the first time (we have two older grandkids, but they weren't officially part of our family until June of 2019, but my daughter was pregnant). It was fun to play with a world where the children really were our future, that they were the best of us, and that they could transform a world full of hate and fear into something that was so much more. Something that was filled with love and intelegence and the need to be better.

Which of your original twelve Prompt stories did you find the most difficult to write?

The short that was most difficult for me was the one for June. It came to me and I had a great story that took a tragic and terrible turn. I didn't realize it was going to be so dark until I got there. I tried to add more, tried to find a happy in it, but it simply wasn't there. There's a content warning on the short because it deals with mental health and suicide. Honestly, it is probably the darkest story I have ever written. It was extremely heart wrenching to write, and I wanted to find something positive. I guess the only positive that came out of it was that there are some things that cannot be fixed.

What book on writing do you recommend?

On Writing by Stephen King. It starts as a biography of how he got to where he is, but the back half of the book is invaluable. He explains so many thing so easily, and it makes writing seem simple. It isn't, but it gives you the idea that it can be. There are a TON of books on writing out there, and many have great pieces, but as the first one to get, I'd highly suggest this one. I have a whole shelf full of books that I use for writing. Some are on the craft, but most are reference books for specific subjects. If you've never written, or if you aren't sure how to craft a story, then this would be where I would point you, at least to begin with.

What advice would you give an unpublished writer?

Read. Honestly, it's the best way to improve your craft. That, and get someone you trust who is pretty good at the written word and have them read your work. Ask them to be honest about how you can improve your work. If all they say is they love your work, then you need to find someone else. Be prepared to hear that your writing sucks, because it will when you first start. Hell, it will when you've been doing it for years, too. There is nothing wrong with that, because you can improve that with practice. Read and write like crazy, as much as you can. And create a space where you can create. It can be anywhere you feel inspired. Oh, and don't just write when you're inspired. It's work, so treat it that way. If you treat it like a job it will give you what you want in return. You can't be like Hemmingway and only write 7 words a day. You will get nowhere if you do that. Treat it as if you were working for someone else. Make your boss (you, the one who pushes yourself) cranky and rude and demanding. Make them push you so that you get more words down than you think you can. Eventually, it will become a habit and you'll be able to give the "boss" the finger and tell them that you're doing fine and to back off. Don't give up, either. When someone says you suck, show them that you are improving. When you get bad reviews (because you will), ignore them, or see what you can glean from them, and put it into practice. Just keep at it.

Do you have a "dream project" as a writer? What would it be?

Ultimately, my dream is to become a writer full time. If I can get my series started with my other pen name, I could see it making me enough to give up my day job. I would love to write all the things and then some, but I don't have as much time as I would like because I am not making enough with my writing to give up that office job. I have wanted to be a storyteller for most of my life, and I've done some things to get there, but it's been in the last decade or so that I've really pushed that side of things. I'm getting my name out there, getting a little bit of royalties, and starting to see advancement in my career, but it's still slow going. My goal for 2021 is to complete the short story projects I have on my calendar, then dive into the full length novels that I have planned. If it's possible, I'd love to be able to move to part time with my office job (if my boss will let me) and put more effort into writing. I'd love to "retire" from office work in the next 5 years, so I have to write to get there.

The original twelve Prompt stories were written in 2019. In 2020 we all experienced a global pandemic. Did the pandemic impact your writing? How?

The pandemic created chaos in my world, just like everyone else. The other thing it did was remove all my creativity. I saw it in many of my author friends as well. So many people were unprepared for working from home, for losing their jobs (my husband was out of work when it started and still is), and for having family around all day every day. It's a struggle for me to get started, and my family is not yet used to me needing space in order to create. It's gotten better as time has gone on, but it still has its issues. I will often be in the middle of a project and one of my family members will begin talking to me. I am working on making sure that they know when I am creating they need to leave me alone. When I was in the office full time, I would have an hour every day to write. I would use my lunch hour to write, and I don't have that now. I still have my lunch break, but I don't have that quiet space to use in order to get into my zone. I've learned a lot during quarentine about what does and does not work for me. I'm hopeful to be more creative in the months to come, and when the world gets back to some semblence of normal, I hope to be ready to tackle bigger projects and get ahead.

DAVID MECKLENBURG

A SCALE ON THE DRAGON

I have lost count of the days. I do not have some blank wall with scores marching across it—one, two, three, four downstrokes and a slash for five. There are blank walls where I live, but I do not own the walls and I'm a middle-aged woman so drawing on them with a Sharpie seems cartoonish, taken most likely from the picture-hoard in my head of someone in a Warner Brother's Looney Tune jail.

I have had a lot of time on my brain to think about such things.

"You seem to have a skill in finding beautiful houses to live in, Ms. Ludenow," the man said.

"It seems that way, but I don't know it's a skill. I've never worked on it. A skill is something you can learn, like calligraphy, Volkswagen repair, or fellatio."

"But you could say those are talents."

"A talent is some innate ability that allows you to learn a skill well. I think of it as a knack."

"A knack for living in beautiful houses that aren't yours."

"Yes."

"'Knack' remains unclear in etymological history. It could mean a special trick or device, which by extension explains its current and useful vagueness. A knack is not necessarily a skill or a talent."

"If you put it that way, I would agree."

It was dark outside and very late for Seattle, because in the June of 2020, as with all previous Junes, the sun went down around 10:00 or so. I was staying in the Mount Baker neighborhood of the City. I am still there, writing this and waiting. The rest of the world, or at least the United States does not seem to be waiting anymore. Many are venturing out to die, or at least get very sick. Some won't and this does not seem to have anything to do with what people call karma, when you closely look at the concept. And yet I know many Americans, both blue and red who use the idea. It cannot be proven or disproven, so it provides a thick blanket of comfort to many, or a shortcut to ending a conversation.

We have always been an impatient country. Many things changed this year. Read any history book or website and you'll know that.

Again, it was very dark outside, and I was speaking with a dog-faced man. I say that because he had a muzzle, furry up to his black, moist nose, bifurcated as are all canid noses. His canine teeth reminded me of candy corn but a special kind—the mistake kind that somehow skipped the layering process of orange, so there is only white and yellow. The sharp tips gleamed white in the light from the streetlamp but yellowed with tartar towards his gums.

He spoke in a beautiful baritone, like all the well-made leather couches you have ever fallen asleep upon. I did not start from the incongruity of this voice coming from a dog-face because I did not stop to think of the biologically dubious construction of his throat, which was bare, masculine, and distinctly human. I am not an expert in acoustics, so I could not know if his voice was impossible in the resonance chamber of his mouth. I had also previously met him in a dream in which he had been naked and moths flew out of his mouth just before he spoke. He handed me an invitation to a wedding. Not mine. Not his. It was for the daughter of an old crush from high school. He allowed me to remember the early deaths of several of my classmates. I have written of that dream elsewhere.

And he was human from the neck down. He was not nude standing in front of me but dressed in a handsome *guayabera* that showed off his biceps. He also wore chinos and a pair of brown Gucci shoes. A large fedora, because of course he would have to wear one in this neighborhood, shaded the details of his face. I could only sense brown, languid eyes. They did not search over me but simply held the gaze of my own. I was not sure of his breed. His ears were folded back underneath the hat.

As I said, 2020 was a year spent waiting. I had been waiting for him for 12 hours that day. I can tell you this with certainty because the message my boss sent me arrived at 2:00 PM.

> At 2:00 AM, you will need to do something for me. There is a man. He will be by the bus-stop. He is unmistakable. He is honorable and will not hurt you. There is no reason to carry a firearm. He will deliver instructions. Please do as he says. Consider it the consideration you bring to our arrangement regarding my house. Besides watering the ferns and giving Leo the rats.

Leo is my boss's boa constrictor. That much is certain. You see, I am living in my boss's house. The reason was and remains simple. The human earth strains under a plague, a pulmonary one known as Covid-19. I trust you are familiar enough with it. I am wordy enough as it is, so let us be familiar with the fact that the world was closed off that early morning in June.

I had been living there since March, when the disease had really begun to take hold of the United States and the rest of the world. The previous year I had lost my job as an executive assistant for a large philanthropic organization. At New Year's I had returned from my uncle's house in Southern California. A friend I had made there, Jack, gave me a tip and introduction for an executive director of an arts organization. They were also familiar with my work at the other organization and hired me.

I had been looking for an apartment. I had been staying at my friend Gretchen's house, but when Covid began to get worse, I was afraid of being trapped there with her, her husband and two children. They are lovely people, but I would have been a monstrously out-of-place fifth wheel as we "sheltered in place." In my sixth day of telecommuting—crammed into a closet that Gretchen let me use as an office—my new boss, I will simply call her Anne, emailed me directly and asked if I would not mind taking care of her house in Washington Park off Hillside Drive East. Anne's husband had emphysema and so they were sheltering in place near Lake Chelan at their large cabin—what I would call a mansion.

The first hitch was having to feed live rats to Leo the boa constrictor. It seemed a fair exchange: to live rent free in a beautiful house, remodeled for not only comfortable living, but also entertaining various wealthy oligarchs who eased their consciences with sizable donations to the non-profit. I did not stay in the main house, but rather the guest house. This is because my uncle's house, which I had just left was also palatial, but I had a rather unnerving experience there. I have written about it elsewhere. The guest house at Anne's was of a smaller scale and more comfortable.

My days are spent working remotely. I wake up and drink some water, then go over to the main house and check through it for any signs of misuse, unlawful entry, or anything else. I make sure the UVB lamps in Leo's tank work, then I work out a bit in the gym. Back in the guest house, I shower. Unlike most people, I will not give up on showering. I am not a fastidious person, but I draw the line against the plague with this ritual. I only wash my hair but once a week and let my bangs grow out until I get bored and I cut them. I've been doing it for a long time so I'm good at it.

After my shower, I eat a simple breakfast, usually muesli, orange juice and black coffee. Then to work. I take a break midday. Sometimes I water plants, sometimes I feed Leo a rat. There is a large hutch full of them, and I have to feed and take care of them as well. Anne left detailed instructions as to the care of the rats, which included population control via segregatory contraceptive techniques.

My evenings have changed. In the beginning, I worked on manuscripts, especially one I had begun some years ago and was finishing for my publisher. I would often go for walks by myself, shadowed in a long sleeve top, leggings, long black coat and boots: the typical clothes of a Seattle-woman, with a new addition of a black face mask. Sometimes I would read. Sometimes I watched streaming television. Sometimes I would take long baths in the beautiful tub. Sometimes I masturbated. Sometimes I would eat marzipan or chocolate. I corresponded with acquaintances and wrote long emails and letters to friends. I tried not to drink or look at social media too much. Other people were drinking too much, posting too much. Most of the dialog at the time consisted of people yelling concepts and memes to reinforce confirmation biases shared amongst their own belief groups. I did not make sourdough starter.

The fact was, I was alone in a beautiful house and I loved it. I did not have to deal with extroverts distracting me and sapping my energy at work. I had it easy and I knew it. The evenings are in the past tense because things have changed somewhat. My days still operate much in the same way, now especially that the virus is surging again.

All good things come to an end quickly while terrible things linger. Cognitive psychology explains this pessimism, naturally and usually in words and Internet articles whose authors seem to ignore that thousands of humans had figured this out a long time ago. If the past has any caché, it seems to be that of a mythical time before Creation, i.e., the individual's own point where memory sticks and facts are learned and digested through a continually developing personal lens at odds or in concordance with the societal lens.

Or, in the Parliament of my Being, the Magical Thinking party warned me this great gig would have to be paid for.

And so, not long after my 50th birthday I got the message from Anne. I spent half an hour looking at it, and then looking out the window. The neighbor, Mrs. Mandalay, sat in her back yard that day because the sun was out. She dressed impeccably in slacks, and a jacket from Nordstrom, I think. She had been living there a long time. As I performed my rituals, she did as well.

Tap, tap, tap, bang!

Mrs. Mandalay struck at the ants on her patio. With a framing hammer. One by one they would come out of their well-developed hills and she would smite them, individually. One day, I had been taking out the garbage and so was she. She was not some filthy old hoarder, although she was retired. Her dead husband had been an executive at PACCAR, and she was rich, healthy, beautiful even with well-kempt silver hair.

"It's a hobby!" she said. Neither of us were masked at the

time and such times made me feel awkward. I fall into the Paracovinoid Persuasion, you understand, seeing the little bastards floating through the air like marine mines from a WWII film.

"Hobby," I said.

"My name is Amanda Mandalay, and you are taking care of Anne's house? You must be Ada. Anne left a note explaining you. It's nice that Anne found you. How is Leo?"

"Fine. Healthy. Hungry."

"Good. Anyway, my hobby. Well, I suppose you should say it's a pastime, but then isn't everything really?"

"You could say that."

"I don't like pesticides, even though it's easier to kill them that way. If I don't kill them, they will take over the back yard and then come through the cracks in my foundation. If I don't do anything, I know that some night they will come into my bed and stuff up my nose and mouth. My ears and ass too. And then I'll suffocate, and you would never know it, Ada, until maybe there was some smell that snuck out through my chimney. So I kill them."

"With a hammer."

"Yes. You see, I don't wipe them out *en masse* with poison or gasoline poured down the holes. Each of them gets to live a life before my hammer kills them."

"It must be meditative."

"Oh, it's much better than praying. I know what you're thinking. This is some crazy old woman's reaction to Coronavirus. Well, ask Anne. I've been the Ancient of Days for a long time before this stupid virus shut us all up."

Tap, tap, tap, bang! Inside my mind, I was winding through thousands of miles, in ant-scale through vast ant architectures below the ground. How unfair it was, really to pour concrete down into them to make the fantastic, amoeba-shaped tombs of their cities.

Half an hour later there was another message from Anne.

> I know this must seem strange. It
> actually is strange, but do not worry. You
> will worry, but I must say that. I think
> once you understand your role, you will not
> be afraid. Anxious, perhaps, but I liked
> that about you during your interview.
>   Besides, Jack spoke very highly of you
> and told me about everything that happened
> at Amancer. While unusual, this assignment
> is nowhere near as dangerous as all of that,
> I assure you.

As soon as I read Jack's name, everything from that strange December at my Uncle's, a house in the desert called *Amancer* came back: the living emptiness and cold air of the desert and the woman floating outside the window. I remembered when she tried to drown me and how she then died of a stroke in a care facility miles away. I also remembered burning the man-faced cat in the incinerator with Jack. (If you are curious, and haven't read it yet, I've written that story elsewhere. Sometimes it even shows up in a book it shares with this narrative.)

> Hello, Anne
>   I'm not exactly sure how to answer all
> of that. How can I be assured of any of
> this?

In a minute she replied:

> Because the world will end if you
> don't. That is not an assurance my dear. But
> it is all I can say. Call a friend if you
> will. Jack, for example. Let him know what
> you are doing. Incidentally, I would

appreciate it if you send your dress sizes
to EMCromarty-Finch02-@gubbernautical.com
        And no, silly, it's not for a coffin.
It's for a suit. Include an inseam, you'll
be wearing trousers. Let them know your hat
size as well.

I called Jack immediately.

"Oh, Anne let you know, huh? Damn. You know, I didn't think they were ever going to make the call. That's sort of troubling."

"What in the hell is this about?"

"It's nothing you really have to worry about. She just needs you to do something."

In many ways that was the last normal conversation I have had in months. I have had other conversations that sounded normal, if you were listening to them in the 3rd or even 2nd person. But my interpretation of them is not normal, in spite of the pedestrian world view I can fake. Everything else filters through the windshield of my life now, save for the wind itself, lest it blind me.

"Mr. Zamora may remain on the line if you wish. This is not entirely a secret meeting," the dog-faced man said.

I looked down at the screen of my phone. There was Jack's name, glowing in the dark. It was the least he owed me for getting me into this situation.

"What is your name?" I asked. "You know mine. You know Jack's"

"Elvis"

"Elvis?"

"You sound surprised. Wouldn't you say 'Elvis' is a good name for someone with my face, regardless of whether the individual is quadrupedal or bipedal."

"Well, he certainly talks like you," Jack's voice crackled over the speaker phone.

"Elvis. Not...*the* Elvis?" I said. I'm not sure where the joke came from, but I felt a little pride in it.

"Sadly, no. There is but one King. But I would also rather not fake my death on a toilet. Seems like a lot of work. Shall we get down to business? The hour is late."

"Yes, Mr. Elvis, and I have to stay up for quite some time trying to sort all of this out. And then work," I said.

"A bit of cheek. Excellent. Today is Monday. Two nights from now, at 2:00 AM you will go to Mrs. Anne's garage. You will find an automobile there, and a passenger. You will drive the passenger to Tacoma. Drive the passenger to the G. Parking lot of the Tacoma Dome. And wait there. The passenger will meet with some associates. You may then drive back to Seattle and do what you will until the next Wednesday."

"And then?"

"You will repeat this. I am assured by Mrs. Anne that there is a credit card in the glove compartment for fuel. I believe she will have further instructions as to the upkeep of the car."

"Why are you telling me all of this?"

"It is our position that not all of us should know the entirety of the arrangement."

"The arrangement?" Jack asked. Elvis looked down his muzzle at the phone.

"Yes, Mr. Zamora. You have already played a rôle in the arrangement."

"Am I finished?" Jack asked.

"I do not know. You are on this phone call. Perhaps not."

"What if I have questions?" I asked. "Should I try and get a hold of you?"

"No. My work is done. But I will stress that this task is very important, Ms. Ludenow. You see you were not the first choice to carry out the driving."

"Why is she doing it?" Jack asked.

"Because the previous driver did not take the necessary precautions and is no longer with us."

"Precautions? Wait, who am I driving?"

"I mean your mask, Ms. Ludenow. That one you are wearing is quite charming. A brilliant crimson, like wine on blood. Shelter in place. Stay safe. Follow the Governor's orders and you shall be fine."

"How long am I going to be doing this?"

"I do not know. Remember, be at the car at 2:00 sharp. I believe Mrs. Anne already has your uniform on the way. Goodnight Ms. Ludenow, and good night Mr. Zamora."

The next morning went as usual. I fed a rat to the snake and watered the plants. Mrs. Mandalay found a new ant-hill to destroy. Her taps sounded irregular, but they were there. In the garage, a huge Mercedes four-door S-Class posed there. Immaculate and powerful, it simply waited for me to paint it with all manner of meaning but I had none. I wished I had a gun. I don't normally want a gun, but I did that day. I made an early dinner and drank the better part of a bottle of wine.

If I had any lingering doubts, any monuments of denial that I had placed in the way of my memory, they all blew away in the wind of a text from Anne.

> Your uniform has been delivered. I believe they left it at the door of the main house. Please see that it fits. Thank you, Ada. We appreciate this very much.

It was a large flat box, the sort you ship clothing in. I took it back to the guest house and opened it. The uniform was a simple black suit made of finely worked gabardine. There was a dress shirt that went with it: white, of fine Pima cotton with French cuffs which I had never worn. Although it looked very much a man's shirt, the buttons were on the correct side for me and the collar (complete with stays) had a graceful, understated feminine flair. There was no label and it all fit me beautifully. A black silk necktie and chauffeur's cap finished it all up and I stood for a while, learning to tie a Windsor knot. It took me a while to get the knot correct and I had a new appreciation for men of business who still wore these things. The entire ensemble would have been too perfect for a costume. I looked my part—an elegant servant.

The next day, I texted Jack:

  Welp, my suit came Jack. You better be awake at 2:00 and on the phone.

  I will A. Just call me and leave it on speaker.

I tried to sleep a little after work, which seemed so ethereal that I can't remember it. Most of it had to do with donors and maintaining the pipelines of their money. I don't really remember the rest of the night except that it crept slow. The lights were on in Mrs. Mandalay's house and I wondered what she did after the evening had set. I ate some dinner, mostly rice and some roast chicken which I threw up about half an hour later. At 10:00, Anne texted me again.

  The remote fob for the Mercedes is in the top right drawer near the south entrance to the kitchen. You only need drive the car.

I typed several answers and sent none of them save for the last:

  Understood. What am I doing?

  You are driving an associate of mine to Tacoma. That is all. How is the suit?

  Impeccable.

And that was it. I got dressed and watched Stephen Fry's *Wagner and Me* on YouTube. I can't exactly explain why, but it somehow dulled the rest of the world and I was able to eat again. At 1:55, Jack called.

"Hello Ada, ready?"

"Jack, what exactly am I doing?"

"I wish I knew. You know me, I would tell you."

"I know. That is what bothers me about this."

"How do you feel?"

"Like shit, what do you think? My stomach's tied up in a monkey's fist."

"Where are you."

"Outside the garage. I haven't heard anyone come or go. I'm going to put you in my pocket now."

"Do you think I'll fit?"

"Fuck you, Jack. Call 911 immediately and…"

"…your uncle. I know."

I opened the side door to the garage, the one that faced the main house and went in. I put on the face mask that came with the uniform: beautiful black silk, triple layered. I turned on the light and there was the car: massive and silent. The rear windows were tinted so heavily that it was difficult to see if anyone was inside of it. The door was shut. I turned to the wall and saw the switch for the garage door next to the light. Upon throwing it, the door began to open slowly, almost noiselessly and I expected the Passenger to be standing there. But no.

I stepped closer to the car and there, on the right side in the back I could see some shadow, some form. It looked like someone sitting there, but the person did not move. I took the phone out of my pocket to check the time and see if Jack was still there. He was, or at least the call was still in service. It was 2:00 AM.

I opened the driver door.

"Hello…" The voice was thin and spidery, but deliberate as though the Passenger forced each word out with a conscious use of the diaphragm. Neither male, nor female, the voice spoke with a distant resonance that reminded me of when I was a child, and I would blow across a blade of grass cupped between my thumbs. "You are Ada."

"Yes."

"Shall we go?"

"Certainly. I have not driven this car. Will you allow me to get used to it for a moment?"

"You have driven a Mercedes before, Ada. I do not believe it will be difficult."

My uncle's Mercedes was nice, but nothing like this thing. It had a V-8 and took Teutonic engineering to a level I had never experienced. I was sure this car cost as much as a house in most of the country. It took a moment, but I adjusted the mirrors, the seat and pressed the start button and slowly pulled it out of the garage and into the darkness of Seattle's streets. The garage door closed automatically behind us.

I was sweating in the suit and tried to catch a glimpse of the Passenger who sensed my curiosity.

"My name is unimportant, but you may call me Möbæum. I am sure you have many questions."

"But I am afraid to ask all of them."

"Perhaps that is for the best. I would not answer you anyway. You know the way?"

"It's not difficult."

The car knew the way after all.

We drove straight down Madison toward the freeway. The

Coronavirus Pandemic had already emptied the streets during the daytime and at night the absence of other cars was even greater. We passed by the Capitol Hill Organized Protest which had quieted down considerably after the beginning of June. I wondered if Möbæum was going to make any observations on the people standing behind the barricades or those before them, but the car was so silent in its path that I could hear Möbæum's even, flinty breaths, but not commentary.

Möbæum was a skinny… person. Dressed in black, the slight figure of Möbæum, perhaps no more than five foot three at most, and with a complicated face mask, seemed to disappear into the leather seats of the Mercedes.

We made nearly every light. Nervous at driving such an expensive car that wasn't even close to being mine, I wondered if I was insured. Given everything else, I assumed my name would be on some card and although the car itself could travel at top Autobahn speeds, I remained at the speed limit. Soon we were driving down I-5, which was almost completely ours.

"The road is so open," I said.

"It is the plague. The roads and streets of Byzantium were clear of horses, carts, and people during the Plague of Justinian. You would know that."

Driving up the grade toward Michigan Street was like going up a long seam on the thigh of a sleeping giantess, once we reached her hip, we dipped down to her waist then up again in the darkness. Antlike, tiny, we scuttled along with our pitifully bright German headlights going deeper into the darkness. I had never driven on the Interstate like this save in empty lands on lost highways that wound deeper into the bunkers of desolation.

"Do you mind if I put on some music?" I asked.

"Not at all."

I did not know what I wanted so I scanned around the bottom of the FM frequency, where the public and college radio stations existed. KEXP seemed good and soon there was a weird mixture of break beats and found sounds, voices, sampled instruments, Hi-hat, or maybe it was simply someone in the universe banging on a freestanding pipe with a kitchen spoon. The music built up in layers and then washed away as the tide of the piece would move across it.

Further south and through the S-curves above the Duwamish into the wide plaza of lanes near Southcenter, I-5 opened; lit yellow, it was like a broad floor emptied of its raving dancers. And like janitors after a rave at 7:00 in the morning, I was among a few other vehicles sweeping through this last remnant of the Anthropocene.

We climbed out of Tukwila and onto the darkened ridge of Highline. This portion of I-5 cuts down by the airport and for once there were no airplane lights, but there were the usual road signs for food, gasoline. Each one seemed haunted and now useless.

Möbæum remained silent. I glanced back a few times when we passed under some sodium light to see if I could tell more about this passenger of mine. *Of mine* seemed ridiculous. The plague, the music, the hour, the reedy voice. I found myself thinking how natural this was. Like the way the gloves fit or the cut of the suit jacket. *I found myself.* I imagined for a moment seeing myself along the road, perhaps near the Kent-Des Moines Exit. I remembered Des Moines. There was a water tower that my friend Joachim and I went to look at to test the durability of Flaubert's quote regarding the intrigue of observed objects. I had been writing about it three weeks ago.

We started to make the west-bound curve near Enchanted Parkway and the end of King County. Bright lights from electric billboards seemed even more impossible with the absence of other cars on the road. I imagined the signs running forever when we were all dead. What a colossal mess that would be at first. Such a stink. But it would go away. And the lights would keep on shining. The admonitions from the overhanging signs from the State of Washington, imploring me to stay home (which I wasn't) and to mask up (which I had) seemed reassuring, as though their existence was evidence that I was not alone in the world.

The music continued, flowing from one soundscape of vast badlands of blackened coal to steppes of sable glass blowing in the currents of abyssal seas. We continued. Möbæum remained silent. There were no cars near me so I could not check the drivers for muzzles.

The music pulsed harder as we moved through Fife and the light show of the Puyallup Tribe's new and massive casino. But that also told me we would be getting off fairly soon for the exit. As I said, the car had an excellent mapping system, and I followed its directions on the display easily to Parking Lot G.

The lot seemed open to the gaze of everyone on the freeway. Maybe that was the point? But it was 2:35 in the morning. No one was out there at that time and they weren't looking into the Tacoma Dome's parking lot.

There was another vehicle in the lot, a large white Sprinter van which seemed odd.

"Pull over a ways, there. I will go to them. You do not have to stay. In fact, it may be better if you did not. At least not now."

"Are you sure."

"Yes. But none of this makes sense to you, Ada."

"No. It doesn't. Was Elvis really a dog?"

"I told you I will not answer your questions. Just remember what you have. Thank you. I will see you next week at the same time. Do not be late."

"Should I open the door?"

"No."

Möbæum opened the door and swung out. Möbæum did not wear leggings so much as sleeves, because how can I describe the legs that came out of the black skirt as legs? They had elbows and a fully formed, gloved hand. Möbæum moved across the parking lot like a bow-legged rider, but there was something delicately beautiful in the deliberation of movement.

I could not see much else. Möbæum's hair was cut into a short bob of black hair that gleamed under the lights. Two people were waiting at the other end. They were tall, dressed in long coats, gray perhaps but it was hard to tell in the monochrome of distance and night. I looked down to find my phone. It was dead. I had forgotten to charge it and the ride must have sapped it completely. When I looked up, Möbæum had reached them and I pulled the car back in gear. That is when they began to stab Möbæum. First, a quick thrust into the gut, then a few more. I punched the gas down to the floor and the Mercedes jerked away into the parking lot. I barely remembered how to get out. I glanced once back at the direction of the stabbing and saw Möbæum's lifeless body before the two silent figures.

I could, at this point describe my actions. I remember them clearly. I raced out of the parking lot and I did not call 911. I couldn't. And what would I tell them? That a Passenger whom I did not know, who had arms for legs—as well as arms for arms, like some playing card come to life—had gotten out of a car that was not mine and was stabbed to death by two mysterious figures. That a dog-faced man and my employer had sent me on this mission?

And what of calling from my employer's house where I sat in a Turkish bath robe I could never afford and drinking several glasses of her Hennessey to get my nerves straight. Did I call the authorities then? Of course not. What is an authority?

I welcomed the morning because I never went to sleep. Did I

call anyone later around 10:00? No, because I had left my phone uncharged, for I was afraid of what it would tell me, who would reach out to me. I was afraid of what I would have to do next. I wondered about "next week." I thought about Möbæum, constantly creating features like ears, nose, jawline, the thickness of Möbæum's lips. I could not decide on pronouns as you may have noticed.

The first tapping-rapping of Mrs. Mandalay's hammer comforted me. I knew what that was, and I could hold it at arm's length: a simple puzzle really in the far larger one I lived in.

Leo moved slowly in his cage, coiling himself in some new position on his branch. I stared at him for a while, trying to understand his knowledge. Writing was impossible, and work seemed a joke. By 5:00 I could not stand it anymore. I weakened. I turned on my laptop and searched over the news for a stabbing in Tacoma. There was nothing, as you have guessed. There was only the single notification that Windows slid in the bottom right-hand corner of my screen. It was an email from Anne.

> Thank you. You have nothing to worry about. Go check the car. You may feed it to Leo, if he will have it. Then have a drink if you have not already done so. It will get easier. Starting next week.

I had been working again at the Hennessey, which was rather effective because I hadn't eaten anything. I tied up the bathrobe as best I could—did I mention I took off the chauffeur's uniform immediately and showered to get whatever that night was off of my skin? Yes, of course I was terrified, but Anne's bathroom was a large one with red tiled walls and an exposed shower so at least I could see Anthony Perkins coming for me. He didn't but I still wished I had a gun.

Thinking about a gun, something with a large caliber and generous magazine, I walked out to the garage. Seattle remained quiet, although it was not desolate. Its people could have been erased for all I knew, save for Mrs. Mandalay who evidently had theological responsibilities to her ants. Swallows dove and shot through the air for bugs. They reassured me as most wild animals did during 2020, whether it was the raccoons and opossums who became brave in their explorations, or even the wild rats whom I thought were searching for their siblings trapped in Leo's livestock complex. Feral cats patrolled the dark, I remembered, keeping a precarious balance on the rats, and yet I suspected they only culled a minimum take because the rats would be needed to help render down the thousands of dead humans who may have surrounded me.

Perhaps. Many of us had such trains of thought during 2020.

I still felt bleary, working off the buzz I had from the 4:30 cognac. The Mercedes waited headfirst in the garage, headfirst because I wasn't about to back it in the previous night. I expected to see Möbæum waiting for me. I expected to see Möbæum bleeding all over the back seat. There was only a package. The package was moving. Something inside of it moved. Some of the movements were precise, and timed in the intervals of mathematics while others, like the unfurling corner seemed organic, random, tired.

It could not have been bigger than a rabbit. That was the first creature I thought of because I was supposed to feed whatever this parcel was to Leo. It was bigger than a rat, for sure. I went back to the house and drank two more glasses of cognac.

What was it? I had drunk enough courage to go back and pick up the moving thing in my hands. I had to set it down on the pathway to the house because I needed to vomit up the cognac and bile I had been working off of. The swallows continued their feast above me. A crow stood on the railing, watching me with interest. The package moved around. Squirmed would be almost accurate, except it was too slow for squirming. Writhed?

I got it inside and sat it in front of Leo's tank. Leo considered us and shifted his muscular body a little. There was a piece of strong packing tape that kept the thick paper from unraveling. I made my plan.

I went and got more Hennessey.

I then placed the thing in Leo's tank and took Leo out. I had no idea what this was although Anne had seemed cavalier in her message. Leo quickly wrapped around my arms and I think his coil about my shoulders felt wonderful, but I was in no shape to enjoy it at that point. I carefully peeled the tape back and then pulled up. The package unrolled.

The creature was like a bag of sorts, with short pinions, six of them sprouting from its abdomen, if I can call it that. The skin appeared moist and moving, but it was only an illusion. I looked closely through the glass and saw that each pore in the skin was plugged with some kind of metal, like mercury, only golden in color. The reflections of light from these metallic pores gave the illusion of water. Some of the pores dilated towards the darkness, the gleam of the reflected light growing in intensity. Now aware that it produced no light of its own, I moved Leo's UVB light around and watched the spray of light course out in gentle stabbings into the dim light.

In this way, I learned the thing was blind. It had no eyes, not even primitive ocelli guiding the undulations toward the light. It possessed pseudopods that could alternatively extend themselves through some vascular expression, or withdraw, like deeply inverted nipples. I was not sure these were either reproductive or gastronomic in purpose. It was likely both, because the phallic protuberances had tiny rings of teeth surrounding a meatus like opening.

I wanted to kill it. Cut it in half with a shovel from the garden shed, but I was worried such an act would simply result in regenerative duplication and it, or they, at that point would crawl out of the earth to find me asleep.

Bereft of its wrappings, it was not much smaller than a domestic rabbit. I placed Leo back in the tank. Like a cat, he ignored the creature and coiled back on his branch. I went to a couch, placed there I realized for Anne's more morbid friends to watch Leo's consumption of live prey. I could see them in elegant dinner attire. Some with long fingernails, expertly enameled and clicking on the rims of the Waterford crystal glasses. Some of the faces were tan, and some deathly pale. Perfect teeth, nearly all of them artificial porcelain, chatted and snicked together in small talk and anticipation. Botoxed foreheads remained smooth and unfurled while Leo sprang at the white rat left to die in the cage.

I blinked. Or rather, I woke up. The house was dark by that point. I had finally passed out on the couch. Leo lay in the tank, a large bulge in his body. The creature was gone. He seemed satisfied and not in pain. It was not trying to dig its way out of him. It was 2:00 in the morning. I went into Anne's massive kitchen and drank as much water as I could. I knew the hangover would be terrible. I figured I should also look for my phone in the guest house. I wanted to call Jack, but by the time I had gotten there, and found my phone and began charging it, I was exhausted again, so I slithered out of the robe and crawled under the bedclothes. The phone began pinging in the darkness, all the messages I had missed. They could wait until the next day. I slept.

"So that was all she said?" Jack asked.

"Yes." There was a long silence on the phone. I could hear him tapping something in the background, perhaps a paintbrush against an easel.

"And the snake seems fine?"

"Yes, he's asleep. Or doing whatever it is he's doing."

"Digesting."

"It all seems so matter of fact."

"An interesting choice of words, Ada. What are you doing now?"

"Looking at a spreadsheet of midlevel donors. Mrs. Mandalay is outside tapping on the concrete with her hammer. Later, swallows will fly around in the dusk eating bugs. You're alive. Anne is... whatever she is."

"Maybe this is just another 'duty as assigned' and you don't have anything to worry about."

"I suppose I don't. And if I did, I doubt worrying about something I can't control is useful. That's Stoicism 101."

"Aurelius."

"A famous practitioner, but I feel more like Epictetus."

"Why don't you get out of there? Take that Mercedes for a drive."

Which is what I did. I drove the car out to North Bend after work and followed the road to Snoqualmie Falls. Just before the Falls, I found a beautiful little park along the riverbank and sat there for a while watching the current. It was not much after the solstice so the light would last until nearly 10:00. There was one other person, a man walking his Bichon, and the light flickered like green and yellow flames on the cottonwood trees just as the sun dipped behind the hills.

It was the sort of place where I could detach the focus of my vision because the river, in all of the Covid silence, was present and reassuring in its flowing whisper. I did not close my eyes; I did not need to. I wondered about Möbæum, and my mind stuttered in memories of the careful, hand-walking from the car. The unreal people, so tall and why knives? The scene seemed mechanical in my mind. What was dream and dreaming? Was it possible to enter someone else's dream and if so, how could one ever be sure?

Doubtless those who have spent a lot of time meditating about this sort of thing have their answers or, more likely, they have read about them on woo-flavored websites and in woo-flavored books. The borrowed reality of reading someone else's writing about something as evanescent and illusory as reality added a layer of unreality that I found distasteful. Vulgar, even.

Music seemed a better way of understanding what I had done. Somehow the rhythm, the time signature, perhaps even the melody of my life, which had always felt boring in the most pedestrian of 4/4 signatures had somehow intersected with other rhythmic lines. Ms. Mandalay, was perhaps an unacknowledged precursor. There were the rhythmic undulations of Leo, leading to the disjointed—to my eyes at first—walk of Möbæum on those strange arm-legs.

The sky deepened into sapphire and I left the little park. I would return to it often over the next few months.

The week slowly returned to what it had been prior to my task of driving Möbæum to Tacoma. Anne did not bring up my short convalescence again and I was paid for Thursday and Friday even though I was utterly useless until Friday afternoon. Leo absorbed the creature without much ado, and the weather was beautiful. Mrs. Mandalay found a new anthill. I finished the last touches on the manuscript I had been working on in the evenings and I approved my illustrator's work on them. He expected more pushback.

"So you don't mind the portrayal of Astrid?"

"No, it very much captures the heart of her. She is…"

"A cruel Goddess."

"Cruelty is one facet. But I think you know that now. We didn't look that good together, by the way."

"Nonsense, you're both beautiful."

"But Ralph really did have abs like that. I like what you did with Matthew's head."

"Hopefully, most people have forgotten about Wegman's Weimaraners. Anyway, your silence comes as something of a surprise, I thought you'd have more to say."

"I think they're very good. Ready to go."

"You don't sound OK. Quarantine got you stir-crazy?"

"Yes, something like that."

"Well, I can see you aren't going to tell me what's bothering you?"

"No, I'm not. It would be difficult to explain."

"I've never known you to throw in the towel to a descriptive challenge before."

"Sometimes I need time to think."

"Well, you have plenty of that right now," David said.

"Don't we all?"

"Ha, yes. I've never been so productive. Anyway, we should celebrate."

"Over Zoom? Hardly."

"No, maybe I'll come over there and we can distance meet. I met a friend of mine down in Tacoma for a nice "socially distanced walk" the other day."

"I'll think about it, David. I'm feeling a little tired, so I think I'll go to bed."

"Alright Ada. You'll send the final submission of the MS? I've already uploaded the images into the cloud. Good night."

Usually, I could tell all sorts of things to David. I don't know if most illustrators take on the role of cheap therapists, but David was good at it. He didn't say much and asked the right questions. But aside from Jack, who was somewhat involved from the start, I did not feel like including David in the new realm I was exploring.

And so the next Wednesday came. I took a long nap that afternoon, made a sensible dinner of pasta carbonara with one glass of Pinot grigio and some sauteed escarole. I had exactly one cup of coffee afterward as I sat outside on Anne's spacious deck. I sat back in a comfortable chaise on the deck and listened to Vaughn Williams and watched the swallows flying in the late light to catch the last of the bugs.

That's why it did not matter that I was buoyed up by warm, tropical water. It was tannic and yet fresh from running down the side of the verdant mountain on my left. The air was heavy with some kind of scent, like rotting fruit, and ripe fruit—a emanation from tender fleshy petals that hung like long ragged trumpets on the enormous, rough-barked trees around me. Their roots dug into the soil and had wrecked the pavement around me although the deep well, from whence I had come still kept something of its pristine ovoid shape.

The night was falling, and I could see the pupating creatures and understood what they were—a phase on the way to something else. Pity there was no dramatic change like that for me. One of them, high in the tree split open and a homunculus batlike creature emerged. It scuttled quickly up in the branches and was gone for there were observant, socially motivated ravens who watched the pupae. I remembered that they would wait for the things to begin emerging and, before the leathery wings were fully extended, the muscles ready, the ravens would peck and badger the homunculus bats until they fell with a wet slap onto the old blocks of stone that had once been a city of men. The ravens would then dine upon the carcass.

I had been sent there to study them. That is why I waited for this hour, the golden hour between the time when the sun was still burning and vivacious in the sky and utter darkness, proceeded by the rushing shadow of Caçachachembourg, the great mountain that proceeded the night as it always did and when the mature bat creatures would fly out to search for nectar. They had to, quickly, and deposit the egg that would eventually hatch into their larval form.

But the water was luxurious to me, and I wished to simply feel my tail move back and forth in it. My scales had never looked this beautiful before this trip. My arms had grown strong from pulling and crawling through the grass here and there were a network of new illustrations that had risen to the surface of my skin.

Anne's text pinged on my phone. I had been drifting in and out of consciousness. I wasn't drunk, nor very tired. My skin was as it always was. I do have tattoos on my right arm, but they were the same: swallows and for a moment I remembered, as I always did when I thought of swallows, of San Juan Capistrano. And Bugs Bunny singing about it. A bat was flying in and out of the canopy of maples and Douglas firs around Anne's house. Perhaps that was it. I mourned the dream. I had been so beautiful there in that world where the creatures came from and now I was back in this one, with two sturdy, long primate legs and descending further into mortality.

I picked up the phone.

```
     All   as   before.   I   wouldn't   recommend
asking questions.
     But    how    about    providing    my    own
answers?
     To your task?
     No.   I   might   try   to   talk   about   the
music. It will get my mind off things. The
Passenger is the same.
     You'll   have   to   find   that   out   for
yourself. You are fond of Heraclitus. I know
that,  I've  read  it  in  your  work.  Does  any
```

The night trudged on and I did not return to dream. Or whatever that had been. I looked at the playlist for KEXP and saw that 2:00 fell in the middle of the *Fortress of Amplitude,* Neve Yamamoto's early morning ambient music show. I read her notes on the show coming up and last week's show. I copied the name "Susumu Yokota, *Dreamer*" and put it in OneNote for some music to maybe download.

There is not much else to say between that point and when I put on the chauffeur's uniform. I still wished for a pistol. I tied the tie—it is instinctual now and I appreciate the ritual of it, and smirk at the men who so ardently cried out against it as a strangulation device—put on my cap and walked to the garage. The door opened almost silently as before. The Mercedes waited there, headlights facing out, for I had backed it in the last time. And there in the passenger seat, I could see in a faint shaft of light, a pair of gloved hands waiting on what appeared to be a lap. There was the same mask, the same eyes. The same bobbed hair.

"Good evening, Ada. You have had much to think about."

"And I will not ask you any questions."

"I think that is for the best."

"How does one know the best under such circumstances? That is rhetorical and not directed at you *per se.*"

"I know. Let us go. We do not want to be late. The swallows. Do they still return to Capistrano?"

"For a time, they didn't. I know about swallows. Then the City realized it was missing tourist dollars and hired a biologist to figure out how to get them back. They cancelled the festival this year, of course, but the swallows returned."

"Then you understand."

"Yes, I do now."

Neve Yamamoto played old Nils Frahm, albums like *Felt* and *Spaces.* The Mercedes almost seemed to fly in that hour upon the road. It all happened as before. Except this time, I remained: with the lights off. The two people gingerly knelt down for a minute or two by the prostrate body of Möbæum. Then, they lifted the body and placed it in the van. The Sprinter's lights turned on, and it moved out the other end of the parking lot and into darkness.

Neve explained meeting Brian Eno in Ulaanbaatar one night and I felt a tinge of jealousy until I remembered my serpentine dream near the mountain of Caçachachembourg that one could reach by way of swallows and Vaughn Williams.

I voted for Joe Biden, but felt very alone in dropping off my ballot. I did so one early Thursday morning after the Appointment in Tacoma. I called it the Appointment by September. The discussions between Möbæum and myself consisted of singular sentences, sometimes non-sequiturs about Heraclitus or Sub-Saharan polyrhythm. I have to look at them in the long game to understand them and even then, it is difficult owing to context.

As I write this: *every day* the virus kills nearly the same number of Americans as those who perished in 9/11. I do not go to many places. The Mercedes needs minimal servicing and they thoroughly disinfect the interior. I order much of my food online.

I finished the manuscript for *Deukollectrum,* a comparative history of my ideas. Certain revisions have no doubt been made as my consciousness alters and adjusts to this new routine. This new life. Throughout the year, I have watched some narrative sketches I wrote appear in a monthly anthology series: the Prompt project. My publisher asked me to write a final story for a personal compendium of those stories, many of which seemed to have occurred to some *other* Ada. Yet I know they are mine.

I speak with Jack sometimes on the phone, or Gretchen, or David or a few of my other friends and the election persuaded me shut down my social media accounts for a while.

Of note, the creature only appears once a month, which seems to suit Leo, who is getting bigger. The remnants of the thing in his shit were repulsive at first—green and brown smearings over what appeared to be biomechanically generated chitinous gears, prongs, and armatures. The stench was comprehensive and profound. I wretched for half an hour the first time I had to clean out the tank. I put the feces outside because the ants seem to relish it. I try to grow colonies here, on this side of the fence in the hope that they will continue to invade Mrs. Mandalay's yard and keep the world from collapsing.

But as with most things in this cycle, whether it is Möbæum's death or the waking dreams I continue to have on Wednesday nights, I have grown accustomed to it.

It is now December. Unlike Möbæum, the humans who continue to die do not come back. At times it wipes out entire families. In spite of the news of vaccines, the world gets very dark now and I do not sit on the deck, but wait in the living room. I watch Leo undulate through his tank beneath his UVB lights. And I write this story. The deadline for it is soon, but I do not know when the deadline for the virus is. Somehow, I know now, in watching the stabbing every Wednesday night, in listening to the cool throaty voice of Neve Yamamoto introducing me to some new ambient composer, in carefully offering the creature's pupa to Leo once a month that the brief grace of a human-scaled cycle is beyond me and everyone else.

For we are all alone together.

Möbæum and I will drive into the darkness tonight and like the days of plague, everything remains the same, which is a dream, an illusion, a single scale on the vast current of the dragon moving its way through the absurd potential of darkness.

AN INTERVIEW WITH DAVID MECKLENBURG

When did you start writing and why?

Before I answer this question and any of the others, it's helpful to understand who Ada Ludenow is. Nearly all of my stories in the Prompt project (and beyond) are either in Ada's perspective or are 'written' by her. For a longer history, you can always visit my website, but I'll just say here that Ada is more than a fictional alter-ego, anima projection, or literary dissociative mechanism. She is definitely not an instrument of appropriation or some ridiculously winsome ingenue. Ada simply is, and the Ancient Greeks knew exactly what sort of Being she is, for her older sisters sang of the Wrath of Achilles and a Complicated Man named Odysseus. (And no, Lady Lovelace was not her namesake. There was a little book that came out by Nabokov the year she and I were conceived.)

So where was I? Oh, when I started writing...

I started writing when I was about 8 or so. Well, at least I wrote one page of a science fiction novel about lizard men. That's about all I remember. My family were a bunch of storytellers (i.e. liars) and highly competitive at it. The unstated fact was that most of what they said were gross exaggerations if not outright fabrications and my aunt was even keen on outright plagiarism (and improvement) upon other family members' stories. But my mother was also an actual writer working on a science fiction novel when I was young. She had a writing group that she would go to and I would often go along, so my initial impressions of what writers were was: women who write and work over each other's manuscripts, support one another through the arduous task of submissions, and finally, drink a lot of red wine and General Foods International Coffee.

Which authors or books influenced you the most as a writer?

That's a very difficult one because I've grown up and through different writers, but the lasting ones? Well, the first is easy: **Herman Melville** was a big influence from when I first read a children's version of *Moby-Dick* when I was seven or so. Melville's interest in the complexities of the human condition and the illusory nature of the world still resonate heavily in Ada's work. And then there is **Angela Carter** and **Jorge Luis Borges** whom I discovered in Graduate School and still return to often. **Haruki Murakami** is another writer who haunts me, primarily because of the way he can weave weird narratives through rather quotidian worlds. Lastly, I cannot leave out **Goethe** because *so many* of my other favorite writers stand in his lengthy shadow, such as **Thomas Mann.** I was fortunate enough to visit Goethe's house in Weimar and saw where he worked and died.

Another author I haven't picked up in a while, but who had a major impact on me is **Robertson Davies.** A friend gave me a copy of *The Cunning Man* after I had gotten out of the restaurant industry, a period in which the only literary authors I read regularly were **Brillat-Savarin** and **MFK Fisher.** But Davies really grabbed me for a while, and

What's Bred in the Bone hit me harder, and more personally than any other book save for perhaps Murakami's *Wind-Up Bird Chronicle*. Both of these books induce the classic reader's reaction of: "this writer's somehow broken a window and stolen into the house of *my* head." And, if anyone is familiar with Samuel Marchbanks and his relationship with Davies, well, Ada becomes much more understandable.

Which authors or books had the biggest impact on you as a person?

I will have to say that **Louise Erdrich** had a huge impact on me as a person. America is a fractured divided place, and her stories about the Ojibway in North Dakota resonate very strongly with me in terms of how people survive tragedy, racism and genocide by rebuilding families with wit, dignity, pathos and most of all love. I got to meet her once after a Seattle Arts and Lecture reading for *The Round House*, and she was as warm, gracious, intelligent and drop-dead gorgeous as she appears in the media. If you love in an "unorthodox" way, and some people can't understand you, it is because they have never read, or could never understand the writings of Louise Erdrich.

Albert Camus helped me get through my own middle-age crisis of existence—he makes so much more sense now that I'm older. Ada is particularly fond of him and *Deukollectrum*, her critique of *The Myth of Sisyphus* along with many other topics derives from her close reading of Camus.

And always in the background there is **Ludwig Wittgenstein** unraveling and glorifying the movements of language. In his mind they shift and flow like massive currents of stars and galaxies through the dark matter of the multiverse, and the clarity of his thought brings these mutable wonders into as sharp a focus as any human could manage. I read him still for inspiration and pleasure.

Which of your original twelve Prompt stories are you most pleased with?

I actually think it's **"The Deception of Fragile Surfaces,"** because I don't normally write stories like that. It was very contemporary, and inspired by film and there was a certain charm in having Ada with a man who was not her lover, but both of them were moving through a kind of romance that was a cover for deeper trauma. It was also the one I had to research the most, such as MGM's purchase by Sony, or working through maps to make sure the locations off Sunset Boulevard were accurate. And then there was watching *Sunset Boulevard* itself. I had never seen it actually, because it's one of those films, like *Casablanca* that "just are." So many people write about them and tell you about them that it feels like you've seen them. But that isn't really the case, so I actually picked up a DVD at Everyday Music in Seattle for $2.00 or something and watched it. And then I had to watch *Mulholland Drive* again. I think the nature of illusion, not in the epistemology, but rather the actual "nuts-and-bolts" or *mechanics* of it—so important for a film director who is working via the illusion of 24+ frames per second—and the industry's marketing of itself and its own dream... well, that's the heady, philosophically recursive stuff that Ada loves.

Which of your original twelve Prompt stories did you find the most difficult to write?

That would have been **"Cantata"** simply because the structure of that was difficult. I wanted something that actually echoed the polyphony of an actual Bach Cantata, so there is the story of Ada in Leipzig, the story of the girl in Felizia, and the strange Player who was made by an AI. Behind all of this is the voice of Ada actually writing it all and summing it up at the end. Making the transitions between those different pieces, and having them harmonize and flow into one another without forcing it too much was very hard, but very satisfying in the end. Hopefully it worked!

What book on writing do you recommend?

I don't really have one. I've been assigned books about writing, but the best piece of advice from them I remember is "read a lot." So, if I really have to point to a book that "started it all," I usually recommend *The Odyssey*, because it's such a terrific weave and weft of narratives and it too is about story telling when you consider that many of its famous parts, like Scylla and Charybdis, Circe, Polyphemus and Calypso are *told* by Odysseus to the Phaeacians. Odysseus is the Lord of Lies and so writers are his children (yes, even the non-fiction ones). How do we know he wasn't making it all up? Go out and buy Emily Wilson's translation. Wilson's done a wonderfully frank job of making it understandable and beautiful in the 21st Century.

However, to be fair, a lot of my friends whom I know and respect love **Anne Lamott**'s *Bird by Bird,* so check that one out.

What advice would you give an unpublished writer?

Don't worry about over-writing, but if you can, find an editor to work with, at least on your first work. I had a long "silent" period between Graduate School and really writing and I was helped out by two remarkable editors. They were just starting out in the business, but pay attention not to just what they say, but how they *see* your work.

What would Joceyln make out of this paragraph. Would Kristen let me get away with a sentence that long? How many "of courses" and "you knows" have I let slip by?

These might seem like mechanical craft things to worry about, but once you can internalize your editor's process, you can often write better the first time and really let the art and emotion of your narratives come out all the faster.

"Oh! But editors are expensive!" Not always. If you can meet one who is going through a certification program, you might be able to get your text as their practicum. **And please do pay them.** They're struggling just like you in this post-Amazon publishing world.

Do you have a "dream project" as a writer? What would it be? Share what you feel comfortable sharing.

I mentioned above that Goethe is one of my most influential writers and like him, I have my *Faust*. It's essentially a story about a Someone who goes to work for An Asshole in a complicated retelling of the Minos/Daedalus/Minotaur/Theseus/Ariadne story. It began a long time ago in 1995, and was set in Mendocino County with a protagonist whom I've long left in the dust. Right now it's moved up to a fictious island in the San Juans and Ada has all sorts of adventures in front of her, but I just need to find the time to write it!

The original twelve Prompt stories were written in 2019. In 2020 we all experienced a global pandemic. Did the pandemic impact your writing? How?

It was wonderful. There, I said it. To begin with, my employment was never in jeopardy and I was fortunate to not have any close relatives, friends, and loved ones come down with Covid (and my magical-thinking brain is crossing my fingers as I write this in November, 2020) I lived alone through most of it, and got to telecommute which freed up a huge amount of time. I started it all out in March by re-reading *The Magic Mountain* by Thomas Mann, and that sort of set me on fire. It was an excellent book to read since it's all about pulmonary disease, isolation, and the decline of a decadent society. And since I wasn't riding the ferry and transit, and had nowhere else to go, I finished *Deukollectrum* which Prompt had somewhat derailed in 2019. Since *Deukollectrum* is also heavily illustrated, that extra time was precious.

However, while Coronavirus gave me the give of Creative Space, it's very difficult to market my writing during a pandemic. I also don't write about race all that much because there are other writers out there who do it far better and my place of privilege works against me. And I don't usually write about disease or politics. So the Big Topics of 2020 were not there for me, and having books come out *during* that time which do not address those issues, along with the cancellation of in-person reading events made getting in touch with my audience nearly impossible. Social media is also suspect for "brand making" considering how toxic it got during the pandemic.

To tie this back into "advice for unpublished writers..." I would warn them that the tedious, odious aspects of marketing will suck a lot of your creative juices. Sorry, that's just the way it is these days and don't expect to have money showered on you. But you know, *writing has never been a great way of making as living* so you should dispense with that myth anyway.

ABOUT THE AUTHORS

JENNIFER DiMARCO

A PNWC and Bumbershoot award-winning poet and Seattle Times bestselling novelist, Jennifer DiMarco first toured nationally as an author when she was nineteen years old. Her resume of publications includes contemporary drama, science fiction, high fantasy, and mystery novels as well as poetry collections and stage plays. For the last ten years, DiMarco has worked as a filmmaker writing and directing more than a dozen feature films, half a dozen mini series, and more than a hundred short films. She lives in the Pacific Northwest with her wife, author and actor Brianne, and their children, author and illustrator Maxwell, and producer and actor Faith. Find out more about DiMarco at www.jenniferdimarco.com.

LAUREN PATZER

Hailing from Tacoma, WA, Lauren has been an information technology guru, actor, writer and film producer among other pursuits. From the earliest days when he could sit up in a chair, he typed happily away at his grandparents IBM Selectric typewriter, writing somewhat less coherent stories than he does now. He feels the best part of writing short stories is the ability to briefly immerse yourself in a brand new world (even if it's modern day America) and tell the reader a complete, entertaining and /or thought-provoking story in just a few short pages. When he's not spending time with his wife, three daughters and grandson, Lauren is pouring over the details of his next pursuit.

HIROMI COTA

Hiromi Cota has been a special operations heavy weapons expert, an adjunct professor, a rave journalist, and the flaming-sword-swinging lead in a heavy metal opera. They (singular) have lived in nations around the world, but have settled down in Seattle with their spouse Randi and their (plural) dog Nasus. Outside of crafting queer science fiction/fantasy, Hiromi writes roleplaying games, produces the inclusive and comedic D&D radio drama podcast "Dear High Elves," programs video games, and gets into sword fights as a member of the Seattle Knights actor-combatant troupe. A reasonably complete list of their work can be found at: HiromiCota.com

AMBER RAINEY

A mom first in all things she does, Amber just happens to also be an author, actor, and award-winning filmmaker. She lives in Texas with her engineer husband, precocious son, and two cats, who vie for her lap while she writes. Amber has yet to find a medium she doesn't enjoy so she writes novels, short stories, and screenplays. Her first novel, *Eternal Willow*, can be found online at Amazon. You can visit www.amberrainey.com and www.tiny.cc/amberrainey for more about Amber and her work.

MARSHALL MILLER

After retiring as a Senior Special Agent/Federal Criminal Investigator, Marshall found a second career in writing and has a published four book series called THE TSCHAAA INFESTATION. These in-depth science fiction/speculative fiction works examine the human condition, and what people would do to survive when threatened with being eaten by an invading intelligent alien species. His thirty years of law enforcement experience and world travel provides him with the basis for the many varied characters which populate his literary works, demonstrating the good, the bad, and the ugly.

ELIZA LOEB

A United States actor, Eliza stepped in to the writing field in 2018, beginning with *Prompt Generation 1*. Originally born on Guam, they had spent their life reading, writing and creating with many artistic influences. Today, Eliza channels their creativity and experiences through their writing and does their best to reach out to their readers with a subtle portrayal of empathy or compassion. Sometimes, by allowing the reader to get close to them through the pages, other times by a means of fiction. Most times with wine that rarely touches the glass. A recently published piece of Eliza Loeb's work can be found on Amazon in the horror anthology *Unnerving*. But for those of you who would like to see the human behind the writer with occasional writing tidbits, feel free to follow Eliza on Tumbler at imelizaloeb.tumblr.com.

SHEILA MENGERT

A transgender novelist, dramatist, and poet, Sheila is also a political commentator. She has a Masters Degree in English Literature from the University of Washington with an emphasis on the works of James Joyce and Virginia Woolf. Her stories in *Prompt Generation 1* are a debut effort for her in a new genre. Her previous books include a non-fiction book on Borderline Personality Disorder and a seven volume epic re-telling of the Sherlock Holmes Saga published under another name. The story of her transition is told in her book *Transsexualism and its Discontents: A Political Profile* available from KitsapPublishing.com under the separate editorial imprint of Trannie-Goddess Press. Sheila is currently at work on an eighth volume sequel to her Sherlock Holmes Saga dealing with The Great European War of 1914-1918 and its critical aftermath in the Peace Conference of 1919 in Paris.

CARRIE AVERY MORIARTY

Born and raised in the Pacific Northwest, Carrie still lives there with the love of her life. She raised two wonderful, if not slightly warped, children who both live close to home. When she's not yelling at her hometown sports teams on the television, she's cheering them on from the stands. She loves nature and spending time enjoying it with her family. And you don't want to attempt to beat her in any board game. They are meant to be played to the death. Find more from Carrie at www.facebook.com/AuthorCarrieAveryMoriarty/ and on Twitter or Instagram @camoriarty13

DAVID MECKLENBURG

Much like his unseen Gemini half/fictional narrator Ada Ludenow, writer & illustrator David Mecklenburg was born in Sacramento, and moved home to Washington to attend the University of Washington. He has worked as a chef, tech support specialist, and capital project manager. You can often find him on the Washington State ferries commuting to and from Bremerton where he now lives. His stories were written "on the water." For more information about David (& Ada) please visit www.hagengard.com.

ABOUT THE EDITOR

BRIANNE DIMARCO

A published short story author, poet, and writer of more than a dozen short films, Brianne has been captivated by the written word from an early age and doesn't even remember when she learned to read. She currently works as a full-time volunteer for Blue Forge Group and is the Senior Editor of their publishing division, Blue Forge Press. Brianne lives with her wife, Jennifer, and their children on the Olympic Peninsula in the Pacific Northwest.